FOR LOVE AND VENGEANCE

AN INTERNATIONAL ROMANTIC THRILLER

When everyone lies to you—trust your gut instinct

If that fails—start over

For your love deserves the best

And murderous terrorist your vengeance

May God have mercy on their soul

FOR LOVE AND VENGEANCE
AN INTERNATIONAL ROMANTIC THRILLER
BY
Johnny Ray

Copyright © 2012
SIR JOHN PUBLISHING
ISBN # 978-1-9409949-28-4

Both the Americans and the Russians think Victoria works for them exclusively. In truth; the Pack, an International Crime Syndicate, brutally controls her while they launder money in America by buying distressed houses for terrorist sleepers. While she executes the perfect escape, staging her death during a shark attack, she makes one mistake—she meets Royce, who worked as a special operative several years earlier, the night before disappearing.

Royce, on the other hand, wants nothing to do with any American led special operations after he had been lied to in order to keep him focus on his prior mission. His girlfriend had been abducted and brutally murdered earlier while they had kept him in the dark. The last thing he had ever expected was another woman in his life, especially a Russian spy. Furthermore, he never would have believed that she would be the one thing that would encourage him to finish a mission that he should have taken care of the first time.

Royce is well trained on how to discover the truth, so although Victoria's apparent shark attack was well conceived, he knows better. He had used the life of a surfer bum for years as his cover. The more lies he uncovers, the more suspicious he becomes until finally he feels like he has little choice. His prior operation was so top secret that even the CIA was told nothing. He didn't need them then, and he sure the hell didn't need them this time either. The last time it was for country—this time it was personal.

As her world falls apart, she has to depend on a guy she wanted to make into a toy. Relying on love rather than her money is a hard lesson to learn, but one that she has to before it's too late and Carlos leaves her and the murderer makes his final move. Converting their passionate sex life to a true love will require admitting secrets that both Carlos and Rachel have to eventually reveal. But will these secrets bring them together or drive them apart forever?

JOHNNY RAY is an award winning novelist who won the Royal Palm literary award for best thriller and is quickly making a name for himself as the master of the romantic thriller. He loves social interaction with his readers and can be found on

Twitter
www.twitter.com/sirjohn_writer

Facebook
www.facebook.com/authorjohnnyray.

He can also be reached by e-mailing at sirjohnnyray@gmail.com

Or you can just follow him on his blog at www.sirjohn.us for updates and future releases.

Johnny Ray's other novels include:

DRONES
Published by Sir John Publishing in 2013

A WAR HERO RETURNS
Published by Sir John Publishing in 2013

JOHN RAIN – THE HAWAIIAN AFFAIR
Published by AMAZON DIGITAL in 2013

MODELS AND LOVERS
Published by Sir John Publishing in 2012

HER HONOR'S BODYGUARD
Published by Sir John Publishing in 2012

STALKING LOVE
Published by Sir John Publishing in 2012

SCANDAL – THE DEATH OF A LEGACY
Published by Sir John Publishing in 2012

THE SALSA CONNECTION
Published by Sir John Publishing in 2012

LITERARY AGENT – BEWARE
Published by Sir John Publishing in 2012

CHAPTER 1

Victoria recognized the expected incoming call immediately upon opening her phone and began to yell, "I don't think this is safe!"

"It's not your job to think." The English overshadowed with a deep Russian accent was barely recognizable.

She slowed her pace along the walkway heading to the beach, knowing one of the Russian operatives must have called to simply let her know that she was being watched. "What happens if I don't make the drop?" she asked in English to challenge her caller.

He converted to Russian. "I don't think you really want to know."

After the connection died, she dropped the phone back into her bag, and forced herself to keep walking. Keenly aware of the presence of both the American and Russian operatives nearby, Victoria stopped for a brief moment at the end of the wooden walkway leading to the beach in order to study the pounding surf caused by a tropical storm off the coast of Jacksonville, Florida. While both governments thought she worked exclusively for them, and not the other side, the Pack, an international crime syndicate owned her. She could almost sense a sharpshooter focusing the cross hairs of a sniper's scope on her head.

No, she didn't see any red dots—yet, but she had been working for both sides too long. She trusted neither one of them to save her from the Pack. While the Americans and the Russians played games, the Pack concentrated on their plan to destroy America and place the blame on Russia later.

Being betrayed by both, she felt like she had no way out. She had to think of a plan, and had to do it now.

As her right hand fought with the wind for control of the heavy surfboard and her left hand struggled with her beach bag, she stepped off the wooden walkway onto the sand. She forced herself to relax, and look normal. She knew they had the technology to zoom in on her face and hands to monitor every inch of her movements. Any moment could be her last. She forced herself to concentrate. The instructions given to her by the Russians were simple: she must drop and cover the canister containing the flash drive with sand after she completed five steps forward and five to the right. Damn, she wanted to glance around, but she knew better.

The cool, yet gritty sand under her feet squished as she counted the steps. She stopped on the fifth, and turned to her right. Without moving her head to the side, she strained to study the skyline of the condos behind her as hard as she could out of the corner of her eye. While she saw nothing, she knew someone, and perhaps even both the Americans, and the Russians, were on top of one of the condos, and monitoring her moves. She wished she knew exactly where the bastards were lurking. If given the chance to escape, she knew she might have no choice but to take it.

Victoria couldn't turn back now, as her feet continued to march in the sand and she counted off the last five steps. Her instincts told her the operation wasn't going as planned. The storm in the Atlantic whistled loud in her ears, making any further contact impossible. She worried about the time when the Russian operative finds the canister, and the transfer is completed, that her future services might be considered unnecessary, and even her very existence considered a liability. An icy shiver racing up her spine suddenly forced her to have further second thoughts about making the drop. She leaned over to adjust her beach bag, letting the board hide her hand reaching into her bag to find the small canister. She studied the canister to examine the seal one more time before holding it high enough to make sure her monitors saw it.

It was now the moment of truth. *Ohmigod!* She finally decided to abort the scheduled drop, and placed the canister back in her bag while it was still hidden behind her board. She quickly stood and kicked her feet in the sand, attempting to convince those monitoring her that she had, in fact, completed the drop. She hoped that both the Americans and the Russians thought she was covering the canister, which was such a small sand-colored plastic container that was designed to keep out the water and salt. As she remembered loading the flash drive earlier with the data, her anxiety started growing. *Damn! If they knew the truth, would they shoot me on the spot?* Still . . . she heard no shots ringing out. They must have assumed she completed her drop. *Good. This will buy me some time.*

After turning toward the water, she walked quickly, and hoped to make it closer to the crowd on the beach who were watching the surfers. She continued to feel the increasing force of the violent waves which were crashing against the shoreline, and producing a salt-filled spray mixed with sand. With the storm out in the Atlantic raging, the high winds kept slapping her face. Despite all of these uncomfortable conditions, this was also perversely why the surfers were here. It was during tropical storms like this that the waves in Jacksonville attracted the serious surfers. As the high gust of winds repeatedly tried to tear the board away from her, the savagery of the storm scared her, but not nearly as much as the terror behind her. She had to think.

Finding a spot next to the crowd of sand sharks, she dropped her board and bag and prepared to *chillax* for a while. She felt safer now that she was closer to them, and especially with the flash drive containing the stolen data still in her bag. She knew if they were going to shoot her, she would be dead by now. She breathed easier for the moment as she reached into her bag, removed her towel, and spread it openly on the beach.

A tall, lean girl in a thong bikini glanced at her and her board. "You're not going out in this, are you?" she yelled in a rough voice over the sound of the surf.

Victoria smiled, and pointed out to the waves. "That's why I came."

"Good luck. The waves are wicked today. It's much more fun to be a *groupie* and just enjoy watching the guys." Her slim legs, which were covered in tattoos, stretched out on a large beach towel. Victoria suddenly realized the reason for the white-framed sunglasses this tattooed girl wore. The sunglasses were not needed for any sun glare protection, since the sun was hidden behind massive clouds. However, the wind which kept hurling torturous sand and salt at the crowd made the sunglasses indispensable in focusing on the guys surfing. She quickly found her glasses in her bag and put them on so that she could give her eyes some relief.

After being able to see better, Victoria focused on the guys working the waves, and had to agree with the other woman. Even from the long distance to the beach they looked great. As she turned toward this girl with a small ass, but huge boobs, she shouted back, "I'm not a great surfer, but I think this is the best way to learn."

"My hat's off to you girl!" The wind roared so loud that the girl's shouting could barely be heard.

"Look!" the girl on the far side yelled.

A lone surfer in the water sprang into action, and started working hard to get on top of the wave. As she strained to see him catch the wave, a new wind gust suddenly hit Victoria, and blurred her vision with mist and sand.

"He's up!" the first girl squealed as she jumped to her feet.

As Victoria's vision cleared, she watched this guy who began working the curl by cutting back and forth, and thus preventing anyone else from frigging his wave. She witnessed the violent crashing surf being controlled by a master who demonstrated his ability to not only stay up on top but obviously wanting to drain it for all it was worth, and even begging for more. From the squeals Victoria heard coming from the other girls, she knew that his muscular body dominated their interest. For Victoria, his performance penetrated her soul, and recorded a dream-like fantasy that was much more powerful than she could have ever imagined. It rendered her into a trance where the world and all of its problems completely vanished. "Wow!" Victoria finally managed to whisper.

After he finished the ride and splashed his way out and onto the shore, he grabbed his board and ran to his towel. Several of the land sharks brought their hands together for him. While the sound of the wind continued to bellow too loud for any applause to be heard, he did give them a quick hand wave and a big smile which was full of brilliant teeth.

As Victoria studied the water dripping down his long, but curly, blond strands of hair that hung shoulder length, she watched him reach for his phone, and stare at it, as if checking his messages for a moment. After he uncapped a bottle of water, he took a long drink before heading back out to the surf. On his way he quickly waved at the girls, as if to politely acknowledge their praise. But Victoria understood, as he glanced back out at the waves, that his mind was consumed with surfing right now, and nothing else.

The girl next to Victoria yelled at her over the wind, "I don't know who he is, but he's *da kine*."

"I'll agree. He looks . . . delicious."

The girl smiled, and glanced back at her sideways. "So . . . are you going in after him?"

"Let's just say that if he wants to give lessons, I'm available." The brief chatting took her mind off her fears. She felt like she would be safe for a while, since the operative would not retrieve the canister until after everyone had left the beach area. "I think I'll take a small walk first, and get my nerve up before I tackle these waves." With the container still hidden in her hand, she quickly walked down the beach a hundred yards, or so. She soon stopped in front of a large piece of driftwood stranded on the beach. This would have to do. She walked over to it, and turned her back toward the beach before counting off the steps. After turning around to face the ocean, she dropped the container. A quick kick of sand covered it. The high winds would cover both her tracks, and the canister, as well, within minutes.

Now she had to think. She had to plan a way to escape from her monitors before it was too late.

***

Royce Cianci glanced around at the other surfers before picking his spot to catch another wave. The wind-driven surf was creating many interesting challenges that he savored. The warm water here contrasted so much with that of the Pacific where he had learned to surf. In Long Beach, he always had to wear a wet-suit to stay warm.

He soon forced himself to dodge his memories of surfing in California, or off the southern coast of France where he had also surfed for three years. Even after his return to civilian life, those memories of him working undercover in France for the General still tormented him.

Considering his new life in Atlanta, he didn't get to go surfing often. While this beach in Jacksonville, Florida was close enough to make a quick run, it was only worth it when a passing storm produced waves like these. Still, he missed

California now and then. France he would never miss.

Royce wished he could have brought some of his clients with him from his company back in Atlanta, but he didn't have the time to arrange it this time. At the last minute he had hoped that maybe some of his buddies would come, but their jobs didn't allow for them to leave on such a minute's notice. In a way, however, it was nice to be here on his own, and not have to cater to the constant yearnings of others. While he loved his job of playing match maker, and he had never minded the long hours it required, there were the times, however, that he missed his life of surfing.

He spotted a wave approaching, building in strength and offering the potential of a great ride. He quickly moved to get in position and up to speed. While his hands dug into the water, he strained the muscles in his back to propel his board forward. The wave was almost upon him. He knew he had to pull harder, or he would be sucked back over the top of the wave. The board shot forward as he made it. He shifted his weight to the front of the board, and used his hands to grasp the sides as he kept balancing the board, which was rushing forward and picking up speed on its own.

He felt the rush of adrenalin flooding his body, as he stood and used his legs to control the movements of the board. With so many of the waves breaking around him, he couldn't see below the surface. While he could feel the eyes of the crowd on the beach watching him surf, he came to surf, and not to simply give them a show. The girls on the beach were like so many of his clients back in Atlanta who were willing to watch, but either too shy, or scared to participate in life. Today he wanted to have fun and forget his tortured past. One at a time, he intended to devour every wave.

***

"Previet. Kak dela (Hello. How are you)?" Robert asked,

forcing his voice to sound as Russian as possible over the phone. He glanced out of the window of his American command post, which was one condo over from where the Russians were watching Victoria on the beach.

"Hello, Robert. Your accent's terrible." Oleg, the Russian intelligence officer answered in a cold voice, which asserted his no nonsense attitude.

"Perhaps, but I do have information for you." Robert knew he needed to get on, and off the phone fast.

"You usually do." Oleg's own Russian accent was half hidden in his coarse voice.

"You've been spotted. The package will have to be picked up later." He knew this would not be perceived well, but he had no time to make excuses now.

"I thought you had your end covered." His harsh Russian accent deepened, as he critically assessed Robert's failure.

"The other CIA officers can be controlled. That's my job. Did you see her make the drop?"

"She's still on the beach, but she had walked where we instructed her to. It should be there."

"I'll provide the necessary diversion. You'll only have a few minutes to disappear." He left the window, and placed his Glock 23 in his side holster.

"If we leave now, you'll have to be responsible for recovering the information."

"It's not going anywhere, and it's best if you stay low for now. She's being watched. Get some rest, and I'll call you soon."

Robert heard the click of the disconnected line. No goodbye. So much for manners.

CHAPTER 2

Victoria returned, and found the towel where she had left it next to the girls. On the far side of her, a new girl had also joined the crowd. Since Victoria had the only surf board among them, their apparent interests were only on the guys in the waves who were showing off.

This newcomer appeared to be slightly over twenty, and wore long baggy pants and a pullover sweater. Like the others, she must be only interested in the guys. But perhaps some of the other spectators were some of her good friends. The girl in the pullover sweater yelled above the wind, "Do you really surf, or is this just your way to get the guys attention?"

"I surf a little, but these waves are much more than I'm used to." Victoria looked out at the waves, as three more male surfers launched at the same time.

The beach crowd jumped to their feet, and waved at the guys. The dark tans on most of the girls indicated that they must be locals who have spent many hours on the beach.

The girl in the pullover pointed to the guy in the center. "That's my boyfriend, Joel."

"Hey, he's not bad." Victoria bounced with excitement.

The girl offered a coy glance at Victoria before laughing.

Victoria quickly glanced back, and smiled in a teasing way. "I meant not bad in surfing . . . of course."

"Sure you did." Her serious face turned into a bright smile. "It's okay. I know he's all mine. We've been together for three years."

"That's great. Do you surf?"

"I can, but not when it gets this rough."

When the three guys finished their ride, the crowd yelled at them, and waved their arms excitedly. As the guys responded by waving back, Victoria thought how great it would be to be a part of this group. She glanced out at the ocean again to suddenly see a lone surfer taking on a wave. After sliding to the bottom of the curl, and back up to the crest, his board dashed rapidly back and forth. While the other guys were good, he, however, was, without doubt, the master. She watched him finish his ride and rapidly paddle back out toward the ocean to grab the next wave.

Victoria stood and walked over to her board, which allowed her one more chance to glance back at the condos. While they were too far for her to identify any signs of being watched, she suspected they were still monitoring her. If not, she would be surprised. However long it took, she knew the spotter would stay until they recovered the package. She also knew that when they didn't find it, they would come looking for her. It would be easy to explain to the Americans why she didn't make the drop as agreed to, but not to the Russians.

She tied the line to her ankle and lifted her board. "Okay, girls. Wish me luck."

"I thought the hunk out there would be too much for you to resist," Joel's girlfriend teased.

Victoria laughed. "I think he has only one thing on his mind. This may be a very short trip." She pointed out at the ocean with the caps spewing white foam everywhere. But it was the heavy clouds that added so much to the dismal stormy weather. "Here goes."

The wind blew stronger, as she approached the water. Again the tropical storm lashing the beach made her have second thoughts about surfing. However, she knew being out in the sea was much better than heading back toward the condos. She needed time to think, and to work out a plan. The water felt warm, and contrasted to the cool gust of wind, which quickly sent small shivers over her body and whipped her hair about her face. As the waves splashed against her legs, she let the board fall to the water. After walking past the breaks, she climbed on top of the board and started to paddle.

The salty water splashed in her face and quickly burned her eyes. Moments later a large wave rolled over her, soaking her hair and sending her a message as to how powerful these waves had become. She knew she had to get out past the breaks where she could ride the smoother curls. At five feet ten, she knew her arms were long enough, but she still lacked a powerful back, which was needed to propel her out quickly. Although she struggled, she did slowly proceed.

A dozen surfers were waiting on waves, as she drifted into where they were congregated. She felt exhausted, and decided to rest on the board to give her aching arms time to recover. She soon watched several guys paddling past her to catch a wave. The white caps that constantly swirled around prevented her from knowing the depth of the water below.

She watched the blond-haired surfer that she considered to be the master in the group return from one run. She instantly felt mesmerized by his powerful shoulders and arms that were thrusting his board back to the crowd. He soon stretched high on his board, and ran his hands through his hair. When the next huge wave built behind them, he swirled his board and dug in with both arms to catch it, apparently not needing any time to recover. He shot forward, and immediately disappeared on the other side of the wave. *Wow!*

Victoria studied one wave after another, as she planned the best location to launch her board. One wave offered promise, but a young guy snaked out in front of her, and thus cut off her attempt. While she knew her board was blocking their way also, she felt like she had as much right to be in the surf as they did. She pushed backwards to keep from being caught on the wrong side of the break.

While each wave looked almost right, she knew she was procrastinating. She saw him, the master, returning again. He rose again on his board to repeat his now signature movement of running his hands through his hair. His ripped body was so beautiful, and just damn mesmerizing. She tried hard to avoid being caught staring, but when he caught her eye, he smiled briefly before glancing back out at the sea.

A new wave was approaching, which looked perfect. It was now or never, as she attempted to avoid what she had often heard referred to as the pucker factor. She steadied her board and turned toward the beach. *Wait . . . wait. Now–go for it!* She dug in with all she had to offer. While she didn't have the speed, she continued to paddle, giving it her best.

When the bottom of the swell had her, she felt the pull. With one more hard push, she quickly settled on the wave. Her hands went to the sides of the board, steadying it as she gained control. "Waaahooo!" As the board rushed forward, she jumped to a crouch position, testing her balance. All was good. She stood, and felt the front of the board lift. While she was almost too late, she managed to correct her balance, and force the board to ride the wave toward the beach.

She rode the board in as far as the wave would carry her. *I did it! It wasn't so bad.* Her heart beat hard, as she enjoyed the great feeling of accomplishment radiating from her victory ride. She glanced around to see if anyone noticed. No one was close.

She turned to work her way back out to the holding pool. While her arms still hurt from the first time, she was too excited to quit. She knew she could rest when she reached the holding area where the other surfers were waiting on the next nice wave. The breakers were the hardest part to get past. She could see why most of the surfers would stop short of these and be able to get back out without using all of their strength. She wished she had now. However, she watched several of the guys heading in to see their girlfriends, and perhaps calling it a day.

She glanced along the beach where she still saw no signs of a pickup operative. But she still knew that he would not show until after she had left the area for good. This surfing was not part of the plan, and had to be driving them crazy. Since she needed this time to think, she knew that she might be out here for a while.

***

Royce enjoyed the waves for what they were as he continued to work one wave after another. He knew they would not last long. The westward winds would be returning tomorrow, and soon this surf would be as smooth as glass. It did feel great to get away for a few days. He now wished he had tried to wind surf. The winds were strong, but he thought he could handle it. Since it would be great to try, perhaps tomorrow he would rent a wind surfing board.

As the day progressed, the crowd of guys Royce had been surfing with all day slowly disappeared. However, this did give him more room to maneuver. He also knew that his arms or back would not last that much longer. He definitely felt the burn building. Still, the storm presented so little time to enjoy waves like this. As he glanced around, he was surprised to see one girl still out on the water. He smiled as he watched her trying to catch the next wave. Another *benny*, he thought at first, but then again she had a lot of spunk to even be out here. He would give her that, and she looked great. In fact, her white bikini showcased a great body. Her breasts were the perfect size, not too small, or too large. And he did notice her white teeth flashing a big smile earlier. Maybe he would talk to her when the day was over. After all, it would be good to have a friend to talk to later.

Eventually, he had no clue how long he had been surfing, but he knew that the daylight was fading fast. He only had time for a few more rides. The *wahine* in the white bikini, who was still surfing, constantly attracted his interest. As he glanced around, he noticed that they were the last two left in the water. He smiled at her, as she returned to where he was waiting on the next wave.

Then—Royce felt the bump. "What the hell." The feel of the shark registered immediately. It wasn't the first time he had felt a bump from a shark in his life. As he jerked around and studied the size of the retreating shadow, his survival mode sent adrenalin rushing though his body. Control. He had to be smart. He glanced over at the girl. He knew she saw the shark also. He glanced around again. They were the only ones in sight, and the beach was over one hundred yards away.

"DON'T MOVE!" Whoever she was, she was in more danger than she realized.

"WHAT DO WE DO?" she screamed back at him. Ten yards separated them.

"Place your hands and feet on the board. Don't move. PLAY DEAD!"

"Ohmigod! It's huge." Her voice trembled, as she complied.

While he knew it was large, he didn't know for sure what kind of shark it was. This was a different ocean for him. He continued to glance around, but saw no other signs of the shark. He saw her crying. "Hey, listen to me, you have to stay still."

He knew she had to be too scared to even reply. He wanted to get closer to her, but couldn't chance putting his arm in the water. "Hang in there. We might be here for a while."

After ten minutes of searching for any more signs of the shark, Royce waved over at her. "Are you okay?

"Noooooooooo!"

"We need to head in. Once we get started, we need to get all of the way into the beach. Move smoothly and try not to attract attention. The shark may still be close. I'll stay next to you. Let me know when you're ready."

When he saw a good wave approaching, he waved at her to turn her board toward the beach. He could see her trembling, but concentrating on his directions. "You're doing fine."

She didn't respond but moved forward, catching the wave. Her own adrenalin must have been kicking in, as he watched her mount the wave. He joined her easily. *Just give us a few more seconds and we'll be out of this.*

Foam covered the beach line, as they splashed in the shallow water coming ashore. She jumped off the board, and ran onto the beach, pulling the board behind her by the line. He followed behind her. On the shore, they both looked back out at the ocean.

"Holly shit! Did you see the size of that shark." she yelled, and pointed out at the sea, as she continued to jump up and down. Royce watched her movements carefully, hoping she could hold it together. The adrenalin had to be blasting through her system right now.

"Yes. I felt the shark bump me. Are you okay?"

"No." She looked back at him. "I'm not okay." Royce saw her weakening, and helped move her to her towel as she started crying into her hands.

He remained next to her, and wrapped an arm around her. "We're safe now."

She continued to cry, as he felt her trembling. He knew it

wasn't a good time to tell her that he had experienced many sharks in the water before. He held her for a long time before he realized that he didn't even know her name.

Finally, she glanced at him, and smiled. "I guess I need to thank you. If you hadn't been in the water to tell me what to do, I know it could have been all over for me."

"You did great." He moved over to her and hugged her around the shoulders again. Being this close to him she looked even better, but now vulnerable. He didn't want her to be apprehensive of a stranger taking liberties at a time like this, but wanted to let her know that she was safe now.

"I need a drink." She lowered her shoulders, and stumbled. Royce moved fast, catching her before she fell. When she recovered, she continued, "Thanks, you might want to make that a double."

"I can fully understand that." He laughed, and brushed his hair back. To him, it was amazing that she could think of a joke line at a time like this. "What kind would you like?"

She forced a small laugh. "I was going to a wine tasting tonight. However, right now I could use anything."

"I like good wine. Where's the tasting?" He stayed close to her, not sure if she had recovered fully, or not.

"It's at new place called the Wine Castle." She raised her head and inhaled. "You should try it."

"I'm not from here, but I think I can find it." He felt her gaining her strength, and released his arm from behind her shoulders. "It sounds like exactly what I need right now."

"Good. I need to go. I hope to see you shortly." She smiled, as her breathing returned to normal.

"Me too. Are you sure you're okay?" With his eyes focusing on her, he looked for any more signs of weakness.

"Yes, and thank you again." She turned toward the condos. "If you could walk me to my car, it would be great."

"I'll be glad to." He reached behind her, and lifted her

board before he examined her body again. She looked great.
***

From the window of a condo down the beach, Brandon watched Victoria and this new guy standing on the beach, as he tried to understand what was going on. Who was this guy she was talking to? The CIA officers working for Brandon had taken some good photos of him, and he had already forwarded them to be checked for any possible matches that he might need to know of. However, Brandon assumed that this might be a chance meeting. What did Victoria have on her mind?

Brandon's phone rang. "Hi, this is Charlotte. We're working on identifying this new guy, but the photos don't match anyone in our files that we can place yet." He rubbed his brow. He knew Charlotte, one of his top officers, was working on it hard, and he relied on her ability to get assignments done quickly and efficiently.

"Stay on it. Have you heard from Robert?" He needed to know what one of his top agents had found out.

"Yes. He had lost the group he was following, and was never able to identify them."

"I see. Let me call him. I may need to get more back up to follow Victoria tonight. I don't want her to spot me." Brandon doubted if Victoria would recognize him, but the less she saw him, the better. While this storm was making his operation difficult to manage, it was too late to abort. He would do what he could to cover for Victoria, but being kept in the dark didn't help much at all.

He needed to make some calls, as he flipped open his phone to make the first one. "Robert, what happened?"

"I arrived here too late. I think they were here, but they're gone now. I'll have a team go through the condo, but I doubt we'll find anything."

"Our girl's on the move, and I'm not sure what she's up

to. I think we'll have to bring her in tomorrow. It'll be too dangerous to approach her now. The Russians may still be watching her."

"I agree. We'll bring her in some time in the morning."

CHAPTER 3

Royce glanced at the entrance to the wine bar, where the heavy oak casings set the stage for a night full of delightful discoveries, as he anticipated tasting some great wines. Thankfully, the rental agent at his condo had given him easy directions to follow. He combed his hands through his hair, and felt the signs of their relentless curls in spite of his attempts to comb them out. The shower had refreshed him enough to encourage him to shave. The clean feeling felt great.

While he wasn't sure how to dress, he assumed the professional casual look would be fine. He had started to not bring the outfit, but changed his mind at the last minute. Now, he was glad he did. The light, tan dress pants matched the deep-blue shirt, and his jewelry consisted of a single ring on his left pinky.

Wow! His expectations of the wine bar changed, as he opened the door. The first word to come to his mind—*swanky*. This would be a great place for him to introduce his clients to each other. He would have to check to see if it was part of a chain. If so, he hoped that they would have a place like this back in Atlanta.

A tall man, dressed in a black company issued uniform, smiled as he waited behind a counter for him to approach. His mannerism appeared to have been polished by many years on the job.

The beauty of the décor entranced him, however, as he continued to study the professional work. From the polished marble on the floor to the exquisite lighting above, an air of sophistication radiated from every angle. The owner had lavished the inside foyer with wine art that complimented the highlighted wines displayed at various locations around the room.

"I understand you have a wine tasting here tonight."

"Yes, we do. We have three different flights or tastings available tonight." He handed Royce a card describing how it worked, as he continued to speak, "We have a ten dollar flight, a twenty dollar flight, and a forty dollar flight."

Royce looked over the list. He saw six wines on the first two flights, and eight on the last one. "It looks like you have a good selection here." He recognized some of them, but others were new to him.

"We do our best to make it interesting for our regulars. They must love it, since they keep coming back." He smiled, swelling with a bit of pride shinning through. "Tonight, we do have some exceptional wines on the list."

"I met a girl a few hours ago, and I was supposed to meet her here. Let me buy two of the forty dollar flights, and I'll let you hold one here for her."

"And what if she doesn't show up?"

Royce smiled. "Then I guess I'll drink a lot of wine to try to forget one beautiful girl."

"Very well." The manager smiled in appreciation of the humor. "We offer one quarter glass tasting, and I'm sure you'll find the gourmet appetizers parcd with the wines to be exceptional tonight, as well."

"I'm looking forward to it. This . . . beautiful girl, that's meeting me here, I have no idea what her name is." He handed his card to the man that he now suspected may be the owner instead of just a manager.

"That's interesting, and I'll not even ask. Please enjoy yourself." He swiped the card and handed a ticket to Royce to sign, as well as the two admission tickets before smiling.

"Remember, all of the wines featured tonight receive a ten percent discount."

He signed for the charge to his credit card. "Thank you very much."

Royce turned to walk through an arched doorway leading to a large showroom which was full of highlighted wines that were sparkling from well placed lights. He studied a dozen or so other customers who were walking around the displays, and making small talk. They were dressed in casual but professional attire, making him feel good about his selection for the night.

As he walked on through the room, and toward the bar where the flights were staged, he saw a different wine consultant standing behind each flight. Unsurprisingly, the circular marble serving stations matched the floor. After smiling at the girls behind the counters, he walked around the room, and inspected more of the decoration. If he wanted to impress a date, this would be a great place.

With the anticipation of the great wines waiting on him, he fought the temptation to start tasting them. He knew he had to wait for his date; after all, she was the one that had told him about this place. Several tall tables scattered around the bar allowed the customers room to mingle and place their glasses. For those wishing to have a seat, several small tables lined the back wall where low lighting accenting them in a cool, but romantic way. The setting defined perfection all of the way down to the classical French music.

Several more customers drifted in, and admired the décor in much the same way as he had. They all appeared to be single. He avoided the temptation to return the flirty smiles of the last two girls entering the room. Since the bar had so many interesting furnishings professionally placed, he soon lost track of time.

When the blonde-haired girl flashed another flirty smile

his way, he returned it politely, but not intently. The room now had many people walking around swirling their wine glasses and laughing.

Making a turn at the end of a wall, he turned to see this same blonde-haired girl with fluffy hair swirled on top of her head standing in front of him. As she grinned at him, her brilliantly white teeth sparkled in the low light. While a string of white pearls around her slender neck added the perfect touch as she moved closer, her bright-blue eyes quickly dominated his attention.

"Hello." He managed to say, as he studied her intense stare.

"Hello." She mocked him back while still smiling, but showing signs of a puzzled mind. "Aren't you *surfer boy*?"

Surfer boy? No one had ever called him exactly that before. He studied her face with new interest. Suddenly it came to him, as he examined her hair. While in the water the hair had appeared dark, almost brown, but now it shinned a bright yellow. "Ohhh . . . my God. You're the girl in the water today."

Her laugh lasted for a long time. "Do I look that different?"

"Yes. Your hair looks very different. I didn't realize that you had such light, blonde hair. It looks great like this." He knew he was talking fast, and trying to make up for his misstep.

"Thanks. I worked on it for a while. By the way, my name is Victoria." She reached out a hand to shake his.

He accepted her hand presented in a professional business manner, and turned it in his hand to form more of a French hold before he gently squeezed her fingers. Her finger nails, which were manicured, and long, indicated she worked as a professional inside girl. "And, by the way," he intentionally mocked her back, "my name is Royce."

She raised her shoulders and squeezed them in close to her, a move revealing her excitement in meeting him. He knew he stared at her, but the shock lingered for several more moments. Her beauty dominated his attention. And on top of that, she loved to surf.

"I'm so glad you found it. I didn't know if you would be here or not." She stepped closer to him, and turned to glance around the room. "It's nice in here, isn't it?"

"It's beautiful. I knew you would be here, so I went ahead and purchased you a ticket."

"You didn't have to do that. I purchased one already." She pouted.

"Don't worry about it. I'm sure they'll let us apply it to a bottle of wine when we leave." He knew he was smiling too much, but he couldn't get over the shock of how she looked so different.

"That sounds like a deal to me. How much do you know about wines?"

He resisted the urge to tell her he had lived in California, home of some of the best wineries in the world or about the time he spent in southern France, a part of his life that he knew he would never tell anyone—that had to remain a secret. And those memories, he desperately wanted to forget. "I enjoy a good wine, as much as most people. How about you?"

"I know wines well, but I would love to know them better."

Royce had the feeling that she knew wines much better than she admitted, as he hoped that he would soon find out more. "Shall we see what they have to offer?"

"Sure. I'm looking forward to it."

They walked over to the counter on the far left. The wine consultant smiled at them, and took his tickets. "We have an extra ticket. I assume we can use it to purchase a bottle later."

"I don't think it'll be a problem. Show it to the cashier on the way out, and he'll take care of it for you." The girl in her early thirties smiled broadly. "Are you ready to get started? We have some great wines tonight."

"Great! What do you have for us first?"

"First we have a great Champagne—a Pol Roger. Then we have a Chablis Blanc from California, a Chardonnay from Australia, a Zinfandel from Spain, a Merlot from South Africa, a Pinot Noir from the Russian Valley in California, and then finally, a rich Bordeaux from France—a Chateau Gruaud Larose, which is sixty five percent cabernet and twenty five percent merlot, with some cabernet franc and petit verdot making up the difference. Most of these wineries I have visited, and I hope I can give you some great insights on these wines."

They accepted their glasses and welcomed the first pour. Royce turned to Victoria as he swirled the champagne in his glass. "Since this is our first glass together, perhaps a toast is in order. What do you think?"

"Definitely . . . and I have the perfect one."

"Oh . . . do you now?"

He saw Victoria raise her glass without hesitation, and announced, "To no more sharks!" She laughed, but maintained a serious look on her face.

As the laugh spread its contagious charm, Royce answered, "If you're going to surf, you have to get used to them, since they kind of come with the territory."

A waiter passed by with a tray of cheeses. The choices looked great, especially since Royce hadn't taken time to eat before coming. He waited on Victoria to make a choice while his stomach started to growl down deep. He hoped she didn't hear it. How embarrassing.

Over the next hour they tasted some great wines and

made several selections along the way. The relaxation and the companionship provided exactly what he had needed tonight. He knew it wouldn't be long before he returned to Atlanta and the long hours of helping others with their problems.

The girl behind the counter smiled as they approached her for the last bottle. "This is the bottle that you'll enjoy the most. I'll admit that I did save the best for last. I want you to take your time and enjoy it slowly since it has the complexities that take a few minutes to fully comprehend."

After Royce reached for the bottle, and she handed it to him, he read the information on the back, trying hard to memorize it. However, with the wine blurring his memory, he knew he would remember little of what he read by tomorrow. "How much is this one?"

"It's eighty, but you receive a ten percent discount tonight."

"That's good. Please reserve us one of these also."

"It'll be my pleasure."

Royce and Victoria faced each other to make a final toast. He lifted his glass, and hesitated for a minute. "To fantastic wines and," he paused to smile, ". . . and to the rest of this fantastic night."

***

Victoria tapped her glass against his. It had been a perfect evening. She could not have picked a better asset for the night; Royce was a complete unknown. He was someone that she knew would drive both sides crazy. By now, they should know the capsule wasn't dropped. She smiled, reflecting on her change of plans. Well, she did drop it, but not in the location they would be looking. She was running out of time, but hopefully she was safe as long as this guy stayed next to her and kept them guessing.

She glanced around the room one more time. She didn't

recognize anyone, but she didn't expect to either. Still, she expected that they would have followed her. "I can tell you love to surf."

"Yes, it's one of my diversions that help me make it through life."

She reflected on his half-way hidden meaning, but couldn't concentrate on it now. "What are you going to do with all of the wine you're purchasing tonight?"

"As usual, I'll share it over good times with friends."

She loved the way his smile made her feel. If only another time, and another place, she thought. "The beach really is amazing with the storm out in the Atlantic. The waves are beautiful right now."

As he looked over at her, his deep-blue eyes haunted her, and appeared to be invading her deepest thoughts, as he asked, "How would you like to open one of these tonight, and walk the beach for a while?"

Perfect, she thought. It would give her more time to work out a plan. "I would love it. But please, let me use my ticket to pay for some of the wine."

He smiled, and motioned to the girl at the counter to box up his order.

***

Charlotte, sitting in a quiet booth in a darkened corner, had decided to handle this assignment personally, as she watched Royce and Victoria at the bar. When she saw them heading for the door, she whispered into her Bluetooth microphone hidden in her blouse, "They're on the move."

Charlotte had just placed her back to the wall to obtain a better view when Victoria turned to survey the room one last time before leaving. She quickly lowered her head to take a sip of wine, hiding her face. That had been too close.

After Charlotte knew they had left, she whispered back into her hidden microphone. "I heard a lot of the conversation, and it appears they just met. They're heading to the beach, and I think all will be good until tomorrow. We can find out what happened on the drop then."

CHAPTER 4

After stepping outside the wine bar, and into the night air, Victoria felt the cool refreshing breeze coming from the tropical storm out in the Atlantic, and welcomed the sobering effect. However, the effect of the wine did dull her worries of the past, and the future, just enough for her to relax. She felt him reach his hand behind her elbow, guiding her along and thus being protective of any missteps she might make in the dark. While not needing the help, she loved the special attention.

His voice resonated smooth and deep. "We can drive my car back to the place we surfed, or go further down the beach if you want. I can bring you back here later."

With a little luck, this might work out great. Unless they had someone watching the parking lot, she should be able to disappear. She wondered what kind of car he drove. "The beach isn't far from here, or my place. If you want, we can take your car to the beach parking lot. Please give me one minute to get my beach bag since it also has a towel in it that we might need."

"Sounds great." He followed her to her car where she grabbed her bag before he then directed her to the back of the lot and to his car—a Porsche Boxster.

"Hey, nice car!" She couldn't remember ever riding in one of these, but always wanted to.

He flashed a smile, as he released her arm and reached for his keys. "It's the one luxury that I allow myself to indulge in."

He opened the car door, and placed the wine he had

purchased behind the seat before offering his hand to her. The low seat and her high heels presented a small problem. Yes, she gladly accepted his hand which he offered to steady her. Apparently, he had been there before–done that. "Thank you."

As she turned to back into the seat, she glanced around the lot where all looked normal. She held his hand, and had a seat. His car still had that new car smell. Now, if they could only simply disappear.

***

Royce whistled, as he walked around to his side of the car. He had looked forward to walking the beach, and now he had someone to enjoy it with. This part of his California life–walking on the beach at night–haunted him, but he knew he would never return there.

The motor roared to life, sending the same sense of excitement through his body that he experienced the first time he cranked it. He loved the powerful feel of the motor, and more importantly, the fact that he had full control of it. Pulling himself out of the intoxicating trance, he glanced at her, and smiled. "I think you need to buckle up."

He heard her giggle with excitement. She grabbed the seat belt, and fastened in, pulling it tight. Her eyes twinkled as he noticed her body tense, reading herself for a fun ride. Good, he felt like he had full permission to let his passion for driving to surface. He dropped the gear into first and hit the gas.

He passed the entrance to the public parking and drove on down A1A to explore the coast line. Soon a different parking lot appeared in which he turned into and pulled to a stop. "How is this?"

"This is fine. It's a long beach, and I have lots of questions for you."

"Oh . . . do you now?" Teasing is an art he enjoyed both

dishing out and receiving.

She sent him a flirty smile, as she quit giggling. The quietness of the moment smothered the harsh realities of the world. Her bright white teeth disappeared, as she pulled her lips together. Wow! He wished he could read her mind right now. However, she remained quiet, mysterious.

He reached behind the seat to hunt for the right bottle. The second bottle brought a smile to his face. "Here, I think this one will do great tonight." He retrieved the last bottle they tasted—the French Bordeaux.

"Are you sure? I know you wanted to share that one with some good friends of yours."

"Yes. That's why I bought it." He slipped it into her beach bag.

Her lips captured his attention—their shape and fullness nearly perfect. The dim light provided by the street lights reflected off her glossy lipstick, which was a beautiful rose colored pink. He knew he stared, a trait he tried to control but often failed. They were so inviting, and too damn intoxicating—he had to concentrate.

He fought off the urge and forced a smile. "Shall we go?"

"Sure. Is it okay if I leave my shoes in your car, and not carry them?"

"Not a problem. I think I'll leave mine here too." He tossed his head backwards, and felt embarrassed, as he realized one mistake. "I forgot. We don't have any glasses for the wine with us."

She laughed. It turned into a giggle. "If you don't tell anyone, I think drinking straight from the bottle will be fine tonight."

That would be different. "Why not? And I'm very good at keeping secrets."

"What about a cork screw?"

"Not a problem." He removed a key ring from his pocket,

which contained an attached, small, collapsible cork screw. "Not too easy to use, but possible I'll assure you."

"Good. Then we're all set." She lifted her bag and placed it on her lap.

As he opened his door and moved around the car to open her door, he noticed that she already had her shoes off. After he kicked his off, and laid them on the floorboard by her shoes, he lifted her bag to his shoulder, and took her hand before turning to the beach entrance.

The walk along the beach in the high winds made it almost impossible to talk. He wished he had a jacket to offer her, but even this early in the season the wind had already obtained some of the summer warmth. The splashing waves and white suds glistened from the lights of the condos behind the beach. He reached over and rolled up the bottom of his pants, knowing full well it would not be enough. Tonight it really didn't matter if they were wet or not. The night presented all kind of special intrigue for him, as he squeezed her hand tightly.

He turned to walk, but stopped to reach inside the bag, and hunt for the bottle. While he fought with the seal, since he didn't have a good knife to remove it, he finally managed to work the small cork screw into the cork, and pull. Nothing happened. He pulled again, and felt it give slightly. One more pull and the cork came out. He quickly removed the cork from the screw, placing it in his pocket. "You know. I don't know how to toast without glasses."

She took the bottle from his hand. "I have an idea. Each time you tell a little about yourself, you get to take a drink." She smiled at him, obviously waiting on an answer.

"That can be neat. Kind of a truth or dare type game."

"Kind of . . . but without the daring. You only have to tell what you want to tell."

"Okay. You can go first."

He watched her raise the bottle as she received the first drink. "I think this is the first time I've ever walked the beach at night. The shark scared me today, and I'm not use to that feeling."

"That can be understandable with a shark that large. I knew it had to be huge when it bumped me."

"You felt it!"

"Yes. Sharks don't like to eat dead food. They'll often bump it to see if it's still alive before they eat." Royce saw the intense look on her face. "I hope you realize that the chances of getting attacked are very slim if you follow a few simple rules."

"I think I understand, but how did you manage to stay so calm out in the surf?"

Royce laughed, almost as if he knew she would ask it next. "I lived on the beach, and I started surfing at six or seven."

"I see. I loved watching you surf today. You have a lot of control, and you appear to never get tired."

He felt the tightness in his arms and back and couldn't agree with her. He wished for the great shape he used to be in. "The storm will be dying down soon, as the winds start blowing in from out of the west. When that happens, the waves will disappear. Tomorrow will be the last day there'll be anything possible to surf on."

"Good, it'll be just for me then."

"I'm glad to see that you're going back in." He smiled at her and continued to hold her hand as they walked.

She handed him the bottle, indicating that it was his time to tell all. He turned the bottle up and tasted the wine. With the full burst of flavor resonating on his tongue, many memories returned. The winemaker had produced a very good wine; perfect for the night. He raised the cuff on his right arm, and pointed to a scar. The dim light made it difficult to make out details, but the rough skin indicated a bad accident or surgery of some kind. "This shark almost made me forget about ever surfing again. It put me in the hospital for a while."

"Wow! When did that happen?"

"I was fifteen, and stupid."

"Why do you say that?"

"I saw the sharks earlier, and thought I was immune."

"I guess you learned a good lesson."

"Yes, I guess." He handed her the bottle.

She accepted it and turned the bottle up again. As she titled her head back and arched her back he examined her breasts, which projected directly out in front of him. As they entranced him, freezing him in place, he stared. Damn—he had to remember to control that.

"I work as a programmer, and if you happen to know, we work all of the time." Victoria had a weak, almost hidden accent in her voice that Royce couldn't identify, but guessed it to be somewhere from Eastern Europe.

"So, you're a computer girl, trying to be a surfer girl." He saw her smile, as she acknowledged the fact that she needed a lot of practice.

"Since I've lived here for several years now, I decided to try it. I wished I had taken it up when I first moved here. I so love it."

"So . . . where did you live before you moved here?"

"I've lived in many places." She smiled as she continued to walk, but never varied her pace.

"Hummm. I hear an accent, but I can't place it."

"Me." She flashed him a teasing, questioning smile. "However, I can hear one also. Let me guess first." He felt her studying his face with an intense quietness, confirming her concentration. "You're definitely not from here."

"Since I'm renting a place here, I think that's obvious."

The teasing tones to his voice brought a smile to her face.

"Since you . . . grew up surfing, I think my first guess would be California."

"I think that's an easy conclusion." He turned to walk, resisting the urge to offer more of his past as he allowed the waves in the surf to splash against his legs. Okay, he had many memories from before—both good and bad. "And now . . . about your accent. I think I hear a mixture of European and New York."

"You're good, but that still covers a lot of territory. My father was born and raised in New York, and he was determined that I also learn English."

Royce felt lucky on the guess, but still, she didn't volunteer any additional information on her past. He studied her deep-blue eyes. "I'm thinking more of the eastern bloc of Europe."

"You're getting warmer." Her smile enhanced her teasing attitude. Royce loved the way she played the game—a game he loved to play so often, and especially when he realized that another person matched his ability at the game. She had him hooked, intrigued, but he didn't want her to know it. He caught himself staring again. *Damn,* he would have to be more careful.

He decided to change the conversation so slightly that he could keep the game going, but cover his burning desire to know more. He reached for the bottle, and saluted her with it before taking another drink. "I enjoy wines, and spend way too much time studying them."

"Why do you say that?"

"Because there are so many things I want to learn." He swallowed hard, trying to decide if he should tell her about his Sunday habit of spending the day at the book store.

She reached for the bottle as he glanced out at the Atlantic, observing the powerful storm shifting ever so slowly out to the east. "I also enjoy great wines, and wish I had time to travel to see the wineries here in America. I've never been to California, and after hearing that you're from there makes me a little bit jealous. Let me see, what else can I tell you about me? Food– I love to cook special meals just for me. If I mess up, I'm the only one disappointed."

He laughed as he turned to face her. "It sounds to me that you don't have much a love life. That is, if you don't mind me being nosey."

Her returned laugh, accented by the affects of the wine carried above the wind. "That would be an understatement! I don't have time for a boyfriend. This night, and this day on the beach, is highly unusual for me."

"That's hard to believe."

"Why?"

"The beach is right here." He knew he left the part of the boyfriend off the statement, but he couldn't resist the urge.

"Yes, the beach is here, but I thought we were talking about my lack of a love life." She grinned out of one side of her mouth, but never took her sideways stare off of him.

"That . . . I find much harder to believe, but let me guess. I know you said you work all of the time, so why do I think there's more to your story than that?"

"Uh huh. So you think you can analyze me?"

He smiled back, increasing his stare. There were times it came in handy, like tonight. "Would you like a free consultation?"

"Do I get another sip of wine?"

"Absolutely. Perhaps, I should have purchased more of this wine. I think you like it."

"Yes, I do, and it's very good. I'll have to remember it and go back to buy some for myself later." She glanced at him, studying his face.

"What are you thinking?"

"I'm wondering how long you're going to be here." She leaned closer to him.

"I think tomorrow will be the last day of good surfing, and I need to head back after that."

"I see. So, in other words, I'm just a one night stand, hummm."

He laughed at the openness, and assumed the wine added to it. "Well . . . it is one night, and we are standing—at least for now." He reached out to steady her as they walked.

"Nothing like stating the obvious."

The fresh smell of the storm, and the faint lights from the condos behind them, kept the world he knew from ruining the moment. "What's obvious . . . is that you don't want to talk about your boyfriend."

"My boyfriend! Like I said, I have no time for one." She laughed again. It was highly unique, and original in both its tone and texture. It was also becoming very familiar to him.

"Okay, is it alright if I ask you a few questions?"

"Why not? I'm not sure I'll answer or not, but you can ask." She took his hand and continued to walk down the beach as the surf splashed against their legs.

"Good. First, let me get the obvious out of the way." As a large wave rushed toward them and he jumped to keep the wave from getting the top of his pants wet, he blurted out, "I assume you're not a lesbian?"

He knew that she would laugh before she responded. "No . . . no, not at all." She swirled toward him, handing him the bottle. "Do I have to prove it?" The laughter was quickly replaced by silence.

He smiled, but didn't know what to expect as she stepped closer. At around five feet ten, she stood tall, but much less than his six foot two. When he leaned closer, as if to call her bluff, she stopped inches from his face, and allowed him time to gaze into her eyes and study the fire that lay beneath them. While they proved much more mysterious than he had anticipated, he still received no indication if this was a tease, or a bluff. Who would make the final move?

With her eyes becoming pools of liquid fire that burned deep into areas of his soul that he had guarded for a long time, he had to look away for a second before he also studied her luscious lips, which glistening in the dim light from behind them. With her presence–unwavering; her expression–unintimidating; and, her patience–hard to understand, he waited until he saw her close her eyes, waiting on his move.

With her permission apparently given, he lowered his head and studied the delicious radiance of her lipstick. He felt her exhale, as the warmth in his face lasted for only a brief instant. He felt the gentlest of touches as their lips met and he tasted the moisture and warmth of her lips. He glanced toward her eyes. They remained closed, and with the expressions on her face resembling that of a person in a trance.

He lowered his gaze back to her lips as he pressed his own lips against them softly, exploring the depth of their fullness. As a flood of old emotions rushed over him, he realized that it had been so long since he . . . . He closed his eyes, and felt the floating of the world around him as he felt her press firmly back against his lips.

Eventually he backed away and glanced at her eyes which were still closed, waiting for more. The taste of her lips lingered on his, with the feeling so intoxicating that he couldn't control his urge to move in stronger. Yet . . . he knew to go slowly at first and not release his full, pent-up urge to ravage her lips; after all, he didn't want to scare her away. As their lips parted, she kissed him again, rendering him helpless in his attempt to go slowly. He plunged his tongue deep into her mouth, exploring the shape, the size, the texture and the taste of a pleasure he had almost forgotten existed.

He withdrew, finishing with a small kiss on the top of her upper lip. He searched her eyes again, hoping they would open. She soon answered his wish, as she opened them, revealing her brilliant eyes, and even in the pale light, he studied their deep-blue color, much like his own.

She remained quiet, apparently waiting on him to continue. He reached over and kissed the top of her forehead instead. "I think I can safely rule out the question of you being a lesbian."

She laughed before she smiled, revealing her bright teeth. "I think the wine must be getting to me. This is very unusual for me."

He reached around and hugged her, as he pulled her closer, much closer, to him. "Now, I'm confused."

"Why is that?"

"Back to the question of why you don't have a boyfriend. It can't be because you're a bad kisser; you're definitely good." He flashed a smile, but never removed his focus off her eyes. With those liquid pools intoxicating him more and more with each passing second, he had to quit staring, or he knew he would soon be falling deep into that pool and without a life preserver.

"Thank you. You're a very good kisser also." He felt her hand reaching around behind him, and increasing the connection between them.

He was falling too fast and needed time to think. "I think I know what it is?"

She giggled. "Okay, tell me. I'm all ears."

"You're married."

Her laughter roared above the wind, which was now decreasing in intensity. "Noooo . . . I'm not married, nor have I ever been married."

He raised an index finger. "Okay, I have it. You have a live-in lover?"

Her laughing continued. "Wrong again."

"Hummm." He twisted his finger just above his lips, as if he twirled an invisible mustache. "The plot thickens. Okay, let me ask you how old are you?"

"You know girls don't like giving their age." She stared deeply into his face, smiling with her lips pursed ever so slightly. "However, I'll make an exception, that is, if you'll tell me how old you are."

"Deal."

"I was born on the tenth of June in nineteen seventy two."

A loud roar escaped, one he wished he had more control over.

"Why are you laughing?" she asked.

"You're older than me."

"Really."

He reached around her to feel the firmness of her body next to his. "Yes, and by exactly one month," he announced.

She turned her head to the side, giving a sideways glance, as she consorted her face into a suspicious expression. "You're kidding me . . . right?"

"I'm absolutely serious." He massaged the top of her shoulder where her skin was irresistibly smooth, and so inviting. He knew instantly that the rest of her skin must be just as silky-smooth. He tried to force his mind not to think about it.

"I'm not so sure I want to be known as the *older woman*."

"I'll tell you what. I think I can keep that a secret." He leaned over and kissed her forehead again. "Now . . . I still find it hard to believe that you don't have a boyfriend. Unless . . . I have it. You recently ended a long-standing

relationship with a boyfriend and are now on the rebound."
He raised his eyebrows in an evil interpretation of the
sinister guy waiting in the shadows.

"Wrong. I haven't had a boyfriend for a long time."

He pulled his hand to his chin, rubbing it slightly, playing
the part of the great thinker. "Okay, then there's only one
answer. You must be the daughter of a very rich and famous
father, and one who thinks no man is good enough for you."

He felt her hesitate, thinking of a response. This time he
knew he hit closer to home, but . . . how close? "Am I
getting too personal?"

"No, not at all. It just brought back memories of my
father. I haven't seen him during the last three years I've
been here." Her distressed face told him he had hit a very
sensitive nerve, and one that he wished he could have
avoided.

"I'm sorry. It sounds like you miss him. Why haven't
you returned home to see him?"

"It's a long story, but impossible. I have no time to do
anything."

"So . . . it does sound to me that you're like so many
professionals who work all of the time and that really don't
have time for a love life." He waited for a reaction, but
received none. Instead, he saw her glancing out at the ocean.

They walked for a while without saying a word, as the
breaking of the waves soothed his frustrations of trying to
figure out her thoughts. His experience in dealing with
clients told him that silence can be the best way to get one to
open up, and tell intimate thoughts about themselves.

She eventually reached for his hand, and squeezed it. "Is
there any wine left?"

"Yes, a little more." He handed her the bottle, and
watched her drank the last of it.

"Perhaps we should add a message to this bottle and then

set it free."

He smiled. "I've never done that, but it could be interesting. The ocean will be receding over the next few days, and with a westward wind blowing the storm out to sea, it could go all of the way to Europe." He had a quick thought as he pulled her closer to him. "With the change in weather, the rip tides will be very strong. Have you ever been in the ocean when this happens?"

"Some, but I'm a very good swimmer."

"It doesn't matter how good you are, if you don't know how to handle them. If you stay on your board and know how to use them, they can save you a lot of energy. If you fight them and don't know how to handle them, you can wear yourself out and die in the surf." He knew it sounded like a lecture, but he had a sudden fear pass over him.

"I understand. Don't worry."

They turned and continued to walk toward his car. As the sky above them partially cleared, revealing the stars and occasionally the moon shinning full above them, the moonlight also reflected on the crashing waves. Out further in the ocean, the light glistened like millions of sparkling diamonds.

He pointed to the moon. "I think we must have someone trying to play cupid for us tonight. What do you think?"

"It would so appear." She lifted her head to study the moon as he, in turn, studied her neck, which looked so lean—so elegant with the white pearls radiating around her neck. He could feel her hiding information about her past, but he couldn't put his finger on it—at least not yet.

"Okay. Let me ask you this. When you're not thinking about surfing, what do you do when you're not working?" he asked.

"I promise, I only work."

"There has to be one goal in your life you really want to

accomplish. If you had the time, what would you love to do?"

"Travel–I want to see this country. That was my hope when I came to America."

"That's not a hard thing to accomplish, just buy a ticket and go."

She threw him a sideways glance. "I wish it was that easy."

"Okay, I'm sorry for pushing, but I'm trying hard to understand who you are. You appear very mysterious to me."

She laughed, as the teasing side of her returned. "Being a one night stand, that might not be such a bad thing."

He laughed back, as the thoughts of getting lucky entered his mind. "I'm enjoying the walk." He pointed south along the beach. "I wonder how long it will take us to get to Miami."

"Forever . . . and will probably take a lot more wine than we have."

"You may be right, but I do have enough to last much longer tonight."

She smiled, and handed him the empty bottle. "You know. I think I'll keep this bottle, and place one of those candles in it, you know, so that I can remember it in the future. What do you think?"

"That could be cool," he replied, as he examined the bottle.

The parking lot lights soon revealed an almost empty lot. When the sand squeaking under their feet ending when they reached the pavement, he felt her glancing around nervously, which also, in turn, made him cautious of the surroundings. While he felt safe, he knew she had some reservations. It felt strange that she didn't act like this on the beach. "Let me see which bottle we'll have next."

After he opened the door, she reached for the bag holding the wines and selected the Pinot Noir from the Russian Valley in California. "I think this one will be very nice."

Upon leaving the car, he felt her rushing back to the beach where her nervousness disappeared as they reached the shoreline again. She had also managed to bring her beach bag with her. While he could see a towel, and a mat inside of it, he had no idea what else she had with her, but it did provide a good place to carry the wine.

They walked for a long time as they listened to the crashing of the waves. She eventually stopped, and turned toward him as she glanced around. "This is where we surfed earlier I think, isn't it?"

"Yes, I think you're right." He reached over and hugged her as he assumed the shark attack from earlier was still bothering her. Her body felt warm and firm. "I think we need to open the bottle, don't we?"

While she smiled, and handed him the bag with the bottle remaining near the top, his phone rang and startled him before he could get his corkscrew out of his pocket He wished he had thought to turn it off. "Hello." He raised one finger to beg for a second while he talked.

She smiled, but crossed her arms and patted her foot in the sand like an inpatient girlfriend. Okay, he knew she just wanted to tease him as he raised his finger again, and mouthed the words, "I'm sorry." He pressed the phone next to his ear, trying to hear above the wind, and the surf. "Oh . . . hi, Beth. How are you tonight," he yelled into the phone in order to be heard.

"I hate to bother you, but I met this guy that's the brother of someone you introduced me to a while back. I like him much better than his brother, and I need you to run a check on him for me."

He turned to Victoria again. "I'm sorry. Give me a

minute. I need to take this call."

Chapter 5

Victoria walked along the beach behind Royce. She knew the old piece of driftwood marking where the tube was must be close. Finally she saw it maybe twenty yards further down the beach. As she headed toward it in a slow, but deliberate pace, she realized that this may be her only chance to recover the container.

After she glanced around and saw no one, she felt safe, but knew she had to hurry while Royce was distracted. Upon finding the spot, she turned and walked off the steps in the hard but smooth sand. It wouldn't be easy, but she had to try as she started digging in with her toes. While moving quickly, she still tried hard to not draw too much attention. She got lucky; she felt it. *Now what do I do*?

When she glanced up, she saw him walking toward her, waving his hand. She quickly grabbed the canister, and dropped it into her bag. While that was close, she felt sure that he never saw it.

After finally reaching her, he put his hand on her shoulder. "I'm sorry again. Duty calls."

She flashed a flirty smile. "Let me guess . . . your wife." She cocked her hip to one side.

The shock registered in his face. "No way. That was a client."

"Hummm. I think it's my time to ask the questions."

He lifted his hands in self defense. "Okay, ask away?"

"I've told you what I do. Now it's time for you to tell me what you do."

She saw his eyes go shifty, as he moved in close to her.

"Well, it's kind of like this: I can tell you, but if I did, I'd have to kill you."

"Very funny, very funny, but if you don't want to tell—it's okay. I can use my imagination."

He held the still unopened bottle in his hand. "Perhaps I need to open this first."

She smiled. "It sounds like you have a story to tell."

He opened the bottle, and placed the cork in his pocket. "Since I'm telling all now, I guess I get the first taste."

"Absolutely. I can't wait to hear this one."

He shifted his focus back on her. "Okay . . . now you have to promise not to laugh."

She laughed anyway, not knowing what to expect, but becoming very intrigued. "I'll do my best."

He lifted the bottle, and slugged a long drink before she then accepted the bottle and his hand as they walked. She could feel him searching for the words. She used the moment to survey the area as they walked past an area that contained fewer and fewer condos. The lack of light from them was perfect. She needed to hide out in the shadows as long as she could.

She heard him clear his throat. "Okay. Like I said, my job's a little different."

She laughed again, and let her imagination roam while the suspense built to a fever pitch. "Spill the beans."

"Okay, I run a business back home —"

"And we still don't know where that is." When he glanced at her, she studied his chin and, of course, the dimples. He had the look; the one she had longed for, but the timing was just so bad.

"I live in Atlanta where I run a small business." He squeezed her hand as he paused for a second.

"And what kind of business is that?"

"I operate an executive level dating service."

"Interesting." She had to think about that answer for a minute, as she wrinkled her nose. "Do you mean you work like a pimp?"

He roared with laughter. "No . . . but sometimes I wonder. I work for very professional clients who don't have time to search for a mate. Also, if they find someone of interest they often ask me to do background checks for them. In fact, the call I received from a client a few minutes ago was exactly that. I work kind of like a life coach, but without a license to practice psychology."

"Now . . . the questions you were asking make sense." Her voice rose in intensity, as it resonated in a higher tone. "You were analyzing me."

"Just a little—sorry. It comes with the trade."

"So . . . how many girlfriends do you have? You can't tell me that after working with all these desperate women that you don't have several on the side."

His laugh resembles a kid that had been caught. "I work with professional men and women. Their main concern is finding someone that's not a gold digger."

"Rather than using a dating service, why don't they simply go to the internet? There are sites everywhere where you can connect with someone."

"Yes . . . but then you have no way of making sure that person's telling the truth. In most cases, the truth isn't even close. People will lie about their age, their weight, their income, being married. Trust me. I've heard the stories from my clients that tried this in the past."

"I can see your point. But with all of these rich, beautiful women running around, I'm sure you have your share of them."

He laughed. "I have a very rigid rule—I don't date clients."

"That's very honorable—not that I believe it, but very

admirable."

She felt him squeeze her hand. "If you have a hard time believing this, you'll have an even harder time believing another service I offer my clients."

She turned to face him, waiting on him to explain. "On some weekends I rent a van, and take several of my clients out to single bars to have a night on the town. I remain the designated driver, or sometimes big brother, if they run into trouble."

"Neat. Kind of a girl's night out . . . hummm." She felt herself being drawn in by him more and more, as he smiled back at her with his cute dimple slightly visible in the dim light.

"Something like that, I guess you could say."

"Now that I have the tables turned, tell me about . . . your girlfriend."

"There's no–girlfriend. I think we're the same in one respect. It appears that we both work all of the time."

As they past the last of a chain of condos, the shoreline had turned increasingly darker. When the clouds suddenly parted, revealing the moon again, she saw him pointing at it. "You know during a full moon . . . the vampires come out."

"So . . . are you telling me you're a vampire now?" She laughed, enjoying the feeling of the free-spirited night.

She felt him shrug as he slipped his arm around her waist and lift his head toward the moon. "Okay, let me ask you another question then."

Victoria watched a few clouds pass by the face of the moon, rendering a magical appearance of perhaps a beautiful fairy tale for one minute, and then moving to more of a cheap beginning of a horror movie at times; in either case, casting an enchanting feeling of mystery and romance. She enjoyed the relaxed feeling of this brief diversion from reality before she asked, "What do you want to know?"

"How long has it been since you howled at the moon?"

What an interesting question, she thought, as she glanced at him, taking her eyes off the moon. "So . . . now you think I'm a dog."

"No, but it's a great feeling, and a feeling of release that everyone needs to experience at least once in their life."

She lifted the bottle and had a sip before returning the bottle to him. "This . . . I have to see."

He reached for her beach bag and pulled out the towel, placing it on the sand behind them. "I think you'll enjoy it."

She had a seat on the towel and rested briefly, as she watched him standing in front of her with the moon glowing off his well sculptured body. She handed him the bottle, and watched him take a long sip. When he raised his head directly at the moon, allowing the bright moonlight to shine in his face, she quickly checked to make sure the container was still in the bag. She had to be careful. Her training alerted her to one fact: he was an unknown, and perhaps a perfect asset, but he could also be a planted operative sent to keep an eye on her. Yes, it would be elaborate, but possible.

He moved in next to her on the towel, wrapping his arms around her. His smile intoxicated her thoughts, as she dismissed him as being anything but a great guy. She smiled, waiting on him to make the next move.

His move was different than she expected when he released her waist and put his two hands together before arching back his head and facing the moon. The howl started low, but grew steadily. She felt herself laughing inside. He really was going to go through with this. "Harowllllllllllllll!"

She laughed loud, much louder than she could ever remember, but she stopped when his face took on a serious tone. He pointed to the moon. "See . . . I'm still human. Now it's your time."

He acted serious. At first, she smiled, but with the wine

getting to her she decided to relax and follow his lead. *How many glasses of wine have I actually had tonight*? It was hard to remember after the wine tasting, which were generous, and the first bottle, and now this one. She also knew that he had one more available for later. It was going to be a long night–a good night. She lifted back her head, staring at the moon above. "Harowlllll, Harowllll!" Damn. It did feel good.

While still knowing very little about him, she felt like she knew the part that mattered–his soul. This bottle disappeared, and after another trip to the car, the next one also vanished as the sun started to rise. She enjoyed his sweet and gentle kisses, making her yearn for more. His control amazed her. He was an interesting guy that always seemed to be smiling.

"My place is very close to here. Would you like to see it?" he asked.

Yes she would; in fact, she would have loved to have seen it many hours ago. His control drove her crazy. "Absolutely, I'm sure it's a great place. Most of these condos are fantastic."

***

As the door cracked open to the condo Royce had rented, Victoria studied the perfect decor she would have expected from a luxury condo on the beach. She instantly had images of huge party gatherings of guests enjoying seafood, and fruity little Caribbean drinks around the kitchen that looked large and well equipped for even a professional chef. A marble top on the island cabinet contained the stove top, and an inside grill which reminded her of her favorite TV program–a cooking show, of course.

While she waited on him to offer to show her more, she glanced around and recorded as many details as she could. "This condo looks great, and much better than the one I'm renting."

"It belongs to a client of mine. She obtained it as part of a divorce settlement. The short story is . . . it belonged to her ex-husband, who maintained this love nest for a mistress that no one knew about until the divorce."

She giggled. "That had to be a shocker."

"Yes, I know it was. I hear about it all of the time. She still owns it for one reason–that mistress lives close to here, and she wanted to make sure that she had a way to keep this mistress miserable for ruining her marriage." He lifted her beach bag, and placed it on the marble counter top. "If you'll excuse me for a minute, I think I've had way too much wine, and I need to go recycle for a minute."

"Not a bad idea at all. Is there a second bathroom?"

"Yes. You can use the first one. I'll go back to the master bath."

"Okay," She said, as he headed for the hallway leading to the master bedroom. She knew she only had a minute, and had to act fast. She had to hide the canister somewhere, but where? She saw the wine bottle they had planned to place a candle in. This would have to do. She pushed the flash drive in as fast as she could. She needed to find a candle to cover the mouth of the bottle quickly. She opened a drawer in the kitchen and located one–good, very good.

***

Royce grinned as he entered the bath room. He had been trying to hold it in for a long time now, and the relief felt great. He had wanted to make a pass at this girl for a while, but needed to wait on this. He whistled softly to himself, as he thought about how beautiful she looked. A quick glance at the mirror reflected the fleeing ability he had in focusing. The amount of wine still circulating in his system dulled his senses, and he knew it.

As he grabbed a towel to dry his hands from the quick

wash, he knew that he could do absolutely nothing about his messy hair. He glanced around the extremely impressive bath with the extra large whirl pool and double shower. He thought about how this one room was larger than the apartment he had back at UCLA.

After stepping out of the bath, he found her setting on the edge of the bed. "This place is huge. You're very lucky to have such a generous client."

"Yes, I'll owe her one for this." He walked over and settled in next her as he studied her calm, but pleasant face. "It has been a long night. Are you tired?"

"Not really. Drunk . . . yes, tired−no."

The passion had been building in him all night. Since she had never offered any resistance, he decided to move forward to what he hoped would be a great night. He eased his arm around her waist where the slim, but firm feeling of her body aroused him immediately.

She titled her head back, exposing her slender, elegant neck. He couldn't resist any longer. He leaned over, and kissed her nape softly at first. She felt so soft, so silky-smooth. When the smell, the scent of her as a woman filled his nostrils, he didn't think it was a perfume; no, it had to be the way she smelled naturally. He nuzzled closer and softly nibbling at her ear. He heard her groan, which excited him.

"That feels so good. I think you've found my weakness," she whispered.

He decided not to admit that it was a weakness of his also. He slipped the strap of her dress off one shoulder. Her short black cotton dress with the small spaghetti strap holding up the top had entranced him all night as they had walked the beach. Beneath the low cut dress, he studied her fully developed breasts that were firm enough to not really need any support. Not long after he first saw her, he knew she wasn't wearing a bra. All night he had forced himself not to stare; however, now he didn't have to pretend any more.

He lifted his head slightly to kiss the side of her cheek and study her face. She had her eyes closed with an expressed look of being mesmerized. He whispered, "Your skin is so soft."

"Thanks." She appeared relaxed.

He could understand how the long walk on the beach must have worn her out, sapping most of her strength, and perhaps all of her resistance, but it had his as well. He placed his hand on her other shoulder, and offered a gentle massage to her skin which was so very soft to him that he couldn't get it out of his mind. He lowered his hand with his movement slow, but deliberate. He felt the top strap of her dress which pulled tight across this shoulder easily give to his draw on the tie. He examined her perfect breasts, loving the nipples perfect size—not too big or too small. He used his fingers to tease and caress as he grazed them over the tip of her nipples, one by one. He heard her moan before she inhaled a deep breath of air.

"They're beautiful."

"Thanks." He recognized her weakness as she responded, and knew that conversation wasn't what she needed.

He played his fingers along the nipples again, and constantly increased the rhythm, and the pressure. When they became firm, and rewarded him for his efforts, he lowered his lips and kissed one of them before taking it into his mouth. Her smell was now enhanced by the taste of her body. He cupped her breast, and nursed it, as he let his tongue explorer the increasing stiffness.

With his hand firmly in place, he raised his head and studied her face, looking for any signs of resistance. He admired her beautiful, almost perfect features. Her lips mesmerized him, and made him stare even more. The lipstick she had used still glistened on them, rendering them so enticing, so inviting. He adjusted his position, and pressed closer to her face, but never removed his attention from her lips.

As he touched her lips, grazing the surface with his, he couldn't resist the urge to lightly lick them with his tongue. Their moisture and their warmth sent strong messages pulsating through his entire body, as his mouth started to suck on the top of her lips, ravaging them. They were full, and much different than any girl from his past. Yes, it had been too damn long.

While holding her shoulder, he directed her back onto the bed. It was amazing, he thought, that she had still been able to sit this long. And he knew the wine probably had much more effect on her than him. The black dress had hung several inches above her knees when she stood. Now, as she lay on the bed, the dress shifted to high upon her legs. Being around many women who enjoyed a healthy life style, he appreciated their efforts of staying in shape by exercising. His mind became fixated on her legs, as he lowered his hand down her thigh, and enjoyed the sensation of her smooth skin. Although, he had no doubts about them being the same silky-smooth texture that continued to drive him crazy.

Since she hadn't hesitated before, he raised his hand smoothly along her thigh, and as earlier, she only moaned. He took that again as a sign and moved higher until he felt her pelvic bone beneath her scanty feeling panties. After his fingers found the way to the top of them, he worked them under easily. She had shaved her pubic hairs, which was no real surprise since she was surfing. As he continued to explore, he heard her moan much louder this time.

As he let his fingers wander more, he still received nothing in the way of resistance. However, he wondered if she had become totally incapacitated, and unable to know what was going on. He had to know. "Are you okay?"

"Uh huh. I'm fine. How about you?" Good, he heard a complete sentence, indicating that while she might have had a lot to drink tonight, she was still able to think clearly to some extent.

He released his connection, removing his hand from under her panties. "I'm fine. I think both of us have had a lot to drink."

"Yes, but I feel so good right now. Please don't stop."

"Are you sure?"

She raised her head slightly and opened her eyes. The deep-blue color melted any doubts he had left. "Do I have to prove it again?"

He recognized the reference to the earlier challenge. "That could be interesting. What do you have in mind?" he asked.

She said the one word he knew he would remember forever. "Everything."

As he raised his body, and rested on one elbow, he stared at both of her exposed breasts before shifting his attention to her dress riding around her waist. She had to be the sexiest woman on the planet. How could anyone say no to that? Still, he resisted. "Are you absolutely sure?"

She reached down to lower her panties. "I'm sure, but please . . . be gentle with me."

He stood to remove his clothes. As he stood, he realized how much wine he had consumed. Damn, she was beautiful. As he watched her slip her dress over her head, he wondered how he ever got this lucky.

Chapter 6

After turning over in bed, Royce raised the comforter to block the morning daylight coming through the blinds before burying his hurting head deeper in the pillows. *Wow*! The bed felt so warm and cozy right now. If there was ever a day to sleep late, this was it. While struggling to gain consciousness, he reached out his hand, but didn't find her in the bed. *Oh boy, what a night.* He glanced around. Where was she?

Various memories of the night before flashed intermittently, as he rubbed his eyes. "Victoria, are you here?" He heard no response. After struggling to stand, he walked to the kitchen. "Victoria." Still, he heard no response.

As he entered the main living area while still staggering from the lasting effects of the wine, a white envelope on the table captured his attention. His heart sunk. *After a night like that—she leaves me a note. A damn note!* He reached for it, and read. "Sorry for having to leave you like this, but it is for the better. You're a very nice guy and deserve someone very special. Thank you for a night I'll always remember, Victoria."

He wondered what time she left. He glanced at the clock on the wall. It was now two in the afternoon. If he hurried, perhaps he could find her on the beach, or out surfing.

***

As Royce jogged over to some men that he assumed were Coast Guard officers, he studied the yellow and black police tape flipping in the wind that held back a crowd of onlookers. "What's going on?"

The first officer studied Royce's board, and lifted a hand to stop him at the tape line. "Sorry, no surfing today. We're investigating a shark attack right now."

"Wow! I understand. I was here yesterday, and I saw a large one. What happened?"

"A couple of young boys saw the attack from the beach, and called it in on a cell phone. They went out to see if they could help, but never found the victim. So far, all we have is a surfboard."

Shock set in as he glanced around and forced himself to maintain control. "Do you know who it was?"

"Not yet. We arrived here about five minutes ago. A copter will be here in a few minutes."

"Like I said, I surfed here yesterday with a girl I had just met. We saw a shark, and left the water. I was hoping to see her here this afternoon."

"Who is she?"

"I only know her first name—it's Victoria."

"Don't go anywhere. We may need to get a statement from you."

"Where's the board you found?" Royce felt his heart racing.

"It's over there." The officer pointed fifty feet to his right.

Royce quickly outmaneuvered the guard and ran for it. He recognized the board as soon as he reached it since it had the name of the rental shop imprinted on one side, and was from the same shop as his. Damn, it also looked like the one Victoria used the day before. "Oh, my God."

"Sir, I'm sorry, but you have to stay behind the line." He stepped in front of Royce, asserting his military training in a firm, but compassionate manner, as he appeared to understand that the victim might be this girl he met yesterday.

Royce stood still, and surveyed the water. How could she have gone back out into the water all by herself after the day before? He dropped to his knees, as his tall muscular surfer body became powerless. While he scanned the water, the pain of the news grew.

A police car quickly dashed on the beach, and was followed by several other unidentified vehicles. After getting out of the cars, several policemen spread out and covered the area. One guy rushed over to where he was and started talking to one of the policeman next to him. "I'm Detective Jacobs–bring me up to date on what you have."

"We're doing our best to contain the area, and need more personnel."

"You'll have several more officers here shortly. Who is this?" Jacobs pointed to Royce, who was still on his knees and looking out at the beach.

"He's a surfer that may know who the victim is."

"Stay with him." He placed a passing hand on Royce's shoulder. "We haven't found a body yet and we can all hope that this is a big mistake."

The sound of a fast approaching copter thundered over their head, and started to work back and forth over the water. Additionally, a truck carrying a small inflatable boat rushed down the beach making its way to the water. Two men quickly jumped out, and hauled the boat into the water.

More vehicles arrived with their blue lights flashing. With the tropical storm out in the Atlantic still pounding the beach, efforts to conduct the search were difficult. A new boat arrived and quickly started searching the area. Royce felt so helpless. He knew it would be useless for him to try to get past all of the men in front of him.

As he stood and glanced around at the men dashing around him, he asked the officer next to him, "Where are the boys that saw the attack?" He quickly spotted them before the officer had time to respond, and darted in their direction.

Another police officer was busy asking them questions as Royce reached them. This officer raised his hand in front of Royce as he watched the other officer who was pursuing him. "Sir, you need to stay behind the line."

Royce ignored him, and yelled over at the two boys, "Tell me what you saw."

The smaller of the two boys backed away with fear all over his face, while the larger boy moved closer to him, as if in a protective brotherly mode.

The guard caught up with Royce and grabbed his arm. "Sir, you'll have to cooperate or I'll have no choice but to remove you from the scene."

Instead of complying, Royce maintained his concentration on the two boys.

"We tried to help . . . we did," one boy answered as they both shook with fear.

"Did you see who it was?"

"We didn't see her up close, but she was very nice. She had on a white bikini."

Royce bit his lip. "What color was her hair?"

"She was a blonde . . . a very light blond." The boy of around twelve started to cry as the other boy hugged him.

"Did you see the attack?"

"No. After we saw a shark in the water over there, we looked for the girl to warn her, but we couldn't find her. All we saw was the board in the surf. We went out there, looking for her, but found nothing. That's when I ran back, and got my phone out of my pack and called 911."

"The girl I was surfing with yesterday was blonde, and in great looking shape." He glanced out at the sea and then back at them. "How long had she been surfing?" He leaned over closer to the boys, but the officer kept him a bay by slightly moving in front of him.

"Not long, maybe twenty minutes. We were resting for a minute until we went out into the surf. We're going to be in trouble when we get home. Our mother doesn't know we sneaked out of the house to go surfing. She thinks the waves are too big with the storm out there." The older boy shivered, as he apparently knew that his mother would be told everything.

The officer continued to take notes, obviously appreciating the help in getting the boys to talk. However, he made it clear that he was still in charge, as he maintained a stern eye focused on Royce.

Royce breathed deeply, trying to control his emotions. "Did you see what kind of shark it was?"

"I couldn't tell for sure, but maybe a bull, or a black tip." The older boy smiled slightly, as he proudly demonstrated his knowledge of the local sharks.

The officer holding Royce by a firm lock on his arm asked, "What kind of shark did you see yesterday?"

"I've not sure exactly, but I think it was a bull shark. It bumped me, but never returned. This girl and I were the last ones in the water late yesterday."

"I hope this is all a bad mistake, and she wasn't out in this." He motioned to Royce to indicate that he needed to quit asking the boys questions.

The crowd behind the police line continued to grow as the officer ushered him behind the tape with the rest of the mob of onlookers. As his head fought to regain clarity from the heavy drinking the night before, Royce searched the breaking waves again, trying to figure out what in the hell had happened.

Chapter7

Royce woke early the next morning, forcing his eyes to open, to focus. He knew that the last two nights of little sleep clouded his ability to think clearly. However, if time ever existed that he needed to, it was now. His thoughts bounced between his haunted past, and the present–his newest nightmare. While he had promised himself that he would never let this happen to him again, this happened so quickly that he had no time to contain the situation.

He closed his eyes. Perhaps he did need to sleep a little more and regain his strength. As his mind floated back to when he first arrived back in the states, he knew very few people had knowledge of the special services that he had provided for his country. Nevertheless, he was proud that he had done his part in the war on terrorism.

He remembered how the news of his girlfriend's disappearance had been hidden from him. Yes, the General was right in assuming that it would distract him. To him, the interest of the country had to come first. Sure, he apologized later, but by then she had been kidnapped for over two months, and the trail was too old to follow. Everyone told him that he was too hard on himself. He had looked for her for a year until she was finally discovered murdered in a house of prostitution in Stockholm. He knew he would always blame himself for not looking harder, and for not being smarter. He cried into his pillow.

He eventually rose from his bed, and forced himself to the shower. Life had changed so much since then. As his mind shifted back to the present, he thought back on the last two days, and the details critical in putting together a plan to find the truth. He forced himself to recall every fact. After all, he had been trained for years to handle this kind of situations.

While in the shower, he concentrated on the events of the last two days, forcing himself to remember all of the details he could. Although he had been through this all night, he wanted to make sure that he hadn't missed any important information.

Royce remembered how he had made it out of bed fully refreshed two days ago and ready to hit the beach. The high winds he experienced the night before definitely would have the waves at their best. He would have loved to have some friends join him, but the storm came in so quickly that he had little time to make plans. While he missed surfing, he never considered the option of returning to California. This was the best he could do.

He had arrived at the surf shop before they opened, and eagerly waited in line with the others. The coffee smelled so good coming from the large cups carried by the guys in front of him that he had to ask, "Where did you get that?"

One young guy, looking more like sixteen, or younger smiled. "Hey man, like there's a place around the corner. You've plenty of time before he opens here."

"Thanks. I wanted to make sure they didn't run out of boards this morning."

"I don't think that's going to be a problem today. Not too many want to take on these waves." He pointed out to the ocean, which was faintly visible past the parking lot. With the salty taste of the wind registered in each gust, he strained to see the Atlantic.

"Great. I'll be right back." He remembered whistling as he walked. This stretch of beach would normally be crowded, but the storm had kept many away, at least during the morning. With many of the locals loving the chance to get out of work and party, he remembered how the liquor stores would be almost bare.

The coffee shop had a walk–up window where a small girl with hair cut very short–almost masculine looking–had opened the glass. Any redeeming smile she might have had was ruined–in his opinion–when she revealed the spike driving through her tongue, as she asked, "You're not going out in the surf today, are you?"

He flashed a smile as he pointed around him. "I wouldn't miss this for anything."

She rolled her eyes. "What can I get you? You guys are crazy."

"A very large coffee would be great." Maybe he was crazy, and he was definitely not as young as he used to be. He was definitely not like the other young guys ready to take on the beast. Yes, this was a young man's sport.

The surf shop had opened when he returned. It was nothing fancy, but it had many boards to choose from. A short board providing lots of ability to work the waves was what he needed. After he hadn't found exactly what he wanted, an older guy walked over to him. "What are you looking for?"

"Like everyone, the perfect shark biscuit. Are these all you have?"

"These are all of the ones we have for rent. If you're interested in buying one, I have some more in the back." He pointed to a door at the rear of the shop.

While his excitement had grown in seeing better boards, he knew that he didn't surf enough to warrant the purchase of a board. However, in the back of his mind, owning one would have been great. "Let me see what you have."

The man, somewhere in his fifties, had looked over Royce, trying to ascertain how good of a surfer he was.

Royce knew that his body definitely showed the lean and strong characteristic of a surfer, but he didn't have the suntan, or rough complexion that so many often had.

"Have you done much surfing before?" he had asked.

Royce remembered laughing in response. "I'm from California originally, and I grew up surfing. I guess you could call it the benefits of a misspent youth."

The man's attitude changed quickly as he smiled broadly. "I see. Come with me."

The backroom operated as both a repair shop and a stockroom. On one side Royce remembered seeing stands of new boards, and in particular, one that had a fantastic array of colors on it. He had anticipated how it would reflect the colors of the rainbow in the ocean, and he also had no doubt it had to be expensive. "This is beautiful."

"It's beautiful when under the control of a master, and is definitely a one of a kind."

"I'll agree." He lifted it from the holder and examined it. "I know I shouldn't ask, but how much?"

"I actually had this one specifically made for me, but I've never used it. I work all of the time now."

Royce remembered handing him the board, and pursing his lips. "I fully understand. What do you have that I can demo?"

The owner had smiled, sharing an understanding that only true lovers of the surf could understand. "I want to know how you think this one handles. It's not doing me any damn good gathering dust in here." He rubbed his hand across the board, examining the feel of the finish.

"No, it's too beautiful. I would hate to get it messed up for you."

"I insist. And if you really like it, I'll make you a special deal on it." He moved to the door. "Come on now, I have customers that are waiting on me." Royce had realized that the owner's attention to the needs of his customers was what had kept him in business year after year. It was very smart on his part to tempt him with a special stick like this.

After he had placed the deposit on his card and lumbered for the beach with the small group of guys, they had quickly eyed his board with envy. "Wow! Oh shit man. How did you manage that fucking board?"

Royce couldn't help making use of the first thought that he had come to his mind from a commercial he loved to watch. He had pointed to the ocean and the pounding surf. "For winds and surf like this I think we need to thank God above, for everything else . . . there's master charge." He remembered lifting his hand and rubbing two fingers together in a dramatic flair. In other words, money had its rewards. While the guys understood instantly, he knew that they would soon be begging for a ride.

However, he had ridden one wave after another, and had never slowed down. The board had performed perfectly. While they were joined by a few other guys with their own boards, most of them had come from this one surf shop. And then, there was this one girl–a girl–right in the middle of them. She wasn't that good, but had lots of spunk, he thought, even trying to ride these waves. Normally he would have been impressed, but he had stayed focused on the waves, draining them for all they were worth, and begging for more. He would have time later, he thought, to find out exactly who she was, and her story–there had to be a story. In California and in France he had seen many great girls surfing, but not here in Florida.

***

While the shower helped him to refocus on the here and now, coffee would help even more. He had to get dressed and check out the many questions he had running through his head during the night. The facts didn't add up. Although his first stop would be the surf shop, he reached for the phone to call his office back in Atlanta first.

"Hello, Executive Services. May I help you?" Alicia answered the phone in her charming voice, making her perfect for the job he had hired her for. His clients expected the best, and to be treated professionally.

"Hi, this is Royce. A problem has come up, and I'm not coming back today like I had planned." He waited for a response, hoping that no major problems had arisen while he had been played in the ocean.

"I see. You must be having fun. Don't worry about anything. We have it all covered here."

"I was enjoying everything until yesterday. I met a girl here —"

"I thought so. That's great."

His stilted laugher didn't last long. "It's not what you think. She may have died in the ocean yesterday. They can't find her body. There's even the possibility that she may have been attacked by a shark." He knew he was talking choppy, but thought that he needed to spit it out quickly.

"That's terrible. I didn't see anything about it on the news."

"I'm sure the story will break soon." He scratched his head. It was strange that there was no major news coverage of the story. Of course, they were still attempting to find out more about her, and if a death had actually happened or not. He felt like the authorities perhaps even doubted the story of the death since all of the events had appeared to be so strange.

"I hope you're okay. We all still think you're crazy to be out surfing in all of this."

"I'm fine, really. The surfing is great. Listen, I'll call you later."

"Don't worry about a thing here. We have several

appointments today, but the girls here can handle them."

"Good. Thanks for taking care of things while I'm gone." She was a friend, and he knew that he could count on her if he needed to. He replaced the phone without saying anything else. He had a lot of stops today, and would worry about sleeping later.

Chapter 8

Finding the coast guard office, Royce walked straight to the front desk. "Hello, my name is Royce Cianci. I wanted to find out if you had any news on the shark attack yesterday."

A guy with a full military appearance, complete with the square jaw, and butch haircut, half-smiled at him. "A search is still being conducted, but at this time, we still don't know for sure that a person is missing. I'm glad you came in. I know you gave us a brief statement yesterday. However, we still only have the surfboard that washed up on the beach. It's the only fact that is giving us some suspicions right now."

Royce glanced around the room, trying to access the extent of how hard they were actually trying to search, as he continued, "I wish I had more information to give you. Two days ago I met this girl out surfing. We went for drinks and walked the beach for the rest of the night. I only know her first name is Victoria."

"I still have the board. Perhaps we can find a name when I return it to the surf shop later today," he added, as his face expressed the inquisitiveness of a trained officer.

"I would love to go with you, if I can."

"That might not be a bad idea. I would really like to get a handle on this case. If you will hold on for a minute, I'll see if I can get someone to cover for me." He turned, walked down a hall, and disappeared into an office.

Royce directed his attention to the various maps covering the wall, trying to ascertain exactly where he surfed two day ago. Bureaucracy will never change. The layout of the office and its cold stiff feeling brought back memories he tried to forget.

The Lieutenant soon lumbered his way back in and watched him studying the maps. "Here let me explain this to you." He pointed to a map of the area where Royce had been surfing. "This is where you were surfing. The normal current flows along this channel, except when these storms come in. Since it's hard to predict where a body would be because of that, this is the area that we're concentrating on now."

Royce knew his smile resembled more of a frown as he worried about her body ever being found. "That looks like a lot of area to cover. How long will you continue to search?"

"It depends on many factors. I've been told to keep searching as long as I feel I need to." He walked over to his desk and retrieved a small case. "We might need this. If you want to go over to the rental shop, you might be of some help."

"Thanks. I hope that I can at least find out her last name." Royce knew that they only had a slight amount of information, but hoped for more. "I still haven't turned in my board. It'll take me a few minutes to stop by the condo and get it."

"Not a problem. I'll see you when you get to the shop."
***

Oleg Markov's face needed shaving, and his eyes begged for sleep. The turn of events placed him in a situation he didn't like. He didn't buy the shark attack story; but, then again, he couldn't fully rule it out either. The information she provided was critical in keeping this project going. He smiled briefly, as he acknowledged the brilliance of the plan, so well executed that no one even suspected the Pack's involvement. While he knew the CIA watched his every move, and fed him bad information, they were such fools–they had no clue.

Oleg glanced around the table, with his eyes piercing each person, looking for answers. "We have a problem. I don't think I have to explain the magnitude of this to you, but what I do have to insist on is answers . . . and I do mean like NOW!" He stood and walked around the room.

Oleg turned to an older man playing with his beard. "As far as I know, you were the last one she had contact with. Think about it. Are you sure she had the information?"

This older man quit stroking his beard, but remained solemn. "She has a blog that she posts in. There's one key word she uses in it to signal that she has it. I don't think she made a mistake in her message." He hesitated in thought. "That's all I have to go by."

Oleg walked around his chair. "What about the drop instructions?"

"We made them very simple and clear. And as far as I can determine, she followed the route perfectly."

Oleg hit the table with both fist. "Then where the fuck is it?"

"I wish I knew. If you remember we were ordered out of the area which delayed the pickup. So . . . one of two things happened; she either didn't make the drop, or someone else helped themselves to it." He glanced sideways, admitting the obvious.

Oleg breathed in deeply before moving over to the next man in front of him.

This young man's quick glances betrayed the lack of confidence possessed by others in the room; he had failed at his job in finding the canister. Oleg knew he had to bring in new faces often to keep from being recognized, but wished in this case that a more experienced Russian agent could have been selected. Now, he had to deal with the damages.

"Tell me. You had a very simple job to do, so why . . . why . . . do I not have the flash drive?"

The new agent's face stayed straight, while his voice remained strained. "I stayed on the beach and not that far away. She had walked directly where we had instructed her to. I waited for a long time on the beach, as I was directed to when our cover was blown. It was several hours before the crowd left and I was finally given the okay to retrieve it. It simply was not on the beach. I have been back there several times, and there's nothing there. I saw no one else searching the area. Unless they retrieved it late in the night, which I doubt, she didn't drop it."

Oleg had his doubts, but knew the agent probably was telling the truth. *If so, why did she not make the drop?* He looked around the room. "Either someone blew our cover, or Robert is lying to us."

The older man glanced around the room with inquisitive eyes. "Have we found out anything about the guy she left the beach with?"

"I've no clue. My guess is that she became spooked and picked someone for cover. We all know that the CIA was monitoring this drop also. We've come too far to have this operation screwed up now." He walked around the back of the table with his hand to his chin as he thought of what to do next.

The older man continued, "I still think he may some information we need. They were seen drinking at a wine bar late before leaving together."

"I agree." He pointed to the younger agent. "Find him. See if you can make a friend." He smiled, the wicked indications obviously well understood.

"I'll get right on it."

"Now about Victoria. Her parents have been invited to be our special guest until we get to the bottom of this. We have warned her of the consequences of failing us many times. Her father, Joseph Zayas, has a very profitable business in Moscow, and it's going to be a shame to see him lose it, as well as his wife, Anastasia" He paused. "You know, I've often thought that Anastasia was much too beautiful to be an engineer."

The older gentleman smiled at the thought of having Anastasia working in one of their brothels. "What do you want us to do now?"

"We wait, and we keep our eyes open. This isn't over yet."

Chapter 9

Royce threw his clothes into a suitcase, and cleaned the basics around the condo. He knew a cleaning service would finish it later. He stopped to reminisce about one of the empty wine bottles on the table as he quickly decided to place it in the suitcase. The candle she placed in it from the night before had burned almost all of the way down with the wax firmly fixing it in place. He thought about how it would give a new meaning to the saying, "I'll keep a candle burning for you."

While the morning that he had spent making love with Victoria was blurry, the memories of the night of walking on the beach remained perfectly clear. Why had he not asked more questions? While he had to get back to Atlanta soon, today he would do all he could to find answers.

***

The owner quickly acknowledged Royce as he walked into the surf shop. His smile focusing on the board soon gave away to a serious nod toward the back. Royce didn't say a word as he followed him without glancing around.

The owner glanced over Royce's shoulder one more time before he began. "I heard about the shark attack yesterday and I hoped to see you soon. Many people have been asking about you."

"About me—why?"

"There's something strange about this shark attack. Let's say I've been around the beach for all of my life and know a thing or two. Now I'm not saying it couldn't happen, but the interest in this girl is . . . puzzling."

"Why do you say that?" He glanced behind his back.

"The questions don't have the tone of concerns for Victoria's health, but about her activities the last few days. You know, man, like where she's been, what she had been doing, and most importantly who you are." He glanced at Royce with his brow suddenly furrowed.

"I see. I hate to ask more questions but I do have a few of my own."

He chuckled. "I heard already about your night together. Hey, she was a cutie." The owner quickly caught himself, lowering his head further before he continued, "And, I hope she still is."

Royce bit his lip. "Okay, tell me what you know."

"Not much. She had been in the shop a few times to rent a board and to ask for advice. She just recently started learning, but from what I can tell she was learning fast."

"I surfed with her the day before she disappeared. She had a lot of spunk, and some natural ability. And I think she had the ability to be very good in time."

The shop owner paused, looking temporarily hesitant. "I'm not supposed to do this, but let me give you her address." He moved to a small desk he used to run his business and started flipping through a small box of receipts.

Royce smiled broadly. "Thanks. I was hoping to learn more about her. I don't even know her last name."

The owner smiled. "I like this girl and I hope she didn't die out there. If you need any help while you're here, call me. I have many contacts that might help." He dropped the receipt on top of the desk. "You know it's a damn shame I keep losing these receipts, especially when some noisy-assed people keep asking for them." He winked at Royce as he walked out to the front of the shop with his intentions clear. The police officer must have already come and gone.

"Thanks." Royce appreciated the unique bond between

surfers, and one that transcended the world. Royce's mind flashed back to his days working for the General, the guy who had sent him to France for three years of his life. His special talent as a surfer had attracted their attention and had also changed his life forever.

Royce retrieved the receipt, and glanced at it before slipping it into his pocket. Her last name was Zayas. He thought that he could find the place she lived without too much help. However, he wanted to make one more stop before going to her condo. He had promised the Florida Marine Police he would come by and check in with them this morning. Hopefully, they would have more information.

Royce walked to the front of the store. "By the way, the board is great, but too beautiful for me. Everyone wants to borrow it." He laughed loudly, mainly for anyone standing around. His instincts and his training clicked in, as he knew he was being observed by someone.

The owner laughed back. "I can understand that, but like shit man, tell me how it handled?"

"Like a dream, man, like a dream."

"I thought so. Perhaps when the next storm comes through I can take some time off to surf with you."

"I would love it. Let me give you my number." He reached over, and wrote down his number and name on a small piece of paper. It would be interesting to see who would end up with it. "It would be great for you to let me know how the storms are building here, and keep me up to date on my surfology. I'm about six hours from here, and most of the time I can get away for a quick day of surfing."

"I'll do it. Thanks for your business."

Royce smiled. "You know, I never asked your name."

He smiled. "My name's Miguel Sanchez."

Royce turned toward the door, but stopped. He shook his head—the name registered. "I remember the name. Don't tell me you're the guy that was world champion for several years in the early eighties."

Miguel smiled, showing reflections of his past. "Those were golden years for me, but that was then, and now is now. It's a long story and perhaps next time you're here we can have some drinks where I can tell it to you."

"I would love to hear it." Down deep, Royce knew a tragedy existed that Miguel hid from most of his customers. Yes . . . he would love to hear the story later.

"Take care." Miguel turned to work on his displays. The conversation ended for now, but only until a better time could be arranged.

***

The station of the Florida Marine Police rested quietly off a main street a few blocks away. A woman officer addressed Royce, as he walked in, "Hello, how can I help you?"

He smiled, knowing charm would be very useful in getting some answers. "My name's Royce Cianci. I'm supposed to come by today and check in with you."

"I understand. Your name was mentioned in the staff meeting this morning. Can I get you some coffee?"

"Thanks, but I've already had enough for today." He felt her stalling him.

She returned to her seat behind a large desk. "The officer in charge of the investigation is out right now. We're still trying to ascertain the name of the girl who was out surfing."

"I see. So . . . I assume they still haven't found a body."

"No . . . nothing has surfaced as of yet."

He continued to feel the stall, and knew he wouldn't get any information on this from her. "When will the investigating officer return?"

"Perhaps in about an hour. I can have him call you."

This appeared to be a wasted trip. "I'm sure he has my

number on the report. Have him call me." He had a sudden urge to make it to Victoria's place as soon as he could get to it. He had the feeling that this officer was working her condo, or would be soon.

***

At his Florida command center, Brandon Wiley shifted in his seat as he studied the team of CIA officers assembled in front of him. The operation was going bad, and he needed to contain the situation—now. It would even be better if the operation could be salvaged, since the work and the man-hours would be sacrificed for nothing if it failed. This would be hard for him to explain to the director, and he didn't like the feeling of admitting failure.

Brandon studied Robert's actions to the reports in front of him. Robert's assessment would be critical. After all, Brandon had accepted his recommendation in bring Victoria in as an agent three years ago. Now, however, Brandon had some second thoughts, as he started asking him questions. "Robert, you recruited Victoria, and know her better than anyone. I need your opinion. Did she break? Is she hiding? Or did she really get attacked in the ocean by a shark?"

Robert glanced around at the other four men in the room. "I think it's obvious that she deviated from the assigned plan. Why? I wish I knew. She was heavily monitored, but she knew she would be. She could have seen something we don't know about."

"What's your take on the shark attack?" Brandon asked pointedly in his strictly no-nonsense style.

"It's still being investigated. There's no body, and it does look suspicious."

"I understand. While I think we all know her file very well, I think now will be as good a time as any to reexamine it. Trust me. I'll have a lot of questions put to me very soon, and I don't like being unprepared."

Brandon knew that the entire room recognized what he was talking about. If his head was on the block, they would also have problems.

Robert spoke again, as Brandon suspected. Robert knew more about this operation than anyone, and had personally recruited Victoria. "We had a very special situation present itself to us. Victoria's background is unique. Her father, Joseph Zayas, is a well known businessman who was born in New York and with connections to the Kennedy's. He mainly deals in Russian Vodka and has built a very lucrative business. On one of his many trips to Moscow he met Anastasia, an engineer working for a company that designed distilleries, and fell in love. At that time in history, his attempts to get an American citizenship for his new wife never materialized. He finally agreed to move his office to Moscow, where he became an exporter rather than an importer. Several years later they had a child, our girl Victoria."

"That part, I think we all know well. I also can understand her wanting to visit America. With an American father, she should have had no problems getting a visa to come."

Robert spoke, choosing his words carefully. "You would think so, but because of her mother's connection to the political parties there, she had problems. This apparently caught the attention of certain people in the *New Russian regime*. They not only offered Victoria assistance, but made it impossible for her to say no."

Brandon shifted in his seat. "It wasn't easy to get approval for this mission. After all, we were admitting a known Russian spy into the country."

Robert leaned forward before he added, "The difference is that we knew this was her first and only mission. When I saw her file, I thought it might be possible to recruit her, and have the perfect way to access information that would be impossible by any other method. I went to Russia to study the situation for months, and she really wanted to come to the States to get away from the politics there. If the Russians thought she worked for them, she would also have information that could be extremely useful to us, and until now, it has proved to be so."

"Robert, it was maybe in the beginning. I now know that they knew we were using her to send false information, and they were sending false information to us as well. The problem now is trying to ascertain exactly what was false and what was true. We also know she's connected to an International mafia cartel which is directly supported by many governments. They have an operation in place and are using information she's providing. It would be good to know, however, exactly what they are using the information for. The best we can guess is that it is some kind of money laundering scheme involving the housing industry. Well we know that is not true, they really want access to seed money we se to obtain assets."

Robert looked around the room. "We all know they would love to have this information on CIA seed money. But that could also expose many of our most coveted operations."

Brandon stared back. "As such, we all know that the information she sends is wild ghost chases. We even know they're following up on them because of feedback from the field."

A knock at the door announced one more member to the team. Charlotte walked to her spot as she held her head high, reflecting an elegant charm. "Guys, I have a bomb shell for you. In fact, I have two of them."

The men leaned forward with their attention expressed in solemn faces. Brandon loved the way Charlotte worked. She was always in control, and always precise in her research.

Charlotte opened the file she carried with her and handed one to each person there. "This is our mysterious guy. His name is Royce Cianci. He's one of our finest. In fact, his file is in such deep cover, I think we're very lucky to have any part of it. He had worked some kind of special operation in France after 911. He left two years ago to return to civilian work. It appears that his girlfriend was abducted in retribution to his activities there, and he wasn't told about the abduction until after his mission was completed. By then it was too late to rescue her. He blamed us for this and left."

Brandon appreciated the straight forth nature of Charlotte for telling the basics and not wasting time. "So . . . what's our mysterious man doing here?"

Charlotte smiled with her perfect teeth radiating a beautiful charm she maintained constantly. "Surfing–he has been a surfer all of his life. As you might guess, his cover was that of a surfer bum, and one that you would never guess to be a special operative."

Brandon quickly acknowledged that it was a great cover. "But why here?"

"The storm brings in the waves. He now lives in Atlanta, where he's trying to start over with his life, and he apparently made a quick trip here to catch some waves. As best I can guess, it was a chance meeting, and I think they both knew nothing about the other's history."

Brandon added a note to the flyer. "Are we sure he's out of the agency?"

"I think so, but with his background it's impossible to know for sure right now. I'll have an answer for you on it soon since it's one of those questions that needs to go through channels. His file is heavily guarded, and in fact, I'm still not sure exactly who he worked for."

Brandon looked over to the first guy on his left. "I think

you need to make contact with this guy—Royce—and see what you can find out."

"I'll get right on it."

Charlotte glanced around the room, regaining control. "Now . . . for the news from the Florida Marine Police that I have just received regarding Victoria. They've found part of her bathing suit. It matches the description of what she was wearing. They found her top with many tears, and with signs of some blood and a few hairs. They're doing a test now to make a match. It appears that she did in fact get attacked by a shark."

"Damn." Brandon hit the top of the desk just enough to show his disappointment. "That does complicate things." He lowered his head, thinking. "I need to have the results as fast as you can get them for me. The news needs to be contained as much as possible on this. I think we also need to send someone to see her parents and give them the news."

As Brandon finished, Charlotte continued. "We also have to find out what happened to the flash drive she carried in the canister. We have no idea if the Russians have it or not."

Brandon motioned to an older man at the table. "We need to go to her apartment and search it immediately. I want it totally cleared before the locals get there, and this operation shut down and erased."

The guy stood. "I'll take care of it now." He left the room.

Robert looked round the room. "If it's okay, I'd like to go to Russia to tell her father what happened. I think I owe it to him. I know the information I give him will be monitored, so I'll do it in a proper manner. I also want to hear what her father knows."

Brandon checked his notes. It might be good to make sure this is contained. "I don't think there's anything else you can do here now. Make plans on leaving as quickly as you can, but call me as soon as you find out anything. I know you have other contacts there. I want to know what they think of this *accident*."

Brandon looked over at Charlotte again. "What's Royce doing in Atlanta?"

She smiled again before batting her eyes softly. "Our mysterious man is now running a dating service for executives. It appears he has found a use for his skills in doing background searches. His ability to flush out gold diggers and other deceptive would-be partners appears to be in large demand."

Brandon whistled softly. "With this kind of skill and knowing his background, he might be a problem. He could easily blow the cover off of this case."

"It is a threat. What do you suggest?"

"A small change in plans." Brandon tried to control a small laugh. "Charlotte, I think you need to take some time to smell the roses."

Her smile faded, as questions reflected on her face. "I'm sorry."

"Yes, it'll be interesting to see who Royce matches you with." His waited, as he studied Charlotte's reaction.

Her smile soon returned, as she understood her assignment.

Brandon turned to the first guy who was next to him. "I hope you don't mind the extra help, but I still want you to find our guy here and see what he knows, or is willing to tell you."

Brandon looked around the room. "As I said, we need to contain this mess and move on."

***

Royce glanced at the address hanging above Victoria's condo building, as his instincts alerting him to several unusual activities in the parking lot. He made his way up the stairs to the third floor, which was also the top floor. There, he saw a man standing in the hallway. The suit gave away the man's background instantly; but, then again, a disappearance was being investigated.

The man quickly acknowledged Royce, and held out his hand. "I'm with the CIA, and my name is agent Brewer. I thought you would show up here soon."

Royce felt shocked, but knew that he should have known this day would come. "The CIA! What are you doing here?"

"Let us go into the room for a minute, and I'll explain things to you."

Agent Brewer opened the door to Victoria's condo, where an older man was examining the contents.

He also reached out his hand. "Hello, I'm agent Mosley."

As the door shut behind them, Royce waited on the agents to talk first, but allowed his eyes to dart around, registering every detail he could. He knew this might be his only chance to do so.

Brewer smiled softly. "I have some bad news for you. I know you just met this girl–Victoria. But we have just received information confirming the fact that she was killed in the shark attack."

Royce felt like his heart had been hit with a large hammer, as his head began to feel a spinning sensation. He forced himself to maintain control and not allow the officers to suspect his weakness. "Are you sure?"

"I'm afraid there's little doubt."

Royce hung his head, concentrating on the previous day. "I only knew her for one day, but she seemed so special. Why are you investigating this?"

"I'm sure you understand there's much I can't tell you. Since I know your background, I'm sure you understand that."

Royce didn't admit anything, as he remained quiet,

waiting for answers.

"What I'm going to tell you is classified information and you'll not be able to tell anyone. Do you understand?" As Royce stared directly into the agent's eyes, registering his understanding without saying a word, the agent continued. "Victoria worked for us."

Royce nodded his understanding again, but yearned for answers that he knew he would never receive right now. He had resources that he could call on later. "I didn't know that."

"We believe you. Since I understand you became very close with Victoria the other day, it's important that I ask you a few questions. I hope you understand."

What was going on? What was Victoria doing? He nodded in agreement again.

"Victoria was in the middle of an operation, where she was also working for the Russians. We knew that . . . and we used it to our advantage. I can't give you much more than that."

"I understand." He paused to look away for a second. "I'm a private citizen now and really don't wish to know any more."

"That's very smart, but she had a small canister with her at the time of her disappearance, and we need to know if you ever saw a small tube she carried with her."

Royce concentrated on the events of the night. "I don't remember anything suspicious, but I had no reason to suspect anything either."

"Yes, I can understand, but I know you're trained in this, so let me ask you straight out. Is there anything you remember that raised doubts about her that you think we should know?"

"Nothing . . . I can think of nothing." Yes he had questions, but he knew better than to ask them here. He also knew that if he remained quiet and waited, he might receive a little more information from these agents. He lowered his head.

Agent Mosley placed a hand on his shoulder. "I'm so sorry, and I know this is a shock to you. Here. I want you to take my card and call me if you think of anything you think we should know."

Royce studied his card before placing it in his pocket. Okay, he had many strong desires to ask questions, but this wasn't the time, or the place.

Chapter 10

"Royce, your appointment is here," Alicia announced over the intercom connected to his desk phone at his office in Atlanta. He looked forward to this meeting with a prospect who had a great sounding voice and most importantly, a great personality. While it has been several weeks since the surfing trip to Florida, the memories of it had constantly haunted him. He glanced around his office, making sure all was in order. Since he interviewed most of the day, he kept it presentable, so that even on a moment's notice like this he could hide all of the files on his desk in seconds.

He walked to his door and opened it. "Good morning."

Charlotte smiled and immediately flashed an intoxicating personality. "Hi." She raised her hand in a small graceful movement of uniqueness that separated her from so many other run of the mill women that came to see him.

"Hello. I'm glad you came." He examined her from top to bottom in less than a second while he forced himself not to stare. She had an elegant style and a certain refinement that yelled money and lots of it. He didn't know all of the name brands of designer outfits, but knew quality when he saw it. He would bet that her extremely elegant dress or the jewelry didn't come off the rack.

"I'm glad also. Since I moved her three months ago I still haven't met anyone special. Not that I'm really looking, but I need someone to go with me on various functions, and I heard you offered a special service here. You've been highly recommended."

"Really. Who recommended me?"

"Several girls at the Atlanta Country Club who invited me to play tennis the other day told me to give you a call." The grace in her movements quickly added to her impressive style. He had worked with her type before. She represented his favorite kind of client–rich and beautiful, but on the inside very lonely, a combination he could relate to very well.

He walked over to his desk and reached behind a chair for her, which she moved into gracefully. He stared at her profile as he walked around to his chair. This was one of those times that he wished he could avoid his rule of dating his own clients. Her dress rose several inches above her knees, revealing firm, slender legs that were tanned to a beautiful bronze color. He still has his eyes on them as he found his seat. Oh no . . . he caught himself staring again–he had to watch it. "Be sure to tell them thank you for me. I know the *Club* well."

"I will. I've never been to a place like this. Tell me what I can expect." She smiled while she never removed the focus of her deep, warm-brown eyes off of his.

"If I had to sum it up in a few words, it would be that I work as a life coach, and help you to make good decisions on people that you invest your time in, and perhaps even your heart one day. My job is to provide you with objective and reliable information on people the closest to you." He studied her face, and features that resembled an actress he loved to see in the movies–Sandra Bullock. Perhaps it was the lips or checks, but definitely the eyes.

"It sounds like you have an interesting job." He watched her eyes glancing around the room, and examining it in detail. For a man's office, he had to admit, it carried a different style, reflecting one of refinement, and an interest in culture. Several paintings of abstracts highlighting wines drew her attention to one wall on the left side of the room. He also knew their massive size made a bold statement. The modern design of the two side chairs balanced the aesthetics, and was custom designed for the spot. Royce knew he had to impress his clients with a style that most men don't care for. The money he had spent with an interior decorator had paid for itself many times over.

Royce reached over the top of his desk to obtain the form she had filled out in the waiting room. "Thanks. Give me a minute to review this."

She smiled, waiting on him to read. He knew before even reading it that she would be easy to work with, and that many of his clients would love to meet her. Now trying to make her happy may be a different story. The information he read confirmed what he had expected. Her inherited money had been well managed. She invested in real estate, and apparently never worked for anyone. She received her education at New York City University, which explained her accent. Anyway, he would still do a background check on her. This rule, he knew he would never break, even if it was tempting to do so.

He smiled at her when he finished. "I don't think we'll have any problems working with you. As you probably know, I do background checks on every client. I also do background checks on anyone you meet and want to know the truth on. Just in case you lose your heart while looking around, it's important not to lose your head as well."

"I understand, and that's the main reason I wanted to come by here. I've heard too many stories in my lifetime of girls being taken advantage of. I use to have my father to look after me, but he died a couple of years ago."

"I'm sorry to hear that." Royce could understand how her father did probably protect her when he was alive, and how she now needed that reassurance of someone else looking over her.

"I was wondering if you have any single mingle parties. I assume you would be at them to monitor things."

"Yes, it's a large part of my job. I'll make sure you're invited."

"If I'm going to place all of my trust in you, I need to get to know you better." She twisted slowly in her chair. With her movements artistically perfect, he knew she must have had some training in ballet.

He laughed, as their eyes focused tightly in on each other. "Yes, I'll . . . by the very nature of the relationship, will know more about you than anyone. It's not a position I take lightly. We'll have some great victories, and may even cry over some disappointments, but that's the way life is."

"Okay, so . . . tell me . . . why do so many people trust you?"

"A reputation is something you build slowly, and I never take it lightly." He maintained a smooth, gentle voice, and forced himself to ignore the urge to dig too deep into her motives for coming to him.

"Can I ask you how you started this business, and a little bit about your history?"

"Sure. I needed a job when I moved to Atlanta, and had originally worked with a travel agency. I soon moved into group bookings, and these quickly led to specializing in singles outings on cruises, as well as foreign trips. To provide security for the group, I started offering background checks for these clients, and it became a very popular service. I don't think any woman likes to make a trip and have it ruined by one jerk guy on the trip." He glanced at Charlotte to see if she understood what his job was there.

"I see. So how did you learn to do background checks?

"It's a skill I learned to do on my own." He glanced at her, hoping that would be all of the answer she needed answered. "I'm not a private detective, and if I uncover anything important to you, I'll direct you to hire your own, that is, if you want to pursue it."

"Thanks. I noticed you have many girls here working for you. Business must be good."

Royce glanced at the door. Yes, he had five girls working for him. He was the only guy on his team, a term he loved to use in describing his company. "Thanks. It has been doing well, and you know the saying *much better than I deserve.*"

Charlotte laughed, but kept dart her attention around the room. "I'm looking forward to this very much."

"I'm glad to hear it." Good, it appeared that would be the end to the questions. "I think the best advice is to get you to one of our social events, and let you meet some of the people in our group. We have the next one this Friday night. I hope you can make it."

"I should be able to. The problem is the amount of traveling I do. I hope it's not a problem."

"Since it's all about your life, just let me know what I can do to help you in this adventure we're starting on."

She turned her head to one side while remaining quiet for a minute. "Let me ask you one more question . . . if I may?"

"Sure. What else do you want to know?"

"What about you? You appear to be very interesting, and fun to be around. Do you attend the social outings?"

"Yes, I do most of them. It makes most of my clients feel comfortable if they know someone is there to rescue them if they get trapped by someone they don't like."

"Does that happen often?"

"No, but it's a good feeling when you have to enter a strange room with perfect strangers for the first time."

"I can understand that. What about you? Do you have a girl friend . . . married? What is your story in all of this?"

This was a question he had been asked many times

before. "I started one rule when I first started this company that a wise man who owned the travel agency I was working for told me. He told me *never, never, never* . . . get involved with clients on a personal bases. I've always followed that advice."

Her smile increased, as the appreciation of that kind of commitment registered on her face. "That must be very hard to do. What about outside of work. Are you the type of guy who has a girl in every port?"

He returned her laugh, but let it die quickly. "It would nice to have the time, but I work night and day in this business. I have no personal life." He glanced into her eyes again. "Perhaps I need my own services, what do you think?"

"I somehow doubt that, but perhaps you do need to listen to your advice sometimes."

She hit a nerve, since he had thought about it many times lately. He forced himself to remain in control. "You may be right."

"I hate to pry, but tell me . . . what do eligible bachelors, like you, do on their free time? Maybe I'm looking in all of the wrong places."

"I have no free time . . . honest."

"Okay . . . if you did have free time, what would you do?"

He thought for a minute, while trying to decide if he should confide in her. While he knew it was best to not give away too many secrets, she had one of those hard to resistance charms. "I love to surf, but since I live in Atlanta, I don't get to do it often."

"I thought there would be a story somewhere if I dug hard enough." She nodded with a sympathetic smile on her face as she continued. "When was the last time you went surfing?"

His mind drifted back to Jacksonville and Victoria. While over the last two week since his trip a lot of his spare time had been devoted to finding out answers, he had very little to show for all of his efforts. "Not too long ago."

"I see. So you really don't work . . . all of the time."

"That was a rare exception. Whenever a tropical storm in the Atlantic produces some nice waves, you have to be prepared for it when it happens. You usually have a very short window of opportunity." He glanced at Charlotte again, while studying her features.

After blinking his eyes to clear his mind, he had to concentrate for a minute—he recognized her face. Charlotte, this woman in front of him now, was at the wine bar in Jacksonville the night he met Victoria. He quickly forced himself to conceal his sudden revelation, and not to show emotions or any surprise give-away looks.

"That sounds exciting. Maybe one day you can teach me how to surf."

"Perhaps we can get a group together one day to do that." He reached over to glance at her data on the form. He would definitely be doing a background check on her, but he knew what he would find. "Have you ever tried surfing before?"

"No, but I think it would be exciting to learn." Royce studied her interest through a new sense of urgency. Why was she there in Jacksonville, and more importantly, why was she in his office now? He remembered the CIA being in Florida to monitor some operation Victoria was involved with. While he still had no information on Victoria, or her operation, he knew not to try to dig too deep too quickly.

"It might be interesting in teaching you. We'll have to talk about it later." He knew not to say any more to her than he had to until he had to check out who she was first. "I'll call you soon, and we can discuss it."

"That sounds good . . . and I look forward to the social on

Friday night." She stood and reached out her hand. Royce accepted it, and studied it for any signs he could recognize.

"Have you ever been to Florida?" He quickly asked as he concentrated on her answer, and in particular at the pupils in her eyes.

"Yes, but it has been a long time ago." Her eyes told a different story–the pupils dilated.

Royce forced himself not to stare. She was here seeking answers, and doing a great job in building trust, while pumping him for information. What did he know that they wanted? "That's too bad; the weather in Florida is great." He stood quickly. "I'll get busy, and I hope to make you a very satisfied customer. It will be great to see how you like the group on Friday night. Is this the best number to reach you at?" He pointed to the cell phone number on the data sheet.

"Yes, that's my cell phone. Like I said, I travel a lot, and I always have it with me." Royce knew that it also allowed her to work on other cases, and fly back to Atlanta when she was needed.

"Very good. I'll see you on Friday night then." He handed her a brochure with the information concerning the outing.

She smiled as she stood. "I'm looking forward to it."

Chapter 11

While reflecting on the last several months, Royce closed the file he had been using to accumulate the information on Victoria, and tossed it to the end of the table where he ate most of his home meals. The more he searched, the more he ran into dead ends. He realized that she had a special gift that most girls don't have. She was much like the girlfriend he had back in California. The memories of the time with her, and the events around her disappearance haunted him almost every night. Now, he had a new nightmare to add to his others.

The clock ticked away, as another night of searching on the internet revealed nothing new. Theo was one of his friends that he had stayed in contact with from his government days. He now worked in homeland security, and would be home soon. Royce knew that when he walked away from the family, his government family, and left the reservation of their sanctuary, he would always be on his own. Until now, that was exactly what he wanted.

He retrieved the phone while whispering a small prayer. Theo answered on the first ring. "Royce, I'm glad you called. I'm sorry it has taken so long, but the file didn't get released until they were sure she had died in the shark attack."

"I appreciate everything you're trying to do for me. What did you find out?"

"Not a lot, but some. Her name was Victoria Zayas." He paused for a long moment. "This is the part that is under wraps. I hate to tell you buddy, but it appears that she operated as a double agent, working both sides of the table. She lived in Moscow and had wanted to move to America for a long time. The Russians made it possible for her, but wanted her to also do some spy work. While her father is American, and it should have been easy for her to move, the American government blocked her attempts for years until they saw a way they could benefit from it. While the exact reason for Victoria's failed visas was not fully detailed, I think it might be due to her training as a computer expert. She has the ability to break into almost any computer."

"I understand, and I've already concluded that much from the CIA officer I talked to in Florida."

"But there's more, since we knew she would be sending information back to them, we offered her a second chance by working for the CIA. Over time, it appears that neither side fully trusted her. In my opinion, I think we have a girl trapped by both sides with no way out."

"My thoughts as well. However, I knew her for only a few hours. Why are they still investigating this case if they think she's dead?"

"They don't know if she made the last info drop or not. They're also considering the fact that she may have given additional data to them that we don't know about."

"I can understand their frustrations."

"I did find the name of the company she worked for. It's located in Jacksonville, Florida. It's called The International Cyber Consulting Group. Her boss in Jacksonville was a Warren Hornbuckle. The company provides internet security for a large number of international companies. Victoria is a C E H—a Certified Ethical Hacker."

Royce laughed. "How in the hell do you use the words ethical and hacker in the same certification?"

"People pay them to see if they can break into their computers. If they can, they then charge a larger fee to plug the breaks in security.”

"So, she really is a computer expert."

"Yes and an extremely good one. It's amazing that the agency didn't use her skill somewhere else. Perhaps in time they would have."

"What can you tell me about her background in Russia?

"Her father's a very prominent Russian businessman now. He was born in New York, but relocated to Russia when he met Victoria's mother. Because of her mother's connection to politicians there, and Victoria's computer skills, she was never, like I said, allowed to visit the States. Victoria has built a very high reputation in the computer industry. Three years ago, she managed to get special permission to come to work for Warren Hornbuckle."

"Thanks . . . that's much more than I thought I would get. If you hear anything else, please let me know. I owe you one, Theo."

"I'm not sure if I'll see anything else since I would think this file will be buried or destroyed very soon."

"I think I'm going back to Florida to talk to her boss. Let me know if you can get an address of where she lived in Moscow. There's still so much that doesn't add up."

"I understand your concerns, but remember this may be much bigger than you need to get involved with, and this isn't your battle. Royce, this . . . this isn't Lynn. There's nothing you can do to bring her back. I hate to see you get hurt again."

"I understand your concerns. Call me when you get it."
***

"Brandon, this is Charlotte. I received a call a few minutes ago from the team running the wire taps on Royce's phone. He still has a few contacts from the past, and he has obtained some information on Victoria. It appears that he'll soon be in Florida, talking to Victoria's boss. What do you want me to do?"

"Nothing. I think this is a dead case now, and it sounds like Royce has no knowledge of what she was directly involved with. Are you sure he doesn't have the canister?"

"I'm fairly sure he doesn't have it. I broke into his apartment and I've been through it with a fine-tooth comb. I didn't see it anywhere."

"Her boss knows nothing of our connection, and I'm sure Royce knows not to leak anything he has found out to him. However, if you think we need to contact him first . . . do what you think best. I'll leave this in your hands, but be sure to keep me updated."

"I will."

Chapter 12

"Hello," Royce yelled, as he knocked on the window of the small coffee shop behind the surf shop in Jacksonville, Florida.

After startling the girl behind the counter, she opened the glass window and smiled, as she apparently recognized him from before. "What can I get for you?"

Again, he forced himself to ignore the spike in her tongue. "A very large coffee would be great."

"You got it." She turned to prepare him a cup. Royce knew that this was the type of place that many locals would use to get their fix early in the morning, and it was a good sign that she recognized him from the one time he had purchased coffee before.

He showed her a photo of Victoria, the one that his friend Theo had provided him with. "Have you ever seen this girl before?"

As she leaned forward to examine it, her smile and quick glances back at Royce signaled that she had. "Yes, I recognize her. She's the girl that was attacked by the shark. Her picture has been in the paper here several times. She also came by several times to get coffee."

"I see. I heard they never found her body."

"No. It never washed up, and it has many people here worrying about it showing up one day, and, you know, scaring the hell out of some kid or tourist."

"You said she came by here for coffee. Did she ever tell you anything about herself?"

"Nothing really. She was always by herself, but often

carried a small bag. You know, one of those that hold a computer inside."

Royce reached for the cup. "Thanks. I really can use some coffee this morning."

"You're welcome. A lot of people want to hush this incident, and I can understand that since it's not one of those events that's good for business. I would think there would be much more coverage on the news since I would love to know more about who she was. Some of the people here are calling her a mystery girl. Why are you asking about her?"

"I met her the last time I was here. It was the day before she disappeared. I thought she was a very nice girl."

"I see. I wish I could tell you more."

Royce walked around the corner toward the surf shop where he found the front door standing open.

Miguel raised his head, as a smile crossed his face. "How are you?"

Royce returned the smile. "Very sleepy." He raised the coffee and patted Miguel on the shoulder with his free hand.

Miguel pointed toward the Atlantic. "There's nothing out there. What brings you here?" He walked around the edge of the counter.

"Questions . . . lots of questions. Have you heard of any new developments in Victoria's disappearance?"

"There's really nothing in the news any more about it, and the sooner people forget about shark attacks, the better it will be for business. However, I think this case is very funny. It's as if this girl had no personal life, no family. You would think the news stations would love a story like this." He lowered his head, and whispered. "I also had a break in after you left."

"A break in! Where? Here?"

"Yes. I almost caught the bastard in the act. I don't think they were trying to steal anything, but they were definitely looking for something. They even went through my cash register and left the money." He turned to where Royce could see the bandage on his knee.

"Wow, man. You got hurt?"

"Yeah, and if I had been a little younger, and didn't have this bum knee, I would have nailed the fucker to the front door."

"So you saw who it was in here?"

"Yes I saw him, but never received a great look at him.

"Did they ever catch him?" He looked around the shop accessing any further damage from the break in.

"No, and I don't think they looked too hard, especially since nothing was missing." Miguel grinned. "I did get one blow to the bastards head however. I know it hurt him, and I hope he remembers it for a long time. What's interesting is that when he yelled out, it wasn't in English."

"What do you mean?" Royce focused on Miguel, while waiting for an answer.

"I think it was German, Polish or maybe even Russian. I don't know exactly. But, I'm sure it was cussing all the same."

Royce resisted the urge to confirm that it must be Russian. "I'm glad to hear that you can still handle yourself."

"How long are you going to be down here?"

Royce looked at him and laughed. "I don't think too long. I know I just met this girl, but I can't get her out of my head."

"I know the feeling, my friend. I lost a lady friend before, and it changed my life forever. I had to get away from everything, and everyone that knew her. They kept bringing back memories of her." He hung his head. Royce knew exactly what he was going through. It was the same reason that he never returned to California.

"On my next trip down, maybe we can have time for that beer you promised me."

Miguel's face lifted, and his eyes sparkled with renewed vigor. "I think that would be great. Let me know when. By the way, I'm still holding on to that board for you."

"Thanks. Who knows, you might have a sale soon. I'll call you next time before I come." Royce walked out of the shop, knowing that he would be back one day soon.

***

The International Cyber Consulting Group's name, written in bold letters on the side of a ten story building, indicated that the size of the company was much larger than Royce had expected. Suddenly concerned that he might not be able to get in to see Victoria's boss, he now wished he had called to make an appointment.

After passing through the massive glass door leading into a marbled-floored atrium with a check-in station guarding further access, he felt impressed with their attention to security. Being a company that promoted security, however, he should have expected as much. He had nothing on him to hide, so he proceeded through the checkpoint. On the other side, a security guard greeted him with a stout grin. "Can I have your name, please?"

"Yes, my name's Royce Cianci. I was hoping to see Warren Hornbuckle." He maintained a firm grin, mimicking the guard, but concentrated on his eyes.

"Do you have an appointment with him today?"

"No, but I know one of his former employees, and I need to ask him some questions. It'll only take a few minutes."

He saw the guard look over his pad. "You need to give him a call and make an appointment."

"I see. I have his number. Give me one second." He pulled out the number he brought with him and started to call, as the guard silently studied his actions.

The call was answered by the main switchboard. "Hello. My name's Royce Cianci. I need to talk to Warren Hornbuckle."

His line switched to different extension. "This is Holly, Mr. Hornsbuckle's secretary, can I help you?"

"Yes, I met one of Mr. Hornsbuckle's employees a while back, and wanted to see if I could ask him a few question." It looked like he was going to get shafted, but he would find a way to talk to him one way or another.

"Maybe I can help you. However, we don't give out much information on our employees here. I hope you understand. Can I ask which employee?"

"I understand. I was a friend of Victoria Zayas." Yes, a very short time friend, but still the truth.

"Hold on for one minute." He heard her click the phone to mute, as elevator music started to play.

A weak sounding man's voice answered, "Hello, this is Warren. How are you?"

"I'm fine, and I hate to disturb you, but I learned a few days ago that you were Victoria's boss. I'm only going to be in town today, and I was hoping to have a few minutes of your time."

"How do you know Victoria?"

"We surfed together and went out one night. It was the night before she disappeared."

Royce heard a grunt, then a small snicker. "So you're the one I heard about. Yes, I would love to talk to you. How long will it take you to come by to see me?"

Royce laughed. "I'm actually in your lobby talking to one of your guards now."

"I see. Give me a minute to clear it for you, and I'll come down and get you."

"Thanks." Royce clicked the phone shut and smiled at the guard. "He's going to clear me now."

True to his word, Warren appeared behind the guards a few minutes later, and signed a pad the officer handed him. "Right this way, Mr. Cianci." He led the way to the elevator.

On the elevator Warren maintained a solemn face as his black strands of hair stuck together in an oily fashion. With his large glasses hanging by a cord around his neck and a pocket full of pencils, he stereotyped the role of the perfect computer nerd that probably had no life outside the office. Royce had worked with this type many times in the past. They were very smart in their profession, but without a clue on how to handle a social or personal life.

They left the elevator and walked to Warren's office without saying a word. Warren's office decorations looked expensive, but not well coordinated. He had computer parts scattered everywhere and three monitors on his desk. Various charts and graphs were taped to the wall behind his desk. Apparently he never had to meet clients in his office, and it was a far cry from Royce's own office where he had to entertain almost all day.

Warren waited for Royce to enter before he closed the door. "I'm glad you decided to come by and see me. I've heard she'd made a friend the day before the attack."

"I spent some time with her surfing a little, and we enjoyed some wine afterwards. I didn't have much time to really get to know her, and I wished I had. She appeared to be a great girl." Royce centered in on Warren's eyes, which were a light gray that didn't appear to match the rest of his appearance.

"We really liked her here. She was extremely brilliant at what she did, and will be impossible to replace."

"She told me she was a computer girl, but didn't give much more detail than that. I found out a few days ago where she worked." Royce glanced around the office. "It seems like you have a very large company here."

"Yes, we do work for companies all over the world." He pointed to a world map on the side wall.

"What exactly do you do, if you don't mind me asking?"

"I can't tell you a lot about the company except that we provide security to a number of large international companies. We try to keep the world safe." Warren faked a smile, but his eyes remained stable, focusing on him.

"I heard she was a Certified Ethical Hacker, and I'm not sure exactly what that is."

Warren smiled. "She had a large number of certifications. We encourage it, and pay for the training and certification test. It can be very expensive, but it increases the rates that we can charge for our employees."

"I can understand that. She appeared tense the night we walked the beach. She must have had an interesting project she was working on." He placed the object of his visit out there to see if he could get a nibble, and waited on Warren to respond.

"She always had interesting projects in the works. Being from Russia, she proved herself to be very useful in helping us. The new Russians, the mafia, and even various governments are extremely well adapted in the internet. It made her services very valuable."

"I can understand that. If you don't mind me asking, how did she manage to move from Russia to here to work?"

"We had to pull many strings. In fact, the American government here was instrumental in helping us find her. We have become highly attached to her over the last three years. She could be found here working night and day, and she hardly ever left the building for long."

"She did tell me she worked all of the time. What do you know about her parents in Russia?"

"Almost nothing, since she didn't talk about them much." He leaned forward and glanced around, before asking Royce a question in almost a whisper. "You were the last one to see her alive, and I know you spent time with her. Did she tell you anything about her work?" Warren's pupils dilated, reflecting his heightened interest in the conversation.

"Only that she was a computer girl. I know you have highly sensitive data you're trusted with, but I sure would like to know anything you could tell me about what she was working on."

Warren smiled out of the corner of his mouth. "Yes it is. I'm sorry. I probably have told you much more than I should have. While she'll be missed very much, I'm very glad she did find a friend, even if it was for one day. She always appeared very lonely when she ever had to leave the office."

"You know . . . it's very interesting that her body has never been found. I don't guess there's any way to determine if she left on her own for a while, and that maybe she didn't die in an attack, is there?"

"I had the same thoughts at first. Since she was a Russian citizen over here on a work visa, I have talked to the CIA many times, and they feel like she died in the attack. In fact, they came by here a few weeks ago to tell me the case was officially closed now." He shifted his eyes back at Royce. "Off of the record, so to speak, what do you think?"

"I really don't know. She seemed happy, and a lot of fun the day we had together. It's hard for me to believe that she died in a shark attack, but I guess I keep hoping for a better answer. I think the CIA would have a much better chance at finding the truth than me, though."

Warren leaned back in his chair. "I don't think I ever asked what you do for a living."

Royce laughed before glancing around. "Nothing like what you do here. However, I have some clients who take what I do very serious."

He had his attention with the small play of drama, as he

watched Warren lean forward. "What is it?"

Royce continued to plaster his best poker face on his face. "I run an executive dating service."

Warren moved back in his seat, while flashing a large grin. "You're kidding me–right?"

"I guess everyone has to do something." He extended his hands, palms up as if to stress the point that he was telling the truth. "It can be very interesting work."

"Perhaps I might need your services here since all I ever do is work. Are you pretty good about getting guys like me dates?"

Royce looked him over again. Warren definitely had to work on his hair, and the clothes could use a lot of work, but he thought this guy may have a good sense of humor underneath it all. He would have to watch him at some social gathering to see how he reacted in a group of people who were not working for him. "I think that you shouldn't have any problems at all, but my operations are a long way from here."

Warren grinned like a rat making it off with the cheese. "I can see why Victoria liked you. You're very different from the guys around here."

"Thanks." After looking around, Royce offered a small prayer of thankfulness under his breath. He knew that he couldn't work in such an environment. His thoughts returned to Victoria. She had such a great personality, in spite of working in such a place where they only thought about work all of the time. "Perhaps we could meet after work today and I could give you some pointers. I'm sure they have some great bars around here."

"Are you serious? I'd love it!" He glanced around, acting suspicious. "I really need to keep it quiet. Do you understand?"

"Yes, confidentially is our specialty." In fact, Royce

understood perfectly well how Warren probably hated being rejected, a history he assumed Warren had to deal with many times before. While sometimes it didn't make sense, it would give him a chance to order a few drinks and maybe get some more information out of him. It would be worth the free lesson on how to be social. "I have a little time before I have to head back tonight. When can you leave?"

"I can leave at five, if that's okay."

"Good. I'll be back then, and I'll wait for you outside. Thanks for the information." Royce stood and left his office. A quick glance over his shoulder revealed the same possum smile. "Oh boy," he thought.

***

A stewardess walking down the aisle smiled at each passenger along the way. Her eyes focused when she saw Royce. "Is there anything else I can get you, sir?"

"I don't suppose you have a map of Moscow that I can study before we land there, do you?"

"I'm not sure, but I'll check for you." She turned and walked back toward the front of the plane.

Royce reviewed the information he had received from Warren the night they went out in Jacksonville. While he had turned this information over and over in his head many times before, he had to assume that Warren really had no idea of what Victoria was actually doing. If he did, he was much better at lying than he guessed. His head was hurting, and sleeping on the plane to Moscow wasn't easy. The little Russian he knew would help, but he had arranged for a translator to meet him at the airport.

A girl next to him leaned forward to catch his attention. "Is this your first time to Moscow?"

Royce thought about the question, as he kept his face level before turning to face her and lie. "Yes, I've never been there before. I hope it's not too hard to find my way around." His special operation had required him to go to Moscow several times, but they were always part of a special mission and he had always used assumed names. He was thankful for the crash courses in learning Russian, but wish he had been trained better now.

"It can be very difficult. Is this trip to Moscow for business, or pleasure?"

"I'm going to Moscow to see some friends of a friend. I have some very bad news to deliver to them."

"What is that?"

"Our mutual friend recently died, and I think that they may have never received word of it. I also have never met her parents, and I would like to if I can."

"This must be a very difficult trip for you then. I'm sorry to intrude." She turned to look straight ahead, which, in turn, offered Royce a chance to glance over at her. She had very beautiful features, including high cheek bones with glowing skin tones, and the kind of girl Russia was famous for. She appeared to be traveling by herself.

Royce leaned forward to see her face better. While he knew that he was staring too much, he didn't try to hide it this time. "No. Everything is fine. In fact, I could use some company."

She smiled back at him. "Good. Do you know any Russian?"

"*Nemnogo (very little). *" He turned his hands over and fluttered them, as he asked, "Is this close?"

She smiled. "I know Russian very hard language for Americans. Don't worry. Many people in Moscow speak English." She shifted her smile to the side of her face, flirting slightly.

"I wish I was better, but I do have a translator meeting me at the airport. I thought it would be good to have someone with me to try to explain Victoria's death to her friends. I don't know if they know all of the details or not."

"It sounds like she must have died suddenly." She turned to face Royce while retaining her elegant mannerism.

"Yes she did. She was attacked by a shark while she was surfing." He looked forward to see the stewardess who was returning with a map.

"That's terrible." Her face reflected the horror of the news. "That's why I never go in the water."

The stewardess reached his seat, and handed him a map. "I hope this will help you some. You should be able to get a better one at the Sheremetevo Airport."

"*Spasibo* (thank you)." He glanced over at his new acquaintance, who was giving him a big smile.

"I think you know how to speak Russian very well." She reached her hand out to him. "My name is Katya."

He received her hand, and felt of her extremely soft and warm skin. "Hi, my name is Royce Cianci."

"I have lived in Moscow all of my life. Maybe I help a little." She pointed to the map.

"That will be great. I'm staying at the Moscow International Hotel near the Kremlin, I think." He reached for his itinerary in the pocket of his white, sports jacket.

"I know where it is. It not far from where I live. I really love the *bijou* boutiques of *Stoleshnikov Pereulok*." She accepted the map from him and pointed to it. "Now, here . . . on *Tvevskaya*, you'll find lots of night life. How long you be in Moscow?"

"For only a few days. While here, I plan on seeing the Bolshoi Theatre, the Kremlin, and Red Square like most tourists." He smiled, knowing that this is what she would expect.

"Yes, they are very interesting, but the city offers so much more to see." She batted her long eyelashes.

"I wish I had more time, but I have a business to run back

in Atlanta." He examined her business suit, which looked very delicate and expensive. "What were you doing in America?"

"I work as model." She shifted her weight, as she twisted to the side to look straight at him.

"I thought that you might be a model. You have great looking features."

"*Spasibo*. I hope modeling agencies think so. For the last two weeks, I traveled to many parts of the United States. The country very strange for me."

"*Pozhalusta* (You're welcome). "Why do you think that, and which cities did you visit?"

"Different parts of the country are so unusual for me. I started in New York, and then flew to San Francisco for several days before going on to Miami. I think I enjoyed it most. The last stop was in Atlanta yesterday." The excitement of telling about the trip registered in Katya's vibrant-green eyes.

The captain's voice broke into their conversation. "– We'll be landing in Sheremetevo shortly. Thanks to some great tail winds, we'll be landing about thirty minutes ahead of schedule." Moments later, the message was repeated in Russian.

"That sounds like great news. This has been a long trip, and I'm anxious to see the sites here."

She reached in her purse, and located a small piece of paper. "Here, I give you my number. If I can help you while you here, please let me know."

"*Spasibo*." He reached in to his shirt pocket, retrieved one of his business cards, and handed it to her.

She examined his card. "What . . . exactly . . . your company do?"

"We help people with the hardest decisions they ever have to make. We run a matching service for executives."

"I know about that type of services here. It's a very big business. I would have to tell you that it's very corrupt business also." She lost her smile as she studied the card again.

Royce knew what she thought. "I'm nothing like the escort services you know that bring rich business men to Russia. Our biggest service is to protect my clients from such fraud. I run background checks on people for them. It saves a lot of heartaches later. I guess you could say that I'm the good guy this time."

The smile returned to her face. "In that case, I think you may have a very busy business."

The plane started descending fast, and the city skyline came into view outside the window. As he leaned over to glance, his head became very close to her. He could smell the subtle perfume she wore. Nice. "Yes. I'm looking forward to this trip."

***

With his visa in proper order, along with the hotel registration he provided, Royce had little trouble in passing the border control. He looked like a tourist on vacation. While he had been well trained in how to slip through customs before, he knew that his visa would be run through the system, and his previous boss would be alerted to his travels.

Without smiling, the agent handed Royce his paperwork back to him while letting his eyes motion for the next in line to come forward. "*Spasibo.*" He said anyway, a habit from in his days in Atlanta.

He headed for the entrance to the main concourse. He was early, and he didn't know if his translator would be waiting on him or not. He passed through the crowd of friends and family members being reunited, as he looked for someone with a sign. When he saw a small woman holding a name card with his name on it, she was arguing with a man in a dark suit. Royce's instinct told him to wait for a minute. His face looked belligerent, as he shouted instructions at her. Royce wished these instructions were louder so that he could understand them above the noise of the crowd. However, no such luck. Since his knowledge of Russian had its limits, he doubted he would understand anyway.

As the conversation continued, Royce studied the man. He knew this man worked as a professional from the fine tailored suit he wore. He also knew the coat was large enough to conceal a gun. Within a minute, he decided that somehow his choice of a translator had been discovered, and someone had planned on monitoring his movements. He walked off to one side, trying hard to avoid attention.

The man left, and walked down the hallway to talk to another large man wearing a suit. Moments later, they separated and moved to new locations. Royce knew that they hadn't expected his plane to be arriving so early.

After he turned his back to them and walked down the hallway toward the baggage pick up, he saw Katya walking directly ahead of him. He quickened his pace until he caught her. "Hi, I think my translator didn't make it. If you live close to where I'm staying, perhaps I can give you a ride in my cab."

"Cabs are expensive here. It's much cheaper to use the metro."

"I understand, but this way we can handle your luggage and you don't have to worry about hauling it with you on the metro. You've been very good company for me, and I insist." He moved in close to her. He didn't know her well, but wanted to do the best he could to appear to be a couple and keep from being spotted. They would be looking for a single male.

"Are you sure I can trust you?" Her eyes flirted with his, failing to hide the fact that she must have found him interesting.

"I'm going to be here for a few days, so let me ask you one question, if I may?"

"Okay, you can ask, for sure."

"If I were to tempt you with a great time, what would you like to do here?"

He could see her thinking about it, and more importantly, she stayed close to him, as he wrapped her arm around his and escorted her along the hallway. "I love to cruise on the Moscow River, and especially when it passes by the Novodevichy Convent. Have you ever seen it?"

"No, but I would love to see it. After I get some rest tonight, and I get over this jet lag, I would love to do that. What do you think?"

"You have my number, and I know you have some business to take care of here first. Call me when you're ready. I'm not planning on working for several days. I also need to rest from the trip." Royce noticed how tall she stood—slightly over six feet tall. *Yes, I can see her making a great model.*

"I'll do that, and I think I'm very lucky to have been given a seat next to you on plane."

"*Spasibo.*" She smiled and continued to hold her head high as she walked gracefully down the corridor. "If you want, we can go down the river during the day and return at night. This will give you some great views of the city. Also, they serve a great lunch of caviar and *blinis* on the boat."

"I'm looking forward to it." He could see the baggage station ahead. Now, if they could quickly retrieve their bags and make it to a taxi before the men spotted them. He would call later and cancel his appointment with the translator's office. Whatever information he obtained from the two friends of Victoria, he didn't want others to have. He appreciated the names he had received from Warren, and knew that he had mentioned these to no one else. He could understand how many people were interested in his trip, and that it was best to keep some cards close to his chest.

As they went outside and glanced at the sun rising high in the sky, several taxi drivers scurried over and joined the other persistent drivers that had followed them, offering their services. Their Russian was rapid and hard for Royce to understand fully. Katya quickly asked questions from several of the competing drivers. He remembered from before that most of the meters in the cabs didn't work properly and that it was better to negotiate a price before accepting a ride. Royce heard one man ask, as he glanced at him, "*Chem platim—ruble ilee dollaree* (Do you pay in rubles or dollars)?"

Royce leaned forward. "Dollars."

The man leaned back and in rough English answered, "one hundred."

Royce nodded his head in approval as he glanced at Katya. "I'll let you give him your address first, and then I'll go to my hotel."

The driver reached for the luggage, and they were soon on their way. Royce thought that perhaps he was too paranoid, but he had learned to be safe rather than sorry. He would make more calls when he returned to the States. In the mean time, he did have a couple of contacts left in Moscow, that is, if he really needed them. He hoped he didn't. He smiled at his new friend. "Tomorrow morning I'll be seeing Victoria's friends, and instead of using the translator I hired, I would love for you to go see them with me. That is, if you feel like it. We could go on a cruise as soon as we finish talking to them."

"As long as it not too early in the morning, I might be

able to help you. Where do they live?"

"I'm not sure, but I know they work for GUM and I hope to see them in their offices."

"Will they be able to talk to you with customers around?"

"I understand they have administrative jobs in a central office overseeing the entire complex, so hopefully they'll have an office we can use. I still don't know if they're aware of the news or not." He hung his head in a small show of respect.

"I see. The offices open at eight, but if you'll let me sleep a little later, I would be glad to go with you. I meet you at the GUM, if that alright with you."

"Yes, that sounds great to me." He slowly breathed out in relief, as this turn of luck relaxed his mind some, but he had many worries still bouncing around in his head.

***

As he began to bring them up to date, Oleg eyed the men around him. "I received word that Royce Cianci is in Moscow. He hired a translator, but later fired her. It appears our mystery man has obtained a new friend on his flight over. Robert tells me that he was part of a special intelligence force, but left it a few years ago. He'll provide us more information when he gets it on him. I'm not so sure about the information that Robert is providing us. Now, why would a guy go half away around the world to say hello to friends of a girl he knew for only one night? Be sure that everyone knows that this guy should be considered extremely dangerous. For all we know, he might be a trained assassin."

"We can have him picked up and questioned. He's on Russian soil and I think we can get any information he has out of him there." The young agent spoke, eager to be of help.

Oleg ignored the young agent. "I can tell he's cautious,

but you would expect that. However his interest in this might do us some good. I want him monitored so close that he can't find out anything without us knowing it at the same time, but I don't want him to know we are monitoring him. In fact, make him believe we lost him."

"Yes, sir. I'll be right on it." The young man's eagerness showed his desire to impress Oleg, but revealing a weakness in speaking before he considered all of the possibilities.

"I appreciate your efforts to make up for the screw up here, but don't you think he'll be back here before you even get there?"

The young agent lowered his head. "I can make arrangements with someone in place to do as you asked."

"That will be good." Oleg turned to study the other men at the table. "Now back to our current problems here. The leads Victoria obtained for us the last time are almost gone. I'm not sure how much longer this real estate crisis will last, but the longer, and the worst it gets, the better. It's close to the breaking point here, and a complete collapse of the American economic system would definitely bring back a time where Russia controlled the world through strength."

Across from Oleg, one of his right hand men, Ivan, raised his head. "The amount of loans we have pushed into early default has generated a lot of cash. We still have to be careful not to let anyone know that all of these foreclosures are related to one central account. The timing on our exit will be crucial, as well as covering all tracks leading to us. A second recession in America would happen quickly when all is in position."

Oleg smiled and glanced around the room. "Greed can ruin a good thing, but in this case, the more greed we have, the better. I think the American capitalist will never know what hit them, and if they do, it will be too late to do anything about it."

Chapter 13

Royce resisted the urge to explore Moscow the night before. He slept for a long time, but still woke early by local time. He needed to disappear for a while, and knew exactly how to do it. With the men following him looking suspicious, he went into the *Gosudarstvenny Universalny Magazin* (the GUM shopping mall), and strolled his way through all three levels while slowly admiring the elegant turn-of-the-century interior. The three parallel arcades centered on a fountain that was overlooked by many stores, or galleries. A glass roof allowed the light in to highlight the various stands, as well as the designer boutiques filling the arcades.

Royce studied some restaurant tables covered by red umbrellas in the center of a walkway. From this point, he knew he could be seen from all over the place. He walked over to the hostess, and pointed to the tables before deciding to practice his limited Russian. "*Ya hachou vonn tam* (I want there)."

She smiled and flashed him a sideways glance. *Okay, I know I have a very bad accent.* She led him to a table in the center and placed a menu in front of him as she waited on him to order.

He glanced at the menu, which allowed him a small indication of what they offered. "*Ya hochoo blinis . . . vareniem, pozhalusta* (I want pancakes with jam, please)."

"*Chto pit' budete* (And what would you want to drink with them)?"

"*Chai, pozhalusta* (Some tea, please)."

She smiled, as she walked away. He smiled at himself thinking he didn't do too badly. A quick glance at his watch indicated that he had two hours before he was to meet Katya. That would be plenty of time to orchestrate his disappearance. By starting at the point he wanted to end up, he knew he would confuse them. If executed properly, this would give him enough time to see Victoria's friends.

After finishing his meal, he ordered one more cup of tea, and asked for his bill. The waitress placed the chit in front of him, and he quickly counted the money out to cover it. "A gde u vas tualet (Where is the toilet)?"

She pointed behind her, keeping a side way glance at him. "Chai budet gotov k vashemu vozvrasheniu (I will have your tea ready for you when you get back)."

"*Spasibo.*" Royce hurried toward the toilet, closing the door behind him. Dropping his pants, he quickly turned them inside out, revealing a light tan color which contrasted with the dark gray he had walked in with. The white coat also reversed to a dark blue, which completed the fast change of clothing. His blond hair, which was previously fluffy from a good hair blowing job, now lay down perfectly with a little water. In less than a minute, he moved back out of the toilet, and headed in the other direction.

Did he think he would fool his monitor—no. Did he want the monitor to think he was trying to disappear—yes. He headed for the exit, and out to the square. He rushed out forward, looking for a taxi. As one appeared, he quickly jumped in. "Ya opazdivau v aeroport, *mozhete dovezti bistro* (I am late for the airport, can you get me there fast)?" He handed the driver a hundred.

The driver glanced at the American. "I speak English. It not be easy at this time of day, but . . . I'll do my best."

"Good." After he sped past the first two blocks, Royce acted like he received a call, and then yelled at the driver.

"Please, stop here."

The driver came to a stop. "I left something at my hotel." He handed the driver a letter. "Please take this to the airport. I have someone that will meet you there. He'll be in a coat like mine, and he will be standing in front of the departing station."

The driver looked at the sealed envelope.

"He's late for his plane. Hurry and he will give you an additional tip as well." Royce didn't wait for a reply, but handed him another hundred before he rushed out of the cab. He knew the driver would like a chance to go back to the airport to obtain his next fare, and receive a nice tip. Glancing over his shoulder, Royce saw the cab disappearing while carrying an envelope with nothing in it.

Royce quickly left the street and waited. Two cars rushed pass him. His timing was perfect. Now, he needed a little luck. He rushed back to the GUM, and disappeared into the first *magazine* (store) he reached where he rushed to the men's clothing department. In minutes, he was wearing a different outfit consisting of black pants, and a white shirt, complete with tie. He folded his jacket, and placed it in his shopping bag. His hair was drying well on its own, as he continued to fluff it. All was good.

He glanced at his watch, hopefully Katya was close. He retrieved his phone, not sure if it was being monitored, or not. She answered on the second ring. "Hi, this is Royce, how are you?"

"Hello, I am fine, and how are you?" Her voice was smooth and spaced, typical of Russians speaking English.

"I'm fine. Did you make it to the GUM this morning?"

"Yes, I am inside now. What about you?"

"I'm here also. Meet me by the fountain, okay?"

"Sure, I'm close to it now."

"Great. I'll see you there." He discounted the phone and

hurried since he wanted to meet her there and leave before they were spotted.

He saw her standing, waiting on him, as he arrived. After glancing around, he didn't see any more suspicious men, so he hurried over to her. "*Privet.*"

"*Privet.* Did you sleep well?"

"Yes, very well actually." He kissed her check slightly, as he tucked her arm under his. "I think we need to go see them before they leave for lunch. I really thank you for helping me." He ushered her toward the stairs, and up to the top floor. The administrative offices were nestled behind one of the store fronts.

She smiled, as they reached the front door. "What are the girl's names?"

He handed her a small piece of paper with their names on it. "The first one is Sasha Goreva, and the second one is a Olya Bulseva. I think this is how to say their names, but I still worry about not pronouncing them correctly. It'll be best if you ask for them."

"So, they don't know you're coming?"

"No. I thought it was best if I didn't call." He watched her face, hoping she didn't ask too many questions.

An attractive girl at the front desk greeted them. "*Dobroe utro, chem mogu pomoch* (Good morning, how may I help you)?"

"*Menya zovut Katya, Ya budu perevodchikom u mistera Cianci* (My name is Katya and I am going to be Mr. Cianci's translator)."

The girl smiled at Royce. "I speak English." She reached out her hand to him.

Royce smiled. This would help very much. "Thanks. I need to see two employees that work here, if I can."

"Which ones?"

He looked over at Katya as she answered for him. "He

needs to see Sasha Goreva and Olya Bulseva, if it is possible."

"May I ask why you want to see them?" Her face remained professional, but pleasantly helpful.

"I knew a friend of theirs that moved to America. They may not know it, but it appears that she may have died in a shark attack while surfing in Florida." He lowered his eyes respectively, but waited on her reaction to the news.

"It doesn't sound like you're bringing good news. I know these girls well. May I ask who this is? I may know her, as well."

Royce glanced at Katya before continuing, "Her name was Victoria Zayas."

He saw the girl fighting to restrain her emotions, as she lifted her hands to her mouth. Her eyes flickered back and forth between Royce and Katya. "I know her."

Royce studied her eyes. "I'm sorry to have to give you the news." Her face reflected a deep concern, or fear, Royce couldn't be sure of which. "How well did you know her?"

"I didn't know her very well, but the two girls you asked for know her much better. Please have a seat to give me a minute to call them, and to find you a room to use." She pointed to some chairs.

***

Oleg heard his phone ringing in his pocket, and retrieved it, as he waived at the men around him to hold their conversation for a minute. "Privet."

As he listened intensely before closing his phone without replying, the men looked at him with expressions of concern written on their faces.

"He's smart—much smarter than we thought. Royce gave our men a slip there, but it will not be long before they'll find him again." He smiled, admiring the ability of this mystery man. "Now, why would he do that? He knows something we don't know." He glanced at the man to his right. "Let him have his fun, but stop him at the airport for questioning when he attempts to leave."

The man smiled. "I'll take care of it."

***

The small conference room had six chairs arranged around an impressive wooden table that Royce thought was oak. Katya's back remained straight, as her charm radiated in this small room.

Royce studied the modern artwork on the walls until he heard a knock on the door.

The girl from the front desk soon appeared, and was followed by two girls in their early thirties who had suspicious smiles accenting their faces. Obviously, they hadn't been told much about why they were called to the meeting.

Katya smiled at them. "*Zdravstvuite, Ya Katya. Ya perevodchik mistera Royce.* (Hello, my name is Katya and I'm Royce's translator.)" She motioned to her left where Royce stood.

"Zdravstvuite.*"* He extended his hand to the first one, and then to the other girl. They had beautiful eyes that darted around. He motioned for them to have a seat.

He spoke directly to Katya, but loud enough for the two girls to hear, in case they understood some English. "Tell them that I met a friend of theirs in America–Victoria Zayas."

As she relayed the information, he saw the girl's nervous reaction, which answered the question of if they knew or not. He had always suspected they had been told something. "It appears that you may know of her accident. I surfed with her the day before her attack, and we spent a lot of time together the night before. I know you might have questions and I'll be glad to answer them for you. I also hope that you might be able to answer some questions for me as well." Royce smiled at Olya and Sasha, trying to muster all of the charm he had in him. He needed their help. They had to have some information that he wanted.

After Katya relayed the information, Royce saw them glancing at each other, passing coded information to each other that they alone would understand. While tears filled both girls' eyes, they maintained their heads high and didn't cry out audibly. He could feel the struggle to maintain control in both of them.

When the room had remained quiet for a while, Olya cleared her throat and talked to Katya in a fast Russian pace. As she finished, Sasha also added a few words. Since Royce couldn't make out much of what they discussed, he was glad to have a translator.

Katya turned toward Royce with a frown on her face. "They've heard of the attack and it has been hard on them. They want to know why you came to see them."

"Tell them . . . that I knew her for only one day, but in that short period of time I felt like I was falling in love . . . and more so than I could ever describe. It's important to me to know more about her, who she was, her life her . . . anything they can tell me would make me happy."

Katya tilted her head slightly, but hesitated before relaying this on to the girls.

Again, Olya responded quickly with Royce understanding almost nothing.

Katya turned to him to translate. "Olya told me that she has known her for a long time, and that they went to school together. She thinks that Victoria never had a boyfriend before. Victoria's parents were devastated by the news. They haven't been seen since her death."

"I was hoping to see her parents while I was here. Do they know how to get in touch with them?" Since his efforts to find her parents had been impossible, this is one of the main reasons he had made the trip.

The two exchanged information again in Russian, and with words from Olya slightly heated at the end.

Katya frowned, as she turned to Royce. "No one knows how to contact them now. You have to remember . . . this is Russia, and sometimes you don't get answers here. Investigators have been here several times asking them questions. Since the body hasn't been recovered, they're keeping the case open. She thinks that they must also think that Victoria may be alive. They want to know what you think."

"I was in Jacksonville when she disappeared. They have enough evidence to conclude that she did die, but for some reason . . . I also have doubts. I guess, I just keep hoping. She really was special."

Royce heard more exchange of Russian that he could only follow a word of here and there. The girls now had tears flowing down their face continuously, but remained sitting straight. Olya placed a hand on Sasha's shoulder. Katya's eyes had several new tears in them, as she faced Royce. "Olya was Victoria best friend. Sasha was a mutual friend. They're too scared to say much, the investigators have told them to tell him if they ever hear anything from Victoria."

"Tell them I understand, and I don't want to get them in trouble. I do have a few more important questions to ask them. Do they have any idea as to what she was working on that is generating all of the investigations, and do they know of anyone else that knows her in America?"

After a quick exchange, Katya answered for them. "Olya told me that Victoria was a computer expert here, and had a reputation for being able to break into any system. However, she wanted to go to America for years, and jumped at the opportunity when it came to her. She wasn't able to say much about it because of security reasons. That is all she knows about her work. As far as anyone else in USA, unless her father introduced her to someone, she knows no one there."

"Tell her thank you for me, and to please take my card and let me know if she hears anything else. I would really like to talk to Victoria's father that speaks English."

The meeting was short, but Royce knew it had to be this way. He would follow up with them later, if he could, through Katya. "*Spasibo*." He rose to come around the table. They both came to him to give him a hug and a small kiss on the cheek before leaving the room. "*Do svidaniya* (Bye)."

As they walked out of the office, Katya apparently knew Royce had a troubled mind, and slipped her hand into his. With her gentle smiles comforting him, he would try to relax the rest of the day and enjoy the sights with his new friend. Tomorrow he would have to return to the States. Royce wanted to complete some more research, and hopped that Victoria's father would call him. He wondered why he disappeared, but knew of several possibilities that he didn't want to acknowledge. Something was definitely going on that he couldn't fully put his fingers on.

***

Royce continued to hold Katya's hand as he walked aimlessly across Red Square. She appeared to know how he was working out various scenarios in his head, and he appreciated the fact that she allowed him time to do so. The pleasant weather was relaxing, as Royce eventually glanced around him. If the men were following him, he acted like he didn't care. He certainly was in the most visible part of the city.

He glanced over at Katya. "I'm sorry for wandering around. Thank you for allowing me to think for a few minutes on what was said in the meeting."

"Not a problem. I know this must be very hard for you." Her vibrant-green eyes sparkled brightly in the full sun.

Royce grinned at Katya, and squeezed her hand slightly harder. "Yes, it has been several months now, and I still cannot put closure on this."

"Perhaps a day of relaxation can help you. I think you'll love the river cruise." She intensified her stare in his direction.

"I'm sure that I will." Royce looked over her again. She had the grace of a ballet dancer and still the height of a super model. "Please. Tell me more about this cruise."

She smiled. "Well, the main route runs between the Kievsky boat landing station, and the Novopassky Monastery. It generally last about one and a half hours, but there are many stops. One is at the foot of Sparrow Hills and the Vorobyovy Gory landing. Another stop is at *Frunzenkaya* near the southern end of *Frunzenskaya naberezhnaya*. Of course, I know you want to stop at *Gorky Park.*" She let her eyes shine, as she appeared to be enjoying telling him the various sites. He realized that she was, in fact, very proud of her city that she knew well.

"That sounds like a full day."

"Yes, it can be. We can get on or off any time. However, we will have to re-buy a tickct each time. I so sorry about that."

"That's not a problem." He enjoyed the way her hand felt in his, and the comforting feeling of having a friend to talk to.

She continued to describe the route of the cruise. "The boat also stops in *Krimean Most,* and *Bolshoy Kamenny Most,* which is opposite of the Kremlin and *Ustinsky Most,* which is east of the Red Square. The boat seats about two hundred people that usually include mostly locals going somewhere specific and not tourist."

It appeared that she has been on this cruise many times before. "I think you could be a very good tour guide."

She blushed. "I've lived here for all of my life." She pointed to where they needed to walk.

He let her lead him, but he knew the way. This was not the first time he had rode this boat. "Are you hungry?"

She squeezed his hand, and pointed to a small café along the way. "We can stop here for a minute, if you wish, or get something to eat on the boat."

"I remember someone telling me that the caviar and pancakes were great on the boat." He referenced her earlier comments.

She smiled. "Yes, they are."

Royce saw the boat operated by the Moscow River Company with its two decks moving toward the station. "Hurry, I think we can make it."

She grabbed his hand and they half-way ran toward it, laughing as they made it just before it left.

She breathed hard and laughed loud. "That was fun."

Yes, it was good to get some exercise and hear someone laugh. They quickly made it to a seat on the upper level. He allowed his mind to soak in the scenery, as they cruised down the river. The clear-blue sky above only had a few white clouds drifting by.

It was perhaps thirty minutes later when a girl approached them, wanting to know if they wanted anything to eat. After he ordered the caviar and pancakes, he glanced at Katya. "Would you like some wine?"

She remained close beside him, holding his hand. "I think that would be great."

He smiled, and turned to watch the scenery some more.

Katya edged closer to him. "I can tell . . . you still have her on your mind."

He blushed slightly. "Yes, she's dominated my interest now for several months."

"So . . . you think she is still alive?"

"I wish I knew for sure. I'm not sure that I'll ever know." He returned his glaze out to the shores of the Moscow River.

She rested her hand on his shoulder, gently massaging it. "I think I understand how you feel. Hopefully one day you will know for sure. Until then, I can be a very good friend, if you want me to be."

Royce appreciated her comprehension of his flight. Yes, a friend is exactly what he needed. He would have to obtain closure somehow before he could think of finding a new love. "Thank you, thank you very much."

She leaned over and kissed his cheek, as he continued to stare at the banks along the river.

Chapter 14

Royce eyes closed again, but he fought the urge to sleep. He would soon be on the plane, and could sleep all of the way to America. The gate to check in his luggage had a small crowd in the line, but all appeared normal. Katya had given him an interesting insight into Moscow, showing him one sight after another until late in the night. He had little doubt that he was being followed. However, he knew that he had evaded them long enough to make the one contact he had come for.

The border control agent in front of Royce motioned him forward. He handed her his paperwork and smiled. She punched the information into the computer screen. The expressions on her face froze as she stared at it for a long time. Finally, she glanced over at him. "Mr. Cianci?"

"Yes."

"I'm sorry, but I've been asked to detain you for questioning." She looked over his shoulder to point to an armed agent moving in on him.

He smiled, somewhat thinking that this would happen. "Is there a problem?"

"Your visa has been flagged. The investigating agent will take you to a room to ask you some questions. Please follow him."

The man in full uniform accepted the paperwork from the desk agent before smiling over at Royce and speaking in English. "Mr. Royce, this way please."

The interrogation room was tiny and perhaps only eight by eight. He had broken no laws, but this was Russia. In fact, he fully expected this interview. With luck, he would receive more information from the meeting than they would. He had to be patient. Questions, in their own way, would speak loudly if he listened closely.

He glanced over the paperwork, and studied Royce. "Mr. Cianci, I see you entered the country a few days ago. What was the purpose of your visit?"

"Pleasure. I accumulated many free miles and had a few days off. Moscow is a very interesting city."

"Yes it is. However, most people that come here stay more than a few days."

"I can understand that since Moscow's a very beautiful city." He smiled, waiting on the agent to proceed.

"There've been a number of inquiries into your trip here. I don't know all of the details, but it appears that the people we follow were following you. Do you have any knowledge of why *certain crime figures* here have an interest in you?"

Royce forced his face to register a surprised look on it. "I have no clue." In fact, that was news to him. While he assumed this was a governmental issue, a new angle had now been added. "Am I in any danger?"

"I think you'd be in a better position than me to answer that one. I hope you don't mind, but a background check is being ordered on you. We should have it any moment, and until it does, you'll have to wait in here with me."

"Will this make me miss my plane?"

"I hope it will be here in a minute. Please make yourself comfortable."

Sure, Royce thought. He had received so little sleep the last few days, and what he had wasn't very good.

His concentration soon shattered when a loud knock at the door interrupted the conversation. A different officer, one in a business suit, entered the room. "Mr. Cianci. It appears you have friends in high places back in America. I have been ordered to release you immediately. We have our suspicions, as to why you came here, but I've a few words of wisdom for you. Be very careful since you can get yourself in a lot of trouble with the wrong people easily here."

"Thanks for the warning. I'll remember it."

"This might be interesting for you to know. In this case, we're not the bad guys to be afraid of. The ones following you are. There may be a time when you would like to ask us for help." He handed Royce a card with his name on it.

He smiled wearily. "Thanks. It's good to know you have my best interests at heart here."

"Have a good trip back to the States. You need to hurry to make your plane." He smiled, shifting his eyes around before asking the first man to leave.

Royce leaned back in his seat.

"This is off of the record, but we know about you and Victoria, and I'm so sorry to have to mention her death. Because she went to America on a *special* work visa, her death leaves many unanswered question—questions that I think no one will ever have now. However, there are many people that would love to have them. So again, I suggest you be very careful in what you're looking for. You might not like what you find."

"I appreciate your concern. Since we're speaking *off the record* . . . can I ask what she was working on that was so important?"

He smiled. "I'm sure you understand that I have told you much more than I should have. It would be good if you go back to your old life and forget this ever happened. Trust me on this."

"Thanks." Royce stood to leave, knowing that this was only the beginning. He had many calls and favors to call in when he returned back home.

Chapter 15

Royce's home phone rang, waking him from a sound early morning sleep. Forcing his head to clear, he answered, "Hello."

"Hello, this is Warren Hornbuckle. How are you?"

Royce rubbed his eyes, this was one call that he had been waiting on since he returned to Atlanta. "I'm fine, and I'm just getting my internal clock reset. I've been trying to get in touch with you."

"I heard. The American office called me. If you remember, I was in line to transfer to the Paris office when we talked in Jacksonville."

"Yes, I remember. So, how is the transfer working out? Are you meeting any girls in France?" He knew he needed to make small talk first.

"The transfer was great, but it's the same old story, I'm working all of the time."

"I understand, but take some time out to make some friends. You might like the French women there."

"Yeah, that would be nice, but I think I need you with me to attract them. It was amazing how you attract women. I could never be as good as you."

Royce smiled. "Thanks, but it's not hard, just be who you are." He waited on the small talk to end—he needed answers.

"Why were you trying to get in touch with me?"

"I returned from Russia last week." He stopped short, allowing the words to sink in.

In a deep tone, Warren spaced his word out carefully. "Why did you go to Russia?"

"I went to see the friends you mentioned that Victoria had in Russia."

"I had too much to drink the night we went out, and I shouldn't have told you about them." He paused for a long time. "What did they tell you?"

"Not much. I think they're too scared to say anything." Royce rubbed his face which needed a shave.

"Why is that?"

"They have had several visits by investigators. You know, many people don't think she died in the ocean." Again, he waited on a response.

"What are you trying to say?"

"The facts aren't adding up, and I can't tell why that is. I think we all know Victoria was working on an important project of some kind. And . . . I know you can't say what it is, but anything that you can tell me would help me very much."

"You're right. I can tell you nothing about what she was working on, but I'll also add that I have my own suspicions. I wasn't aware that I was being considered for this promotion to Paris, but it came quickly after her disappearance, and my files in America have been turned over to someone else."

"I understand. Perhaps I shouldn't be chasing this crazy idea, but the more I do . . . the more interesting it's becoming. The Russian authorities warned me against pursuing it."

The phone remained quiet. "Royce, I know you love to travel. When was the last time you visited France?"

Not long enough, was his first thought. He had worked hard in France, and did his duty to home and country, and all that. It had cost him the most important thing is his life–Lynn. "It's been a while." While he did make one trip to France that would show on his passport, the rest would be covered deep in a file somewhere in Washington where an elite group of military officers were the only ones that knew about his mission.

"I think I can use another consultation on how to meet women. They're still a mystery to me."

Royce laughed. "I'll see what I can do."

"I have to go now, but call me when you can work it out."

Royce replaced the phone on the receiver, wondering why the sudden brush off, but more interesting–why did he leave the door open?

***

Oleg read over the numbers. Their number of forced foreclosures had increased by over sixty percent from the previous year. Business was fantastic, in fact, it couldn't be any better. If he could only find a way to keep the data coming in. The last batch of loan analysis provided by Victoria was almost exhausted. However, they had enough old leads to stay busy while they waited on a new batch. Soon, it would be time to reunite the housing crash, and this time finish the job of destroying America.

He examined the paperwork on one of the purchases recently acquired. "This was a good job, and one I wish we could duplicate all of the time."

His young assistant glanced at the file. "That purchase will lead to many other bargains; especially, when we resell it to an affiliate for half of that price. Two years ago it sold for one point one million, but we purchased it for seven hundred thousand. Soon we'll have it worth four hundred thousand, effectively lowering the value of all properties in the building. The pickings will be very good. We have the names of all of the owners, and we will convince most of them we're their savior."

"How is the guy that we managed to get into Warren's

old position working out?"

"He's working hard, and knows we mean business. However, Victoria locked the files up so effectively that it'll take him some time. He does have plenty of incentive, much like Victoria had."

"I hope so since we need some fresh accounts to work on. We also have some of our old accounts missing, and my boss doesn't like having some of his money disappearing. You may need to place more pressure on him."

"I'll stay on it." He smiled at his challenge. "I also need to ask you about Joseph Zayas. He has been on *vacation* for a while now at our expense. People will soon be asking questions of how long will it take for him to get over the death of his daughter."

"I agree. He needs to be returned to Moscow. If Victoria was going to contact him, or if he knew anything, we would know it by now."

"I'll take care of it soon."

"We also need to talk to the appraiser, and make sure he can accommodate us with more of these appraisals. We need to keep him busy."

"Don't worry. He's getting very wealthy from working with us."

Chapter 16

As he walked in, Royce saw Alicia examining his face. "Well, tell me, did you wear out Moscow, or did it wear you out." She stopped to wink. "You look like you need to go to bed."

"Thanks. I look that bad, huh?"

"Worse. Why are you coming in? I know you must be exhausted. I promise we can handle everything for one more day."

Royce smiled. "I'm sure you can."

"So tell me about your whirlwind trip to Moscow. How was it?"

"I met a girl there, and I did visit many of the sites I wanted to see. It's really an amazing place." His eyes felt heavy, and perhaps she was right. While he needed more time to rest, and the harder he tried to sleep, the more he kept second guessing what was going on. Lynn had died because he didn't find her in time. Since he still hadn't convinced himself that Victoria died as he was told either, he had to know for sure.

"I see . . . so Moscow did wear you out then. Why didn't you stay longer? It looks like you could use some more rest."

Royce blinked his eyes. "You know, I think you're right. I think I'll take off a few more days."

***

As Royce walked into the Jacksonville condo, memories of Victoria being there with him flooded his mind. He owed his friend a big favor for letting him use it again, and especially on such short notice. Flashbacks of her moving around the room, the drunken memories of staggering into bed, and them making love until they passed out haunted him. His feet stayed glued to the entrance where he was unable to explore such a love nest that was preserved in his memory.

Since nothing had been changed since his visit, he wondered if it had even been rented since he left it. He spotted another bottle of wine they had enjoyed on the beach, and another candle firmly in place in its mouth. A smile crossed his lips. Victoria must have worked on several of these the night they spent together. Embarrassed about leaving it, he walked over and lifted it. The candle had burned down close to the mouth of the bottle, and covered it with a bright red color.

He carried his bag into the bedroom, and opened it to place this bottle inside. This one promise he had made to Victoria, he intended to keep. His imagination envisioned the numerous candles that would be offered in memory of their time together, and the effect it would have on the side of the bottle over time.

He decided to remove the candle for safe keeping later. Thinking that a small amount of the candle had fallen in the bottle, he swirled the bottle, and examined it. He soon turned the bottle toward the window. An object of some kind definitely was in the bottle. He smiled, as he remembered her joking about putting a message in a bottle and setting it free.

Excited about the possibilities, he turned the bottle upside down, and watched a small object fall out. What the hell! He raised it above his head, and examined it with care. It appeared to be a small flash drive of some kind. Alarms went off in his head. He glanced around the room, and rushed back to the front door to lock it.

The intense questioning of the CIA and the Russian authorities were becoming clear. Since this had to be what they were looking for, he had to know what was on it. He hurried back to his bedroom and opened his overnight bag containing his computer. With the flash drive connected to a port, he turned on his computer.

***

Miguel's surf shop only had a few customers renting boards and gawking at his prized merchandise, as Royce entered. A smile curling out of the side of Miguel's face sent a coded message that left little doubt that they both knew Royce would return.

Royce waved slightly before heading to the back shop where the board he had admired still rested on the same spot. When he lifted it and felt of the balance, it had the same effect of bringing back memories of the day on the surf, and the day he met Victoria. His mind drifted with his immediate surroundings disappearing completely.

"It has to be hard to let something so beautiful go." Miguel soft words broke the tranquility of his daydream.

Royce smiled, letting reality focus again. "Yes, it's a great board."

Miguel's stern face and deep set eyes penetrated Royce's, matching his ability to drive home his domination of piercing inquisitivity. "I wasn't talking about the board."

Royce frowned, Miguel had developed an ability to see inside him that very few others had ever obtained. "I remember one saying I will never forget, *Dreams never die unless you let them, and reality never dies as long as you have a dream.*"

"Makes sense to me. So what brings you back here this time?"

"The truth. I want the truth on what happened." He locked eyes with Miguel.

"I wish I could tell you my friend. I can tell you the feds are still investigating this. In fact . . . they were here yesterday, asking questions about the attack."

"Yesterday . . . what kind of questions?"

"They wanted to know if I had heard of any new developments in the case, or if anyone has been asking about her?"

"Did you say anything about me coming back?" Miguel didn't answer, but raised his head in a questioning look, as if to say, "You know I didn't."

Royce continued to study the board. "Thanks, you know I appreciate it."

"Not a problem. I still think something stinks in this."

"Me too." Royce glanced at the board again. "I was wondering about one thing. Do you think you could make one small modification for me on this board?"

"Perhaps. What would you like?"

"If you add an *in memory of Victoria* to the board, something that you think she would approve of, I'll buy the board."

"Are you sure you want to carry that with you? It's a lot of baggage you might not want one day."

Royce smiled. "It's a message I want to send loud and clear. Please put a sold sign on it, and feel free to leave it out front. It might help you make some more sales."

"Be careful, my friend. I think there's much more to this story than we know."

"I think you're right." Royce smiled, and raised his head. "Kind of like chasing a storm: if you want the best waves, or the best of anything in life, you have to be willing to take chances."

Miguel gave him a knuckle bump. "You're so right."

Royce headed for the door. "Do you have time for a few beers tonight?"

"If you're buying . . . absolutely. Give me few hours to close up shop, and to change clothes."

Royce laughed, knowing that would be interesting to see. "I'll come by later tonight after you get all of the boards in for the day."

***

Leaving the shop, Royce turned the corner, looking for his red Boxster. He soon saw a man in a dark suit leaning against a telephone pole next to it. Royce expected such, as he walked straight toward his car.

He smiled at the CIA officer, trying to remember if he knew him from his past. "How are you?"

The agent smiled. "I'm not doing so bad, and just working steadily. What brings you back to Jacksonville?"

"I decided to buy a surf board." Smiling with an intense, expressed look of exquisiteness on his face, he pointed in the direction of the surf shop. "Why do you ask?" He decided he had nothing to lose in being direct.

"Curiosity." With a large grin, he stepped closer.

"I'm sure you heard the phrase *curiosity can kill the cat.*"

The agent smiled. "That's very true advice to give, and to live by."

"Works for me." Royce looked off into the distance. "Would you like to get to the point and ask me what you want to know?"

"I think we both have one question we would like to have answered. Victoria may have died in the shark attack, and then again, maybe not. Officially, it has been ruled as a death. That's very unfortunate for many people."

"If it's been *officially* ruled a death, why are you still working on it?"

"I think you know there's a limit as to what I can tell you, even if you used to work for the government. You left our little reservation, and no longer have clearance. You know that."

"I know the rules of the game. I also know how *things* are hidden from even those on the inside, you know, in the interest of the greater good." Royce stared straight at the agent with his focus intent on memorizing every feature of his face.

"I read part of your file and I know you blame the government for your girlfriend's death."He paused briefly. "And yes . . . it is all about the greater good."

"I guess some *things* never change." Royce kept his eyes connected to the agent in front of him, as he attempted to penetrate layers of armor. Royce had been well trained in this technique. "In such as case, I don't think I have anything else to say to you right now."

The agent handed him a card. "I'm really not such a bad guy. Call me if you need to talk, and for what it's worth, off of the record, I'm truly sorry in your loss. I only found out about your past a few days go. When I heard you were coming here, I thought it would be good to make direct contact with you, which is something I rarely do."

Royce looked at the card and whistled. "I've heard of you. They say you're one of the best."

He smiled. "You know what they say about rumors. It's best to discount them completely."

"I'll keep the card. Nice talking to you."

He smiled. "Call me sometime. I don't think this is the last time we'll meet."

Chapter 17

As Royce walked in to his office in Atlanta, Alicia smiled at him. "How are you?"

Her voice, which was both friendly, and flirty as usual, made him return the smile. "I'm tired, but ready to get back to work. I know I must have a ton of people wanting to know where I've been."

"Yes, you've started a rumor mill circulating. Everybody thinks you have a new sweetie, and I'm sure you'll get asked a lot about it." She glanced at him sideways, letting her eyes twinkle with a certain flair of teasing that she had developed perfectly.

Royce smiled back. "I see I have my work cut out for me. Now . . . you don't know anyone that would start such a rumor, do you?"

"My lips are sealed." She pushed back from the desk that she occupied in the front entrance. He had hired Alicia to handle the front desk because she did flirt with everyone, and it was a decision he had never regretted. As far as the rest of his work, she probably comprehended many aspects of his investigations, as well as the seriousness of the faith many of his clients placed in his services. He knew his clients understood that when they first see her. Everyone had a place on his team.

He stretched. "I'm glad to be back." Again, he had to force himself to control his staring. She had long, shapely legs, covered by a short dress. The push back from the desk had exposed her legs all of the way to her panties. He knew he should say something about it, but hesitated, totally lost for words.

She batted her eyelashes, apparently reading his mind, but not wanting to push it too far for now as she crossed her legs slowly. "There are a lot of notes on your desk, let me know what I can do to help."

"Thanks. I think I need to dive into them and do the best I can today. Are any of them in here that extremely important?"

"I think all of them might be important, but one interesting man from Russia has called several times, and wanted to talk to you. It must be someone you met on your trip."

His interest suddenly became aroused. "Who was it?"

"Some guy named Joseph Zayas."

Royce turned toward his office. "Thanks. This could be important to me. I'll call him first. Please hold my calls until I finish." He walked into his office before she could ask questions. It was eight in the morning in Atlanta and four in the evening in Moscow. If he had called from work, Royce wanted to reach him before he went home.

A man answered the phone on the first ring. "*Helo* (Hello)."

"Hi. Mr. Zayas, this is Royce Cianci. How are you?"

"Hello to you. I have been trying to reach you."

"Yes, I understand, I've been out of town for a few days."

"I'm so sorry to have missed you when you came to Russia. Sasha Goreva called me and told me that you came to see her."

"Yes. I didn't know how to reach you, and I also didn't know if these girls had heard the news about Victoria." Royce stopped cold on the mentioning of her name. "Mr. Zayas . . . I'm so sorry about Victoria. I was surfing with her the day before she disappeared."

He waited on a response. Time passed slowly, as he hesitated to speak until Joseph had. "Thank you. It has been a big shock to me and her mother. We only returned home a few days ago. Her mother took the news very badly, and I had to get her somewhere that she could remain out of sight for a while. I hope you understand."

"I can understand it fully. How is she now?"

He received a long pause. "She is better now, but barely."

"I met Victoria the day before she disappeared. She appeared to be a great girl, and I would have loved to have known her better." His heart felt the love of this father for his daughter, and he realized what he must be going through. The not knowing for sure and the inability to recover her body must have been beyond terrible for him and his wife.

"I never knew she had any interest in surfing. How long has she been learning to surf?"

"Not for long, but she appeared to be learning very fast. We were in the water the day we met, and saw a shark. It scared us both, and we left the water. That night we went out tasting wines, and talked for a while. The next morning is when she went surfing on her own and disappeared. I don't know why she went surfing on her own, and especially after seeing the shark the day before. That's the part that doesn't make sense to me." He rested for a minute, letting the father reflect on the information. He heard the faint cry of a man that loved his daughter.

"I understand. Please excuse me. It's hard to think of my daughter being eaten by a shark." Royce waited for what seemed to be forever, as he let him quietly weep on the phone. Finally he continued. "Did you see the attack?"

"No, I arrived after it happened." Royce voice remained slow, and steady.

Joseph's voice became much lighter, as he asked, "Are

you sure it was her?"

It felt like Royce's heart suddenly jumped to his throat. "I can't say for sure, but believe me; I've asked myself that question many times. There hasn't been a body recovered, and the only evidence we really have is her surfboard."

"I understand. She loved being in America. It was a dream she had most of her life. I never would have believed this kind of thing would happen to her there."

"I could tell she liked it, but it appears that she worked all of the time."

"–Yes." Joseph butted in, eager to speak. "But this job she obtained was the only way she could move to America. I really advised her against it, but she had her mind determined to go."

"I do understand. Let me ask you a question, if I may." Royce kept his voice as respectful as he could manage.

"Sure, what do you want to know?"

"Do you know anything about what she was working on?"

Royce waited, as the total silence on the phone seemed to take forever. "She worked as a computer specialist."

There was much more to the story, Royce knew it. The silence indicated as much. "Yes, she told me that."

"Royce, this is Russia. You have to remember we don't ask too many questions here."

"I'm sorry for asking, and I do understand. If I hear any more news, I'll be sure to call you. Also, if you hear anything from sources in Russia, please feel free to call me as well. You can call me anytime. Please let me give you my cell phone before you hang up."

"Thanks, I would appreciate it very much." The faint crying disappeared. "Until I hear that her body has been recovered, I'll always hold out hope for her."

"I will . . . I will also."

"She'll always be missed. Her mother blames herself for Victoria's death."

"Why does she do that?"

"It's because of my wife's previous connections here that made it so hard for Victoria to get a visa. That's why Victoria accepted the position she had in America." After a small pause, his voice strengthened, as he continued, "She worked for people she shouldn't have worked for—people that have been here many times asking questions. I hope they don't bother you there."

Royce saw no reason to concern him. "Don't worry, this is America, I'll be safe here."

"Don't be fooled into thinking that. You need to be on your guard. Perhaps it might be best if you forget about her. I don't think she would like to know that she got you into trouble."

"I don't think she did. I can take care of myself. Tell Anastasia that I'm truly sorry."

"I will. Take care, Royce."

***

Royce walked to the door of his office to make sure he had locked it. The small flash drive hidden in the bottom of his office bag seemed to be the answer to so many questions he had. Now, if he could only open the damn thing. He trusted no one—absolutely no one with it. His eyes roamed around his office, as he unplugged the connection to the internet before connecting the flash drive.

Access denied flashed almost immediately. There had to be a way to get into it, or she wouldn't have left it for him. He played with it for an hour, which frustrated him more and more as he tried everything he knew. He had to turn to someone, but whom?

In reality, Royce knew only one person that might be capable in opening it, and he lived in Paris now. Did he trust

Warren? No! Did he have a choice? Hell no! He searched for Warren's number, and dialed it with deep reservations.

Warren answered after several rings. "Hello, Royce. How are you?" Caller identification was a great invention sometimes.

"I'm fine. I was thinking about you. How are things going?" A little small chat never hurts, he thought.

"Everything is good. I was hoping to hear from you again."

"I'm glad to hear that because I need your help. I don't know too many computer people, and I lost my password to a program that I use. Is there an easy way to fix it?"

"It depends on how it's protected. Let me have access to your computer, and I think I might be able to help you."

Royce pulled the flash drive out of the computer, shutting it off. He wondered if calling Warren was a mistake now. "I appreciate it, but I have too much confidential information on it. For all I know, you'll be calling all of my beautiful clients here."

Warren laughed. "That would be tempting, but then I would also have to figure out what to say."

"I haven't been to France in a long time. Perhaps it would be good for me to make a trip there to see some friends. How busy are you going to be next week?"

"If you make the trip here, I'll make the time to see you. This city has some interesting places that I can show you."

"I'll think about it, and let you know."

Chapter 18

Royce flipped through the books that he had purchased at the bookstore during his lunch break, but nothing helped. Why couldn't he open the damn thing? She left it for him for a reason, which was very obvious—but why?

A knock at the door startled him. He closed the screen, and hid the flash drive using a plan he had devised to make sure no one knew he had it. After making it to the door and opening it, he saw Alicia standing silently, but obviously waiting on him.

She peeked around the door with a sheepish smile. "What are you doing in here? Watching porn?"

He returned her smile with a frown. "Not hardly—too much work for play time."

She walked over to his desk and glanced at the closed screen. "I see. Remember if you ever need some *playtime,* let me know. I think I can be much better than the computer." She flashed her eyes playfully.

Royce whistled low. "I'll keep that in mind, but right now I think someone's trying to break into my computer, and I have some sensitive information on it concerning our clients. It wouldn't be good to have it become public knowledge."

Her face squinted. "I can understand that. You know I would love to be in here sometime when some of these clients spill the beans."

Royce smiled. "I bet you would." He turned his computer on, allowing it to connect to the internet.

As the computer came to life on its own, Alicia's mouth

opened wide. "How is it doing that?"

"I think someone is trying to remotely access the computer." He pulled the internet connection plug.

"That is weird. I've never seen anything like that. Who do you think it is?"

Royce rubbed his chin, as he thought of several possibilities. "I wish I knew. Whoever is doing this is very good and never leaves a trail to follow. Since this is the first time that I have absolutely no doubt, I think I need some professional advice."

"I agree. Who do you know?"

"I know a few people. Close the door for me and let me make some calls."

She grimaced, as she proceeded to the door. "That's spooky."

Royce suspected that he might have this problem eventually, and now he expected that it would only get worse. It was time to make some calls.
***

Charlotte walked over to Brandon. "I know he'll be on to us soon, but I also think we're not the main one hacking his computer. We have evidence of many other attempts to break into his data files."

Brandon smiled at her. "You know. I think what you need is a date. You do like the Atlanta night life, don't you?"

"It does have its rewards, especially when you have the right guy showing it to you."

"Enjoy yourself, Charlotte. And this is one time you don't have to give me all of the details. Just give me the ones I want." He winked, and turned his chair back toward his desk.
***

Royce walked into the restaurant, scanning the

surroundings from top to bottom. Charlotte had called, and had wanted to have him meet her for a late night diner. She sounded very desperate, but his guard was up and he was ready for a night that could become . . . very interesting.

Charlotte waved at Royce as he approached the hostess. She was dressed to kill, so to speak, with the little black dress, pearls, and hair professionally styled. Boy, she must need information from him, and much more than he thought. But what was it? Oh yes, the flash drive.

He glanced down at his casual tan slacks, and open shirt. Perhaps he should have worn a tie, but that wasn't in his style for a late night out. The sports coat helped, but left a much mismatched status compared to her stunning outfit.

As he approached the table, she twisted in her seat, allowing the black dress to rise above her knees and reveal her legs. He knew the movement was intentional, but he appeared not to notice, and blocked his eyes from staring. It wasn't easy, but he managed. "Hello, Royce. Thank you so much for coming tonight." She stood and walked around the table to kiss him slightly on the cheek.

"You're welcome. You sounded desperate on the phone, but you look fantastic tonight." He intensified his focus on her eyes.

"I have to apologize for earlier. It has been one of those days that I wish I could forget. I knew I'd be here tonight, and I didn't want to spend it alone. Not after being taken for a fool by a jerk yesterday." She lowered her head, as an attempt of an embarrassed frown drifting across it.

Royce smiled. "I think I hear the *tell-tell* signs of a boyfriend problem."

She smiled, glanced around, and stared back at his focused eyes. "I don't think I would call him a boyfriend. A jerk would be more like it."

"I see. I kind of thought so." He fought the urge to laugh,

and hoped it didn't show.

"It's worse than you think. He's married. Can you believe it?"

Royce relaxed. This was going to be an interesting night. "I understand. You found this out yesterday?"

"Yes . . . from a mutual friend. We were supposed to go to a party in San Francisco last night. When I confronted him with the truth, he admitted it, and he even laughed about it. I guess he felt like I was going to be another notch on his bed post." A small tear formed in the corner of her eye that she dapped with the corner of her napkin. Royce thought about how she had really missed her calling as an actress.

"Well, look at it this way, at least you found out about it now rather than later. It's also a prime reason for using my agency, and letting us complete background checks on those you trust your heart, not to mention your life with."

"I guess that maybe I should have told you about him, but he lives in San Francisco, and not Atlanta."

"It doesn't matter. I have contacts all over the world."

"That's interesting. Do you like to travel?"

Amazing recover, he thought. "Yes, I do. How about you? Where do you like to travel?"

Her smile radiated with a new life. "I've travelled most of my life, and I love so many places. However, it gets boring if you don't have the right person with you." She shifted her eyes away from him momentarily, then darted them back in his attention. "Don't you think so?"

"Yes, I do understand the difference. So . . . tell me where you would like to travel," he added, allowing her to volunteer any information that might be useful

"I think Europe. There's so much history in Europe to learn from."

"You're right, but where do you want to go in Europe?" He decided to push.

"Well, I like Western Europe–maybe London, or Paris . . . or even further, like say St. Petersburg, Russia."

"That covers a lot of territory. Do you know anyone in Europe?"

"Yes, I have friends in many places, but no one special."

"I understand, but back to your problem at hand–tell me about this guy you had an affair with." He concentrated on her eyes. They immediately dilated, as he expected.

She closed her eyes, nodding her head forward. Too late, he thought, since he had already discovered the truth. "I do have some information about him that I would like to verify. However, it's back in my hotel room."

"Hotel room?" He allowed his voice to act surprised.

"Yes. My new place here is being renovated, and I only stopped by Atlanta long enough to check on how it was coming along."

Very convenient, he thought. "It would be good for me to check him out, and give you the full details. You never know when someone like this can use information about you in an indiscriminate manner later."

"I would really appreciate it if you would look into it." She batted her eyes softly. "I think it would also be good to hear more about you. You have to have an exciting life, working like you do. Do you get to travel much, Royce?"

"Not much, but I love to when I can."

"Where have you been lately?"

Go for the throat, he thought. "I visited Moscow recently." He knew she knew it, so why not admit it. He wanted her to ask questions, and especially if the questions tipped her hand on what she knew.

"Moscow . . . that must have been an interesting trip."

"Yes, it was a good trip, but I only had a small amount of time to enjoy it. I had a problem arise back home, and had to attend to it."

"Oh, what was that?"

"As you know, I have many clients that need . . . shall I say . . . personal attention. It was a small crisis, but needed my immediate attention."

"Kind of like me, hummm."

"Yes, kind of . . . "

She leaned forward, the low cut dress falling away from her breast, exposing more cleavage. "Do you have friends in Moscow?"

He forced himself to avoid staring again, as he glanced away, trying to appear relaxed and in control "Yes, a few, and I manage to make a few new ones on every trip."

"I see—a different girl in each port." She shifted her eyes, waiting on his response.

"I did make a friend this last trip." He knew she was going to be a hard target to crack, but she did have information he needed.

"I can imagine you make friends very easily." She batted her eyelashes slowly. "Can you tell me one more thing?"

"Sure, what do you want to know?"

"What kind of activities do you like to do, outside of work? You know, what do you like to do in your spare time?"

"It's well known that I love to surf, but living in Atlanta doesn't allow me many opportunities to do it often. I think I mentioned this before."

He watched her gaze over his body with her eyes caressing, or perhaps a better description would be even undressing him, as she covered all of the important areas. He again forced himself to control his urge to laugh. "I definitely can see the surfer body." She quickly added a sexy purr for an added effect. "Where did you learn to surf?"

"California." He assumed she already knew that also, but

played the game. He wasn't sure if she knew about his work in France, but assumed that she might not know.

"I love the beaches of California."

"I did, at one time." He started to add to the story, but the pain of the thoughts stopped him short. He saw no reason in going into it.

"Do you have friends that you go surfing with?" She was fishing. Why? What did she know that he didn't?

"I have a few, and always make a few more each time I go." He shifted his eyes away from her to scan the room. He knew he had to keep baiting her.

"I see. Have you made any new ones lately?"

"I thought I had a very good one, but she died suddenly." He studied her eyes. He hit home again, as he studied the dilation.

"Oh, what happened?"

"She died in a shark attack." He let his head sink—he knew how to play the game as well as she did.

She quickly raised her hand to cover her mouth, as if in shock. "I'm sorry. How terrible!"

"Yes. The reason for the trip to Russia was to tell her friends and family."

He saw the smile in the side of her lips being hid by the look of surprise that she forced on her face. He knew that she thought she was getting the information she was after. "How did that go?"

He decided to avoid the answer, and instead shrug his shoulders before glancing away for a minute.

She finally continued, obviously not wanting this moment to get away. "I can imagine that was hard information to deliver to the parents."

Again, he didn't answer, as he thought how golden the use of silence could be.

It worked. She glanced around the restaurant, and raised

her eyes, indicating how she was deep in thought. "I know you're tired, but I would love for you to have the information on this guy in California to check out. I'm not going to be here long. I do have great room service, and perhaps I can talk you into a small night cap." She let the chair push back slightly from the table exposing her shapely legs again.

Since she had information he needed, he quickly decided that perhaps she might let it slip if he did have a drink or two with her. She knew more than he had previously assumed, or she wouldn't be working him so hard.

***

Royce reached for the door handle with one hand, and extended the other one toward Charlotte to obtain the key. She smiled, and handed it to him. The electronic key turned on the traditional green light to indicate it was approved. He pushed it open, allowing her to walk in first as he closed the door behind him.

The suite was enormous. The large California king size bed in the center of the room which was covered with a plush comforter of swirled golden patterns, and perfectly matched the curtains running the length of the far wall. She walked over and tossed her black shawl on the bed.

A large couch was situated in front of the sheer curtains that revealed the skylights of Atlanta outside the window. The top floor had the additional height to provide interesting perspectives. "They have a full bar in the refrigerator, and if you don't see what you want, we can order from the bar downstairs." She walked over to the couch before turning to face him.

Since this room was expensive, they were sparing no expenses in pumping him for information, but why? "Let me see what you have."

Charlotte slithered into the side of the couch, letting her

dress rise, as she pointed her knees directly at him. Her white panties flashed like a beacon—so obvious. She had left plenty of space next to her for him to sit.

Royce opened the refrigerator, and studied what was inside. She was right; it was stocked with everything that they might want. He glanced at a bottle of champagne, but only smiled. The bottles of vodka would be a better choice tonight, and the bottles of tequila maybe even a better choice. He retrieved several of each. "Do you like yours straight up, or over ice?"

She smiled, as he knew the game had started. Now, it would be interesting to see which one held their liquor best. As he walked over to her, he wondered how many times she had watched the *Mrs. Robinson* movie, and tried not to laugh while he thought of it. "The Greg Goose is good. I hope you like it." He poured her glass first, and then opened one for his own glass.

She accepted her glass, and tapped his glass as soon as he lifted it. "Thanks for keeping me company."

"You're welcome." He tossed the drink, and waited on her.

She tossed her drink. He watched her trying hard to avoid revealing the burning sensation of the vodka going down her throat. She closed her eyes for a minute. He knew she had to regain her thoughts. "That was . . . good."

"I think so also. You want another?"

"Sure why not?"

"Where is the information that you have for me?"

"It's on the table over there. You can take it with you when you leave."

As Royce glanced at it, he knew that would be a long time from now before he left.

Chapter 19

Royce glanced at his watch, as his flight to France bumped from air pocket to air pocket. It was almost as bad as the screaming kid behind him. His eyes peeked open to see a stewardess making her way down the aisle. What the hell? He motioned to her.

She smiled. "May I help you?"

He knew she spoke French and decided it was time to slip into the mode of a Frenchman. "*Le Vin rouge, s'il vous plaît* (The red wine, please)"

She smiled, acknowledging his French, as she left and returned to her station. His three years of service in France had polished his French. However, memories of how he was used still burned inside of him.

He knew as soon as he booked the flight, the CIA would be monitoring his trip. After all, this was his old stomping grounds, and he was no longer part of the family. He knew how the French were notorious for losing paper work and he had prepared several copies of his passport with extra photos to present to the local Parisian Prefecture. He knew he would be asked if he wanted to pursue getting his *Carte de Séjour carte verte* (the equivalent to an American Green Card). The French were as weary as the American is guarding against illegal emigrants.

He had concluded several things. One—Victoria must be alive. Two—she had to be a victim of the system, much like he had been. And third—he wasn't going to fail again. This time he would not back down.

Hiding the information from the flash drive was the

hardest part. He knew he would be searched–extensively. However, it was his best key to finding the truth, and if anyone could open it, it was Warren.

The captain's voice followed an announcement bell. "I hope everyone had a pleasant flight this morning. We should be landing at the Charles de Gaulle International Airport shortly. We'll be approaching from the west, and should have a good view of the city from the right side of the plane as we approach the airport. We'll be using terminal 2 C today for those familiar with the airport. An attendant will be standing outside of the plane to assist with those needing help."

Royce knew to take the CDGVAL connection to the T1 train to Paris after making his way through customs. He had little doubt he would be followed, and making fast moves would be his best way to disappear. With pick pocket artists common, he guarded his wallet and knew to stay alert.

After the plane landed, he waited until the rest of the plane to exit before him. Being at the end of the passengers exiting had certain advantages. Only those making connections with love ones would be left at the welcoming gate. Also, the customs and immigration people would have plenty of other targets to inspect before he reached them.

He approached customs and handed a tall, lady officer his papers. She punched in his information and smiled. "Mr. Cianci, how are you today?"

"Fine . . . thanks."

"It appears that I'll need you to take your luggage with you to a holding room. Someone will be with you shortly."

He smiled. "I see. How long will this take?"

"It shouldn't take long." She pointed to a man wearing a dark blue suit.

He opened his badge as he approached. "I'm with the CIA. You'll need to come with me."

"Yes, Sir. Is there a problem?"

He turned and smiled. "I hope not."

They walked along a corridor before entering a small room. Royce walked in, forcing himself to show little emotions. He hadn't broken any laws, that is, as long as they didn't find the data stored in the flash drive. "I hope this doesn't take long."

Another officer joined them in the room, who immediately opened the suitcases and overnight bag that Royce had carried with him. He searched every aspect of the luggage, looking for any small hiding place. He produced a small metal detector, and searched again, but still nothing unusual surfaced. "I'll have to search you as well." He motioned for Royce to stand.

Royce obliged him with a smile. "Can I ask what it is you're looking for?"

He smiled at Royce. "This will just take a few more minutes." He finished, and signaled to the agent that he thought he was clean.

Royce had a seat.

"Royce, there's a phone call that you need to take. I'll be outside waiting on you." He pointed to the phone on the table, and closed the door behind them, leaving him by himself.

Royce glanced around the room, looking for a monitor. The phone rang. He reached for it, saying nothing.

"Royce, this is General Ralph Klinkenberg."

His head snapped backwards as he blinked his eyes. The voice of his old boss surprised him. But, then again, he half-way expected it. "Sir, how are you?"

His coarse voice, reflecting a life of yelling to subordinates, identified him immediately. "I'm fine, but that's not the question here. Royce, what in the hell are you doing in France?"

Royce smiled. So much for niceties. He hadn't changed at all. "You know the city of light, the city of romance."

"Cut the bull shit, Royce."

"General, you're the one with all of the answers. What do you want to ask me that you don't already know?"

"We have a lot of investment in people you know in France, and I'll not idly stand by and let you destroy it. I'm as sorry about Lynn as anyone, but nothing you can do will ever bring her back."

Royce remained quiet for a minute, as the thoughts of his life with Lynn raced through his mind. "Yes, there's nothing that can bring her back now, but a lot that could have been done then."

The phone remained quiet. "We've had this discussion many times before. You know my response."

"Yes, Sir, and I think we'll always agree to disagree. However, to ease your mind, I'm not here to cause problems."

"Remember, when you left the family here, you also left our protection. If you get into trouble in France, there'll be absolutely nothing I can do for you. And I don't have to remind you that you left some enemies in France that would love to find you."

"Is there anything else, Sir?"

"I see you're as arrogant as always. However, you did do your country a big service in breaking open this case."

"Thank you, Sir. Is there anything else, Sir?"

"The *Pack* is still in operation. Be careful."

"Yes, Sir, but it's not my battle anymore." He decided to put the General's mind at ease. "I'm not planning on staying here long."

"Watch your back, watch your back, son. You were one of my best and I hated losing you." The phone line went dead.

Royce knocked on the door, and the agent returned. He leaned toward Royce, and looked one last time over his paperwork. "I see you're scheduled to be here for three days. That's not a long time to do much sightseeing."

"You know, you have to do what you can do." Royce smiled, and crossed his arms.

The agent examined his cell phone. "I'm not sure if you can use this much here or not."

Royce smiled. "You never know. Anyway, I don't plan on making many calls here."

He flipped it open and scanned the menu. "I see you're not one to store much music on yours."

"I'm not too much into the music downloads." He smiled back, watching the guy's eyes.

"I think that'll be all for now. Enjoy your trip."

Royce proceeded through the rest of the check-in without any problems, and retrieved his luggage as he hurried toward the T1. He glanced around, knowing he would be followed. He checked his reservation sheet.

***

The Accor Hotel chain in Paris did provided the perfect accommodations, as well as good prices. It was also exactly what he needed to accomplish his new mission. However, he had many stops before he turned in for the night. He removed the clothes he brought with him, and hung them in the closet. While his wallet contained the bare essentials that he needed, the *plan d'arrondissement de Paris* (Paris map book) provided exactly what he needed to plan out his day. He smiled, thinking of the hell he was going to cause several people before the day was over.

He walked out, and glanced around at the crowds making their way along the street. The Paris officials, true to their determination of making the 1st, 2nd, 3rd and 4th *Arrondissements* (neighbourhoods) completely car-free in the near future showed signs of their work along the way. He kept his eyes down, watching for the hazards of walking–dog poop.

He smiled, and glanced around him. It was time to see what kind of shape his tail was in. He found a *vélo Liberté,* part of *le Vélib (*Freedom bike program) where you can rent bikes for a very modest program. Royce knew that the special credit card he ordered before leaving the States carried a smart card that would work. The cost, one euro for the day, was the best bargain in Paris. The trick was to get to the next station in the thirty minute time period, and have no charge at all. He felt like he was in shape, but glanced behind him to see if his tail was following. It was really hard to tell.

Royce sweated heavily from the hard peddling as he headed for the *Rue de Rivoli*–the perfect test for a tag-along–before proceeding to his next stop the *Marché aux puces de St-Ouen (Porte de Clignancourt*) (Clignancourt flea market). He knew his lead wouldn't last long, and in the streets he would be found soon. He headed for a stall full of second hand clothes, looking for the right look. He purchased what he needed, and shoved them into his day pack.

The next purchase–the *Paris Pass*, a pre-paid card to around sixty attractions. This would give him plenty of time and opportunities to access the extent of his tail. He had seen the sights many times before, as he recalled his trips here when he worked for the General. Nothing much had changed.

He headed into a train station, showed his pass, and walked back to the next car. His exit, just before the train departure, left little room to doubt that the last of his tail didn't make it off in time. Too bad. The toilet on the other side of the corridor was almost vacant. Perfect. He changed to the flea market clothes, fluffed his hair, and removed the pencil in his pocket. A few scrapes added an interesting three day growth to his face. The sock hat perfected the look he was after. Now, he had to make it to the northeast where the low class immigrants lived. No one would want to follow him to this part of Paris.

***

Royce hid in the short foyer entrance, doing his best to avoid attention. He wished he still had the key, but knew there was absolutely nothing he could do now but wait.

He heard the shuffling of feet on the pavement, and lowered his head, waiting on the occupant to show up. The solid body–the size of a refrigerator–moved in his direction. *"Bonsoir* (good evening)." He raised his head to see a small smile creak across his friends face.

"Ça va (How are you)?" He glanced around before moving to the door, and unlocking it. "I knew you would be back."

"Oui (Yes). Ça va bien, et vous (I'm fine, and you)?" Royce followed him into the apartment. "I need your help, Charles."

Charles raised his eye brows as he switched to English. "Is this personal, or is this company business?"

"Personal for now, but where it leads to . . . I'm not sure." He walked across the kitchen to the refrigerator. "Did anyone tell you I was coming?"

He turned his hands over. "I'm retired. This is a young man's game." He lowered his head. "I do have good hearing, however."

"Good. I need to talk to someone and not have a small army following me around."

"It seems to me that you do a pretty damn good job of disappearing."

Royce smiled. "It's a little different when they know

where I'll show up. It'll be better to arrange a more private meeting."

"So you're still trying to find out exactly who is responsible for kidnapping Lynn."

"That's information I'll always want to know, and that's what part of the army of tails here think I'm after. Yes, I'll never forget the hell I was put through here, and you know about it, and why I left the service. However, I have a new mission. I met a girl who either worked for us, or for the Russians, but the best I can tell, nobody knows for sure. Her name is Victoria Zayas. Do you know anything about her?"

He smiled. "I've heard of the name, and I understand the CIA posted a worldwide alert on her a few months ago, but I also heard she died in an accident in America." He turned sideways, questioning Royce's interest in the name.

"I was in Jacksonville when that shark attack occurred, but I don't buy it." He removed a half-open bottle of wine from the refrigerator, and located some cheese.

"You think she's here?"

"I don't think so. But have no way of really knowing. I need to talk to her boss, a Warren Hornbuckle that transferred here last month."

"He works here in France now?"

"Yes. I need you to get me in to see him tomorrow night. Late night at his office would be good."

Charles smiled. "I guess I owe you that much."

Royce poured the wine into two glasses. He noticed a faint smell of vinegar, reflecting the tell-tell signs of the hard life his friend must be living now. "To old times . . . may they be forgotten."

Charles lifted his glass. "If it was only that easy . . . my friend."

Chapter 20

Royce pushed the heavy floor buffer out of the truck, moving forward quietly. Most of the employees at the International Cyber Consulting Group building had already left. A tall man at the entrance stopped them one by one to clear them into the building. However, all he really checked were the photos with the faces. After all, they were janitors only hired to clean the floors and toilets.

Royce knew his French was good, but it was far from perfect, and with an accent that was hard to fake at times. If asked any questions, he planned on answering in Spanish, the same native language as the crew leader, and one that he had a much better chance of hiding his English accent. Fortunately, the guard eyed him, but waved him on through.

They started on the second floor and worked up. Warren had his office on the sixth. Royce had no idea if Warren had received a message about him coming, but he would soon know for sure.

The elevator opened on the sixth floor as he scanned the foyer. He heard no music playing, and the main lights had been turned off. He clicked on the master switch for the floor, and pulled the buffer after him, making his way along the hallway. Halfway down, a door opened. An older woman glanced at him, and surveyed the machine before she re-entered her office, closing the door behind her. The look on her face clearly indicated she wanted peace and quiet and could care less about a shiny floor.

He continued down the hallway with the buffer squeaking until he turned a corner. Where was his office? It had to be here close. One door was cracked open, but was still blocking his view. He heard music coming from inside as he moved forward, allowing him to glance around.

The song was American, and perhaps Bon Jovi–a good sign. Royce checked behind him, and saw the office of the inquisitive woman still shut. He found a plug, and turned on the machine. With luck any others on the floor would react the same way as she had, closing their doors. While the marble floor covered the hallway, the individual offices were covered in an expensive looking carpet.

He peeked around the door, Warren had his head stretched forward, focusing on a computer screen. His hands were covering his ears, attempting to avoid the sound of the buffer. His intense concentration allowed Royce time to close the door behind him.

As Royce entering Warren's office, he startled him and watched him jerk his head in his direction. Warren opened his mouth and was preparing to shout at the intruder until he saw Royce raise a finger to his lips. His face first registered a disgusted frown, but softened, as Royce lowered the sock hat off of his head, revealing his image. "Royce–what the hell are you doing here?"

Royce lifted his finger to his lip again before he glanced around at the door. "I need to talk to you."

Warren pushed back deep into his over-sized executive chair, as questioning looks covered his face. "Okay."

Royce continued to hold up one finger to indicate he needed one minute. He opened the door, turned off the buffer, and glanced around to see if anyone else was around. He pulled the buffer into Warren's office before closing the door behind him. "I'm truly sorry about all of this."

"What's this all about? You should have called me. Why are you being so secretive?" The questions poured out, raising the high tenor tone of Warren's voice.

"I need your help. I don't know who else to trust." Royce walked around the large desk to shake his hand.

A smug look crossed Warren's face. "Why? What have you found out?"

"I found a flash drive hidden in a wine bottle that Victoria and I drank the night we met. I don't have any idea what's on it, but for some reason, she wanted me to have it or keep it for safe keeping. I was hoping you might be able to open it for me."

Warren mimicked Royce in his paranoid glancing around the room. "Do you have it with you?"

"I know you have confidential issues involved, but all I'm worried about is finding Victoria and discovering the truth."

"So . . . you think Victoria's alive."

"I don't know for sure, and I don't know if she's dead either."

"Yes, Victoria, as you would suspect, was working on several very high profile cases for us. You do understand that."

"I understand, and I don't care to know anything other than what may have caused her to fake a disappearance."

"I know what you're saying. I'll try to help you as best I can, but it all depends on what's on the flash drive."

Royce knew that was the best he could hope for. He pulled the phone out of his pocket. "It's amazing what you can hide in a phone these days." He opened the back and retrieved a small chip, replacing it with the one hidden, but not connected to anything on the inside.

Warren raised an eyebrow. "Interesting. That's smart."

"Here, I'll let you finish the download to your computer."

The download opened on his computer in seconds and a file named *Freedom* appeared on the screen. Royce watched Warren play with it for several minutes, as his face squinted with each failed attempt.

Royce's impatience caused him to constantly look over his shoulder. "How long do you think it'll take to open it?"

A smile spread across Warren's face, almost as if he was presented with a challenge. "You have to remember, Victoria's one of the best in the world at what she did. In fact, she may have succeeded in making it impossible to open without the proper code."

"I see, but that's what your firm specializes in, isn't it?"

"Yes, but you don't need to stand over me." He pointed to the small sofa on the other side of his office. "Trust me, I've slept on it many times for a few hours rather than going home. It's not that bad."

Royce nodded. He acted like his head hurt, and that the lack of sleep and jet lag was catching up with him. He knew that his constant peering over Warren's shoulder was probably hampering him. However, in this environment, sleep is one luxury he would put off for later. "I appreciate the offer, but I'll wait on you."

Royce stayed busy walking around the office. It reminded him of the one in Jacksonville. The room, originally designed for an executive, had been rearranged for a guy who was mostly interested in just concentrating on a computer screen in front of him. He suspected that Warren was a master at his craft, but only made it into management because of his computer skill and not his managerial ability.

He occupied his time walking around the office, as his background in investigating kicking in. His eyes darted over to Warren to see if he was being observed. He wasn't. He knew chances were that nothing of importance would be left in the open, but he would never know for sure if he didn't at least attempt to snoop.

The French paper Mondo was spread on the sofa, and computer parts were scattered all over the place. Books that were half opened covered many flat surfaces. On the wall Warren had stapled various projects he was working on. That's what he really would like to study, but knew he wouldn't get too much of a chance until later. He would bide his time.

He roamed the room, trying hard to give the impression that he wasn't concentrating too hard on any one item on the wall. He closed his eyes often, making it appear that he was much more "sleepy" than he really was. The truth was: he had slept all day at his friend's apartment, leaving his pursuers to hunt for him in vain.

Halfway down a wall, he recognized a name—one that stopped him cold. Raptor was a top enforcer in the Pack and wanted worldwide. Was he a client, or was he someone Warren had been asked to locate for someone else? He had to know. His mind flashed back to his last assignment in France where he came close to assisting in his capture. That was also when he learned of Lynn's abduction. He had little doubt that this guy was responsible. Could it be that Victoria and this guy are connected somehow?

While maintaining his guard, he decided on a new approach. "I think you have your hands full, and I haven't had any sleep in two days now. If you don't mind, I'll take you up on the use of the couch."

Warren waved at him, but kept his focus staring at the screen, and his fingers working the keyboard.

In a few minutes, Royce started snoring lightly, and just enough to be heard, but still not loud enough to be aggravating. His eyes were closed enough to appear that he was asleep, but remained open enough to allow him to see faintly. Warren did glance over at him several times.

Thoughts of Raptor continued to race through his mind. No one knew exactly who he was, or what he looked like. They did know the results of his anger when he enforced his dominance over the operations of the Pack. Royce knew much more about the Pack than he ever reported. Some information was best to save for the right moment.

Organized crime has become more and more sophisticated over the last ten or twenty years. Respectability is almost laughable, he thought, but it appeared to make sense to the upper echelon that viewed life much different than the average politician or businessman. Government wasn't one to set the rules that they would follow, but one that was used to foster control over others. They considered themselves to be far above the dismal working of politics, or the laws of pathetic governments.

The one problem that the Pack solved was the internal fighting between rival groups, or organizations. No one person was allowed to dominate the Pack. In fact, membership was never discussed. Meetings were set up strictly when necessary. The network extended from China to Russia, but operated mainly in Central Europe.

Royce allowed his mind to shift to old memories, as he reflected on being recruited by the General personally while he had been surfing in California. While he had loved his life then, and one that it hurt even now to think back on, he forced himself to avoid the same type tears he had cried in the past over her. *Lynn, I'm so sorry.*

The General, his prior boss, had just warned him that the Pack was still in operation. It would be great to have his help now, but he knew that it would be impossible. He was on his own–totally.

***

Brandon shuffled papers on his desk, as the perfect order on the desk-top reflected his attention to detail. Perhaps he had been working at a desk for too long, he thought, but he knew that it was necessary work since he reported to the director of the CIA, and only worked high profile cases.

Charlotte knocked on the door, but entered before he could answer. "We may have a problem. Royce is in France, and may be accidentally stumbling into an operation we have working there."

"What the hell are you telling me?"

"I talked to General Ralph Klinkenberg. He called to ask for an off-the-record assistance. Royce worked for him."

Brandon whistled. "So that explains his classified history. What kind of assistance?"

"Apparently he likes Royce and he feels like he owes him for his sacrifice in the past. Royce had worked directly on tracking down the Pack."

Brandon blinked before he shouted, "Are you telling me that Royce is working independently and trying to take on an old operation? And . . . why would he do that?"

"I don't think he is. I think he went to see Warren Hornbuckle, Victoria's old boss from Jacksonville, who has been transferred to Paris."

"Humm, okay. Again I ask—why would he do that?"

"I wish I knew. I do know that the General talked to him yesterday and warned him about going it alone. He said that Royce acted like he wasn't, but he has his doubts. He placed a tail on Royce that didn't last long."

Brandon smiled, thinking about the one in Moscow he had ordered. "I have to admit, the boy is good when it comes to disappearing."

"If Royce found the missing flash drive, it makes sense that he would ask Warren to help him with it." She waited for his response.

"Sounds to me like the boy may be getting himself into one hell of a mess."

"It's worse. The General told us that he knows that he wasn't the only one following Royce. Since it wasn't us, take a guess who it might be. Also, consider the fact that if he's abducted by the Pack, and has the information from the flash drive with him, what they could do with it."

Brandon leaned forward, his heart pumping hard. "I hope you're packed, we're leaving now."

Charlotte smiled. "I thought so. And I am. Are you?"

He smiled. "Where is Robert?"

"He's currently in Germany, but on his way to France as we speak. I left him a message to call us immediately."

Chapter 21

Royce never moved as he pretended to sleep on the Warren's sofa. With his eyes constantly studied him, and his intense work on the keyboard, he would have thought Warren would have given away some tidbit of information by now. Perhaps this ploy wasn't going to work. It had to be very early morning by now, and he wasn't sure how the janitorial service manager covered for him. Perhaps he was still in the building, but he knew he would have to leave soon.

He reached up and rubbed his eyes before glancing over at Warren. "Any luck?"

Warren smiled, sliding his fingers through his slick black hair. "I think it might be impossible. We'll need the code."

"Is there any idea what this is at all?"

"I wish I could tell you."

The door swung open, and Robert entered the room. Royce recognized him from Jacksonville. He was the CIA officer asking question after Victoria's shark attack. "Hello, Royce. You travelled a long way to return this to me." He quickly raised his hand and banished a small handgun.

Royce's face squinted. "How did you know I was here?"

Warren grinned. "E-mail."

Royce felt stupid. He didn't think about Warren doing that, as he slid back into the couch. "Is there any chance that one of you can tell me what's on that file?"

"Information. Lots of information." Warren turned to face Robert. "All useless unless we have the code."

"So . . . you don't have the code to unlock the

information."

"This'll take some time. Victoria's very good at her job."

"Time is one thing we don't have, my friend." He handed Warren a new flash drive. "Download it to this one for me—now."

Warren looked puzzled. "I don't think anyone will have a better chance at finding the code than me."

Robert raised his gun, pointing point blank at his face.

Warren smiled out of the corner of his mouth. "If you want a back up copy, all you have to do is ask. I don't think I've ever disappointed you before, have I?"

Royce stood still, listening, trying to understand. It didn't surprise him that the CIA wanted the information stored on the flash drive. What it contained, he still had no clue, and it looked like he would never know now.

Warren handed the flash drive back to Robert. "It's a large file. Trust me, she secured it well."

"I would expect nothing less." Robert turned to Royce. "I appreciate you being so helpful. I knew it would turn up at some time, but I was hoping that you would have turned it over to me directly, and saved us all some embarrassing moments. I guess life does have its surprises. Who would have ever guessed that you would be the one she picked, out of all the surfers in the world."

Royce remained quiet, waiting on Robert to volunteer more information. Why was he holding a gun on him and Warren?

Robert turned to Warren. "I also need you to erase the copy you have on this computer."

Warren looked shocked, but staring down the barrel of the gun, he decided to comply. "I don't understand. How do you plan to open it without the code?"

"I think Victoria's still alive. When she hears that we have the data file, she'll reappear. She has much to lose . . .

her family . . . her new lover boy." He pointed in the direction of Royce.

Warren smiled when he finished. "You're not the only one interested in this file, what will the others say?"

"You have no clue who really hired you, do you?" Robert smiled. "You've been very useful until now. Thanks to Royce here, you've become a liability. That's one thing the Pack can't accept."

"I'm not sure who it is that you call the Pack. Most of our work has been for various government agencies."

"To be so smart, you can be such a dumb ass." He raised the gun higher, pointing it directly at Warren's head. "Just so you know, moron, the Pack is run by the various government agencies that have their hands tied by politics back home, but are so willing to cooperate with various syndications of special interest. It does provide the means to get results."

BAM! The gun recoiled in Robert's hand as Warren's head exploded, splattering blood on the wall behind him.

In more of a knee jerk type reaction, Royce rushed toward Robert, but he moved faster, leveling the barrel at Royce. "You're alive for one reason right now. I may need you to convince Victoria to contact me."

"What makes you so sure she's still alive? You're the one that convinced everyone else that she had, in fact, died."

Robert smiled. "The best way to keep everyone else out of this is to let them believe that. Now, I'm sure you also have an additional copy of this somewhere. Would you like to tell me now or later?"

Royce remained quiet as Robert glanced at his watch. "It's a good thing I was in Germany when word of your trip surfaced. While it allowed me to get here first, we now need to disappear. If you had gone anywhere but France, I would never had known about your background. Damm, you had a file impossible to obtain."

"So . . . where are we going?"

"You went looking for Raptor for a long time here. This time, I think he would like to meet you. He does have a certain flair for entertaining special guests. I'm sure you will in particular like to hear how he took special interest in a sweet little thing for California."

Royce closed his eyes briefly. *Lynn, I'm so sorry. Please forgive me.* He opened them, blinking several times. "I'm looking forward to it." He forced himself to smile.

As they stepped out of the office, two other men joined them. The first one surveyed the room. "I don't think will look too good on your annual review."

Robert smiled, but spoke in Russian. "Oleg, you know, I think the Pack will not be asking for any referrals anyway."

So, that was it. Robert was defecting to the Russian side or going to work directly for the Pack. Either that or he had worked for them all this time.

They proceeded down the stairways, one level at a time. On one turn, Robert stopped and faced Royce. "I can see where you entered here undetected, but how in the hell were you going to make it out of here? Did you think Warren would help you get out?" He shook his head from one side to the other. "I can see why you didn't make it, boy."

As they reached the second floor, and moved toward the exit, a large box hit the first guy on the back of his head. Robert turned, and fired three shots while the third guy moved in behind him.

Royce delivered a blow to the back of the head of this third guy, dazing him. Next, Royce shoved his head into a wall before he could recover, shattering his skull.

Robert quickly swirled to point the barrel directly between Royce's eyes. Royce stopped, his face frozen, but his eyes darted to one side long enough to see Charles on the floor, covered in blood.

"It looks like displaced loyalty cost you one more life." Robert glanced at the flash drive. "I know that Raptor would love to see you, but perhaps he would be happy just to know that you're dead." His fingers tightened on the gun.

Royce knew all he needed was a microsecond to make a move. Suddenly, Robert's phone vibrated. He stepped back one step, the phone vibrated again. Robert lifted it from his coat pocket, saying nothing, as he flipped it open.

Royce waited, as Robert smiled, and time seemed to be moving in slow motion. "Hello, Victoria."

***

General Klinkenberg shoved through the exit, shouting to his men following him. "Is the copter on the ground yet?"

"Not yet, Sir!"

"They have one minute before I'll be on the pad. Do you understand?"

"Sir, yes Sir." A subordinate raised his phone, indicating that he was in contact with the pilot.

"I need to get onboard one of the strike eagles now. What's the name of the pilot again?"

"Colonel Davidson, Sir."

"Good man. I know him—and the two escorts?"

"Colonel Davidson picked out the pilots for the other two strike eagles, Sir. I can get the names if you want me to."

"Never mind, I trust Colonel Davidson." He rushed in front of his men, making his way onto the pad as the copter landed. "Make sure the French know I'm coming, and be sure to tell them we're coming in loaded for bear. If they try to make a run for it, we'll appreciate any help, of course, but plan on using all possible means to stop them from making it back to Russia."

"I'm on it, Sir."

The General entered the copter without taking time to

salute.

***

Brandon had settled into his seat aboard the agencies jet, and hoped to grab a little rest on the flight when his phone rang. "Sorry to bother you, but you have an emergency call coming in from General Ralph Klinkenberg. Shall I put it through?"

"Yes, this could be interesting." Brandon answered, as he smiled at Charlotte, indicating that he wanted her listening in on this call.

"Brandon, I received a call a few minutes ago from an operative in France. I can't go into all of the details of this operation now, but it appears that we have a mutual target. When is the last time you heard from Robert?"

Charlotte was monitoring the call playing over Brandon's speaker phone. An inquisitive glance crossed her face. "It was before we left. He was in Germany. I would guess he's on his way to France right now."

The General recognized the extra voice. "For your information, Charlotte, he's already in France, and he has just shot one of my operatives in Paris—a man that should be living out his retirement now, but will never get the chance. I think he may have died talking to me since he managed to tell me he had been shot. The French police are on the way to The International Cyber Consulting Group's building as we speak."

"Since I know Robert, I hope you can back up that acquisition."

"Brandon, I have the words of an operative that recognized him after he had been shot by him."

Shit! "Well, I'll be damned. We're in route now, General, and I'll get back to you shortly. We have assets on the ground in Paris now also."

"Brandon, I'm on the way to France as we speak, and I'm

not planning on taking time to knock on the front door before entering. Call me back shortly."

"Really!"

The General laughed. "As you know, it's not smart to stir up a nest of *hornets*, especially when they're loaded with venom." The phone line died.

Chapter 22

"Well . . . hello, Victoria, it's good to know that a cute little thing like you didn't become a shark appetizer. I thought you would show up soon enough." Robert motioned to Oleg and Royce to keep moving.

Royce, however, locked his focus on Oleg's eyes, forcing himself to avoid concentrating on the gun in his face. He needed one or two blinks, one moment of a break in concentration, or one small error. Oleg's reflected stare signaled that he understood it well. Still, both allowed their concentration to include the conversation between Robert and Victoria.

"As you may know, Royce has found the flash drive." He glanced over at Royce. "It's too bad you couldn't pick a better asset. He brought it to Warren, looking for a little help."

Being pushed along, they finally reached the front entrance where a man guarded a hostage at the front gate. Oleg glanced at Ivan. "Do you have everything we need from him?"

"Yes."

Oleg raised his gun, shooting the guard point blank. "Put him behind the desk, and let's get out of here."

"Look, sweetheart, we both know you did a number on the data file, and I need the password to open it." He motioned for them to keep walking. "Listen, I'm a little busy right now." He hurried to keep up with the rest. "Call me back in about ten minutes. For his sake, I hope you can provide me with what I need." He closed his phone.

As they all moved to two waiting cars in the front of the building, Royce needed two things. He had to escape, and he had to take Robert's phone with him.

Robert glanced over at Royce. "It looks like your girlfriend purchased you a little time, but for your sake; well I hope she does the smart thing."

"You know I don't have the slightest clue what's on that data file. Can you, at least, tell me what's so important on it that makes a man sworn to protect his country turn traitor?"

Robert smiled. "I know you probably hate me for this, but remember that very few things in life are exactly as they appear."

When they pulled out of the parking lot, a flurry of cars appeared down the street, and headed directly for them. Their car sprinted for the exit, as the one carrying Oleg's bodyguards turned to face the onslaught. All four doors opened with men jumping out and opening fire immediately. The men from the back seat moved to the trunk, where they removed a small rocket launcher.

The release of the rockets lit up the still early morning sky with the resulting explosion shattering all doubts as to the faith of the responding officers. Oleg's men smiled at each other briefly before throwing their weapons back in the trunk, and jumping back in their seats to chase after Oleg's car.

***

Charlotte answered her cell on the first ring. "This is Charlotte." Her eyebrows arched upward. "Oh my God! Do what you have to do to contain this now. We're on our way, but it'll still be several hours before we make it to France. I want a command post set up at the airport by the time I arrive in Paris. Do you understand?"

She closed her phone and glanced at Brandon. "We lost three men."

He lowered his head. "Damn." He retrieved his phone and dialed the Major back. "Sir, we have a situation here. We just lost three men trying to stop Royce from being abducted."

"I'll be airborne shortly. Until I arrive, do what you can, but . . . I might arrive even before you do. We're going to be lighting up the sky soon."

"Thank you, Sir. We'll be talking to you soon."

***

Royce watched Oleg roll his eyes upward, and as if he was in deep thought about the flash drive that he constantly played with. The brief moment allowed Royce time to touch his phone from outside his pants. He pressed the record button on the side that he used to make notes on all of the time easily.

"So . . . it appears that you have information you wanted, but even Warren couldn't open it. And . . . without Victoria's help, it's useless. Am I guessing right so far?"

"I don't think you have to be a genius to figure that out."

Racing along the streets Royce was thankful for being in *la Ville-Lumière* (The City of Light) as he easily recognized his location. He could see the Eiffel's tower on his right, as they headed to the south-west, and out of the center of Paris. "I'll admit that I'm no genius, but at least I'm loyal to my country."

Robert laughed. Oleg laughed. However Royce didn't laugh, as he hoped his phone would record the conversation through his pants. "I hear a Russian accent."

Oleg smiled. "So much for years of practice." He glanced over at Robert. "Royce, it's not our fault that America has given us such a perfect opportunity to make money, and one that we cannot ignore."

"Really!"

Oleg ignored Royce's sarcasm. "The housing market, and

well really the real estate market in general, is what made America become so wealthy and arrogant over the years. Take that away and the whole country will fall apart at the seams."

Royce raised an eyebrow expressing an interest in knowing more. "Yes, the real estate market has seen better days, but I still don't have any clue how you fit into all of this."

"We buy the deals at bargain prices, making sure that the spiral is continued, but most importantly, it gives us ownership to a large number of homes, and places we can transplant many people. It also gives us a way to move money easily into the United States. No one even questions where the money comes from when they're so desperate to save their ass. It's the best way ever contemplated to avoid money transaction problems."

So the Russians were buying real estate at bargain prices. Somehow Royce knew that the Pack was involved in this, but decided to conceal his knowledge of this for now. He glances out of the window and saw them approaching *la Perpherique* (A multi-lane highway around Paris). "Can I ask where we're heading?"

Oleg smiled. "Somewhere we can have a little privacy, but I think it'll be a quick meeting. It all depends on how far away Victoria is. By the way, I think it's time to call her back."

Robert smiled, as he looked at his phone. "You don't really think she left a call-back number for us, do you? Don't worry so much. I'm sure she'll call in a minute."

"I hope so." He glanced at his watch. "We'll be at Orly shortly, and the sooner we get in the air, the better."

Royce fought the urge to smile. So . . . the Orly International Airport is where they were heading. "I can't believe that all is this over real estate purchases. Deals are all over the place, and there's no reason to be secretive about it."

Oleg glanced over at Robert. "Yes, there's much more. Like your government loves to track money transferred to America, we also have an interest in tracking American money here. The illegal seed money the United States uses here causes a lot of problems for us. It's best to be one step ahead of them."

"I see . . . and Victoria was part of this?"

"Ahhh, Victoria. A rare find, and a girl with a very special gift. She does have the ability to find her way into the most protected sites. You know, if she had used her head, she could have had a very rewarding career. However, I see that she has some misplaced loyalties. It's too bad."

"I'll have to say that I only knew her for one night." He kept a cold stare on Oleg.

"Yes. I've wondered about that night. She must have been fantastic for you to keep pursuing this so hard. Either that, or you're one dumb bastard." Oleg smiled over at Robert.

When Robert's phone rang, he smiled in the direction of Oleg. "Hello."

Oleg reached for the phone. *Vica, kak dela* (Vicki (a nickname for Victoria), how are you)?" He glanced over at Royce, and switched to English for his benefit. "I have your boyfriend here." There was a short pause. "Yes, he's healthy, but it totally depends upon you if he stays that way for long."

Robert leaned forward, trying to hear her voice.

"We have a plane located in a hangar at Orly. Since you know where it is, I suggest you make it to the airport as fast as you can. It will be interesting to learn what you've been doing." He closed the phone.

***

Victoria closed the phone. She was in the *Le bon Marché de Paris* (The Parisian mega-store) located in the 7th *arrondissement* (district). Perhaps with a little luck she could get their first, but she had to hurry.

How could I have been so stupid? After reaching down to her stomach, she patted it and smiled. *On the other hand, how could I have been so lucky? Why won't they just let us just disappear?* Okay, she knew she had what they wanted, but she assumed they should be able to have other ways of obtaining it.

Memories of their time together had never left her thoughts. She hoped he didn't hate her when he found out the truth. Surely he would understand, especially since out of all of the people she could have chosen, she had to pick one with a history. While her research on him was shaky, it was enough to convince her that he had a past much like her own, but he was allowed out.

She checked to make sure her hair fit under her hat and that her outfit was perfect. This was a totally different look for her. It was expensive, but she knew it was effective in covering her identity. She had a plan in place, but knew she had to modify it along the way. With a little luck all of this could be behind them soon. If she had known what she was getting herself involved with at the beginning, she would never have placed so many people at risk such as her Dad and Mom that she adored, not her friends, and now she had placed an innocent guy in danger. It was time to correct her errors of the past and make those responsible pay, but most importantly, she wanted the one item she had dreamed of all of her life—the right to live in America as an American. While she didn't want to forget her Russian heritage, she wanted to be able to experience both sides of who she was.

The more she had researched Royce's history, the more she had fallen in love with him. He had been mistreated by the government, and abandoned, but, in spite of it all, he had managed to keep a good outlook on life, and above all, he had managed to help others find love. Now he needed her help, and much more than he could imagine. These people will never let him go alive, they had too much at stake.

Chapter 23

"Bonjour." The pilot at the airport smiled at Victoria as she approached him.

Victoria had her dark glasses in place while doing her best to appear arrogant, rich, and spoiled. She attempted to hide her knowledge of French, and most importantly, her identity, as she spoke in rapid English. "Is the copter ready?"

"Oui, Mademoiselle." He pointed to the copter, which was slightly outside a hangar.

She peered over the top of her glasses, indicating her intolerance to his use of French. "I'll need it in a few minutes. My schedule is very tight." She turned her back to him and walked away as she opened her purse, retrieving the disposable phone she had purchased for this meeting.

From the corner of her eye she saw him shaking his head, but walk toward the copter regardless. She knew that he must have thought he would be well paid for a quick trip around the city to pacify a bored American businessman's wife. If he only knew what kind of wild joy ride he was in for. Her research indicated that he had been a pilot for one of the French elite attack forces in his earlier years, and she was counting on those skills today.

She punched in the number to Robert's phone and glanced at the sky above, hoping for—no pleading for any help or guidance. Robert answered immediately. "Hello, Victoria. I hope you're close by, we've very little time."

"I'm not too far away."

"Very good. Once we get airborne, it'll be very

interesting to hear your story. You've caused us some problems, and some concerns we need to discuss."

"Robert . . . I know you want the code to the data, but . . . I want something also."

The line remained quiet for a while, but he finally responded. "We don't have much time to discuss this."

"I understand. Here's the deal. You want the code, and I want two things."

"Let me guess. Could that be a certain guy we have with us?"

"Yes, of course, but you know that already."

"And what else is it that you want?"

"My freedom."

"Do you think that's really possible?"

"It's possible if you allow it. I guess it really all depends on how much you want the code."

"There's no way I can guarantee that, and I think you know that."

"I think you need to work on it, but for now, I want Royce set free. He's not involved in this and it's my fault for involving him. That is one point I won't negotiate on."

"I see." He whistled. "It appears you must have had more of a one night stand than I thought."

Victoria bit her lip. If he only knew how much. "You can take it or leave it, but if anything happens to him, just remember that you have nothing else that matters to me, and therefore nothing to bargain with."

She heard muffled voices on the phone. "Okay . . . so how do you want to handle this?"

"How long before you're at the hangar?"

"Perhaps a few hours. Why?" She thought about saying more, but needed to time this perfectly.

She knew they were perhaps already at the hangar, but played along. "I'll call you back in ten minutes with the details. You give me what I want, and I'll give you what you want."

More muffled voices. "We'll have very little time to make anything happen. If we don't get the code when we arrive, you can say goodbye to lover boy here." The phone line went dead.

Victoria looked behind her before she walked over to the pilot. "We'll need to leave in about five minutes and we'll have one more . . . special passenger."

He looked inquisitively at Victoria. "One more passenger?"

"Yes, I'll explain in a second when we get airborne." She handed him a stack of one hundred Euros. "Will it be a problem?"

He accepted the money and smiled. "I can be discrete, not to worry."

Good, she hoped that he would think of it as a love connection, thus explaining the need for secrecy. This would keep him from asking any more questions for the time being. "That's good to know. I hope you're as good as I heard. We need to disappear as soon as he's on board, and I don't like having my photo taken. You do understand?"

"I think I understand perfectly."

"Very good." She hated using him, but he would be well compensated.

She walked away from him and called Robert back to ask. "Are you close?"

"Perhaps. What do you have in mind?"

"Let Royce go. Tell him to walk straight out toward the runway using the taxi lane."

"And why would I do that?"

"I'll transmit the code to you in an e-mail as soon as he's safe."

"And if you don't?"

"I guess you'll have to trust me. The second part of this is my freedom."

"Victoria, you're in way over your head. I think you know not to fuck with us, and I'll only say this once. This had better be on the level."

"I fully understand. Let me know when he's walking out, and make sure he has a phone where I can contact him for further instructions."

"He has a cell phone, and I'm fairly sure you know the number. We'll let him take it with him, but we want the code before he disappears."

"Fine. We'll do it at the same time, but he has some walking to do, so don't make this difficult."

"He'll be leaving in a few minutes. For your sake, I hope you use your head."

Victoria turned to the pilot. "I'm ready when you are."

He smiled. "I'm at your service, Mademoiselle." He opened the passenger door for her, and watched her entering the copter. "Where are we heading?"

"The corporate hangars across the runway. He'll be walking toward the taxi lane.

An inquisitive expression crossed his face again, but he apparently knew to keep his thoughts private. "As you wish."

The pilot contacted the tower speaking in French. "I have one more passenger I need to pick up on the other side of the airport. Requesting permission to circle airport."

Victoria pretended to not understand the French, remaining in her arrogant stance, as she retrieved her phone and dialed Royce.

"Hello," he answered almost immediately.

Her mind raced, trying to think of what she was going to say to him. Hopefully she would have the opportunity to explain everything soon. "Hi, Royce. I'm sorry for all of this, but right now I need you to follow my instructions precisely. Do you understand?"

"I'm listening."

"Are you walking away from the hangar?"

"Yes, they told me to walk out on the taxi lane toward the runway. They have a small army of guns pointed my way."

"I understand. It'll be all over in a minute. I promise." She bit her lip, hoping that was the truth. She checked her watch. The General would be arriving soon, and the timing had to be perfect.

The copter lifted off, and flew around the central part of the main runway. Victoria felt the control the pilot maintained on the copter. Yes, he was very good. He flew around to the other side without any further contact with the tower. When a man walking on the outskirt of the hangar came into view, she pointed to him for the benefit of the pilot. "Please, give him a few minutes to make it out closer to the runway. He needs to disappear from the sight of the hangar. You do understand." She smiled at him for the first time.

"Yes, I think I do. If you want I can circle the airport once."

"I think that'll be good." Royce needed to get as far as possible from the hangar.

Finally, they completed their circle around the airport. This'll work she thought, and with her adrenalin pulling hard, she called Robert back. "Okay, the code is located on a site I've set up. I'll e-mail the address to it as we pick Royce up."

"For your sake, I hope you're right."

She motioned for the pilot to pick him up. She knew they had no intentions on letting them leave, but she knew one thing they didn't know.

When the pilot landed close to Royce, and he headed for

the copter, she sent the e-mail, knowing they would attempt to verify it immediately. She felt Robert, or perhaps one of his men, focusing the cross hairs of a sniper's rifle on her.

VAROOM! The roar of the copter quickly disappeared under the much louder sound of strike eagles making a flyby of the airport. The General had arrived.

The startled pilot looked at Victoria. "What the hell was that?"

"Reinforcements. We need to make a run for it now."

He didn't take time to ask question, taking off low and fast.

***

Robert also saw the American combat jets–the strike eagles. What the fuck was going on? He hadn't returned calls from Brandon, and had wanted him to think that he was still in route to France. As he glanced at the rest of the group rushing behind Oleg to the jet, he knew that this changed everything, but surely the Americans didn't think they could lead an attack on French soil.

He retrieved his phone, and hit the speed dial button for Brandon, who answered on the first ring.

"What's going on? I landed in France, and heard we have several strike eagles running havoc here?"

Brandon voice remained smooth, but demanding. "Robert, I've been trying to reach you. Where are you?"

"I'm coming into the airport, trying to track down members of the Pack. What's with these jets?"

"The General has information on the Pack being here as well, and he's fully intent on stopping him from escaping this time. If the French don't take care of business, he's fully prepared to do so."

"Oh, shit. He can't do that."

"Yes, he can, and he's prepared to do so. He has about half of the Air force behind him. He struck out on his own, but he's a very popular General, and the word quickly spread. He means business. Stay where you are, I'll call you back shortly."

Oleg looked at him and yelled, "What's going on?"

"We have company."

Oleg ran toward the plane. "We'll be airborne in a few seconds. They won't follow us toward Russia." However, when he turned around Robert had vanished.

***

The helicopter pilot flew halfway across the airport before banking, and the pilot changing his course. He glanced again at the strike eagles climbing in the sky before yelling at them in French, "Sorry, folks, but I'm making a small change in plans." He pulled into the front of the hangar before Royce and Victoria knew what he was up to, making a bumpy landing.

They both saw the betrayal, but it was too late to react. Oleg's right hand man was standing outside the copter, pointing his pistol at them. Behind him several other men were backing him up. The pilot dashed from the copter, yelling at them to hurry.

Victoria and Royce moved through the door slowly. They had to bide their time, as the sound of sirens screamed from many directions. "Hello, Victoria. Glad you could join us." Oleg's right hand man smiled, and raised his pistol toward her head. "You've caused a lot of problems. Now move it, we have to get out of here."

As the other men dashed toward a small jet, and scrambled to make it onboard as fast as possible, Oleg's right hand man remained in the rear to escort Royce and Victoria on board.

Royce winked at Victoria and stopped. The right hand man quickly moved up closer behind them, as if to push him further. Royce swirled and kicked out, connecting with his face. As he staggered with shock registering on his face, an additional new kick sent him flying backwards to the ground.

When the gun bounced on the concrete, Victoria scrambled to retrieve it before several men rushed back to the door of the jet. After retrieving the gun, Victoria raised it and fired three fast shots, sending the men scurrying inside for cover. The door closed behind them, and the engine started humming. From the far side of the hangar, the helicopter pilot returned, running in their direction.

Royce hit the right hand man one more time, and turned him toward the onslaught of men coming in their direction. Victoria pressed the gun to the back of his head. The men stopped running. "Drop your weapons or he dies now," Royce yelled.

After the men slowly looked at each other and complied, Royce and Victoria moved backwards toward the entrance. As the sounds of the sirens were getting closer, the men decided to make a run for it, leaving in various directions.

The right hand man suddenly surprised both of them with a few tricks of his own, as he stomped Royce's foot, and elbowed him. Victoria aimed at both of them, but knew it was too chancy to take a shot. Seconds later they broke free for a minute, and Victoria targeted the gun on his head.

"WAIT!" Royce stretched his open hand toward Victoria. "Don't kill him yet." He stood in front of him. "I need some information."

Royce grinned. "I know who you are, but it's been a while. You may also know me better as Sand Dog."

The man's eyes widen. "I was wondering what happened to you. I heard you had a breakdown after hearing what happened to your girlfriend." A sinister smile crossed his lips.

"You should know not to always believe everything you

hear, but, then again, you might be right. I might be crazy." He spun and kicked his face again, splattering blood across the hangar."

He stood. "You ass hole. You don't know who you're messing with."

Royce kicked out again, aiming for the right knee. The sound of a bone breaking registered above all of the sirens approaching even faster. "I don't have much time to ask you this, so I need you to think fast." He kicked out again, aiming for ribs this time.

The man lifted his hand. "Enough. What the hell do you want?"

"Raptor, where is he?"

He looked straight at Royce–defiantly. "Screw you!"

Royce kicked out again, aiming for his balls. "Damn."

"Tell me." He prepared to kick again.

"Okay. He's at his estate on the 12th. I'm sure he'd love to see you." He spit some blood. "Fuck you."

Royce kicked again, and grabbed his throat. "I need a number."

He mumbled a number before he appeared to pass out.

Victoria grabbed his hand. "We have to get out of here."

They turned and began to run out the back door, as the private jet travelled out of the hangar with the engines revving high. After Victoria and Royce turned to see the right hand man stand, and remove a pistol from his ankle holster, Victoria fired first, two shots to the head and one to the chest, sending him reeling over backwards.

Royce grabbed her hand and smiled, but the approaching sirens left him little time to rest. "I have an idea. Don't worry, I'll be back for you," he shouted, "I have one more mission I need to take care of."

After Royce rushed through the side door, which was still left open, he started the copter while scanning the area around him. He lifted his hand to stop her as she tried to make it onto the copter. "Stay here, you'll be safe now. I have one more thing I have to do on my own, I'll explain later. I promise I'll be back."

"We're not going to get far in this," Victoria shouted, as she watched him handle the controls.

"I don't need to get far, just a little closer to the 12th."

"You're not really going after Raptor, are you?"

"I may never have a better chance." He reached into his pocket, and found the General's number. "I'll leave you in good hands."

She studied his face. *Who is this guy?*

He lifted into the air before she could say another word.

***

Robert studied the situation as best he could from the far side of the airport. He knew that Royce and Victoria had been recaptured by Oleg and would be onboard the jet taxiing toward the runway. That would be one plane he had no intention of on being on when it was fired upon.

With all of the players subsequently killed, including Royce and Victoria, he might have a way to get out of this mess. He had to play it smart and hope for the best. As he watched the copter making a wild dash out of the airport, he assumed that it must be the rest of the men making a run for it.

Chapter 24

Oleg scanned the sky above him, knowing they were above him somewhere. They have to be nuts. He yelled to one of his men, "When we get airborne, find out what happened to Robert. I think our need for his services is over."

The pilot turned to Oleg, looking for instruction as he flipped the channel to the tower over to the cabin speaker. The tower controller yelled his instructions in French. "Pilot, you haven't been cleared to approach the runway. Stay where you are."

Oleg yelled over to the pilot. "How long will it take to get airborne?"

He smiled. "In less than a minute."

"Do it. When we get airborne tell them we have diplomatic immunity. By the time they figure out who we are, we'll be outside of the country."

"What about the Americans?"

"Don't worry. I don't think they'll attack a Russian jet that is totally unarmed, and over a foreign soil."

When the pilot reached the end of the runway, and turned toward his take off position, a strike eagle approaching from the other end stared in his face. Unimpressed, he opened the throttles in full defiance.

The soon mid-air collision was avoided by meters, as the pilot lifted off the runway. While Oleg knew they were no match for a military attack plane, he felt confident in his ability to bluff, and out maneuver them long enough to establish their diplomatic immunity and escape back to

Russia.

Two American strike eagles soon appeared on both sides of them. Oleg smiled when the controller had turned the microphone over to a senior man yelling commands into the speakers. Oleg extended his hand to receive a cockpit microphone from the pilot. "This is Oleg Markov with the Russian government and we're under full diplomatic immunity. Since we're under attack by an American strike eagle, it would be nice to know what you're doing about it."

The commander answered. "You're not authorized to be in the air. If you don't alter your course, we'll have no choice but to fire upon you. Our jets will be airborne in seconds. We're also conferring with the Americans now to determine what they're doing here."

Oleg opened his phone to a text message sent to him by Victoria, and smiled before he flipped open his laptop and plugging in the flash drive. While the code activated the screen immediately, he didn't see what he expected. "Damn her!"

"What is it," one of his men yelled, as he looked over his shoulder.

"We've been had!"

Oleg retrieved his cell phone, calling his right hand man, hoping he was still alive.

"Royce here."

Oleg smiled. "I assume my man isn't with you."

"That'll be a good assumption."

"There'll be another day, my friend."

"I'm not your friend."

"You can tell Victoria that the Americans will soon know of her double crossing activities, and as far as you're concerned, I think Raptor will take care of you soon enough."

Royce laughed on the phone. "If you wish, be my guest

to call him. On the other hand, give me a few more minutes, and I'll deliver the message for you . . . personally."

"You can't be that crazy."

"Maybe–maybe not, but I'm coming to see you next, and that . . . you can count on."

"Anytime, anytime." Oleg disconnected, but smiled. This Royce had more guts than he thought.

However, he had more immediate problems now as he opened his phone again, dialing his contact in Moscow. "Hello, this is Oleg. We have a problem. There's an American combat plane on our tail."

"I know. The Americans contacted us a few minutes ago. They claim that you're part of an international terrorist group known as the Pack."

"I don't think I have to explain all of this to you. You know how it works."

"They say that they have proof. This is one piece of embarrassment I'm afraid that we don't need, and will not accept. I received your downloaded file. How could you have been such an idiot?"

"What do you mean?"

"Victoria has infected our entire system with a virus."

"A virus?"

"Yes, all of the real estate assets we have in America are now lost. Additionally, all funds used in these operations have disappeared. We might be able to recover some of the homes we purchased, but only at a significant cost of being discovered."

"I see. We've a lot of work to do when we get home. But for now–get these damn jets off of us."

"I wish I could help you, but this time you're on your own."

"What?" The line went dead.

Oleg dropped the microphone and patted the pilot of the

shoulder. "We have a change in plans again. Head south and try to stay close to civilian populations until we get out of this."

"Why? Where are we heading now?"

"The best place I can think of now, and the one that they'll not go—Iran."

The pilot banked the jet, heading south as the strike eagles followed closely.

The speaker cracked, and a new voice, an American speaking in English, boomed across the cabin. "This is General Ralph Klinkenberg. Do you hear me? I sure the hell hope so."

Oleg reached for the microphone. "Hello, General. You're a little out of your territory, aren't you?"

"My territory covers anywhere terrorists are that want to threaten the United States. I'll give you one warning. Land the plane now."

A new voice echoed on the box from the commander at the airport. "Enough of this, the French Air force will be intercepting both of you in minutes."

Oleg smiled. "Sorry about that General, but I think you're being overruled, and I think you don't have the guts to shoot down a Russian jet on a diplomatic mission."

"On that point you're wrong. In fact, I received permission, or even better, a request to stop you at all cost by Russian intelligence."

"Damn, that was fast."

The pilot changed directions quickly, looking for anything close to civilization, and cover. "I know of a small landing field that I think I can make. We'll have to make a run for it as soon as we land. It's our only chance."

"Go for it."

The tower commander echoed over the box again. "General, you have no authority to be here, please step down now."

Oleg smiled. Perhaps there was a small chance after all. "Make it quick, we don't have much time."

An unidentified voice broke the silence. "General Klinkenberg. I've been apprised of your target, and in the interest of international peace, I think it's best if I take the shot, Sir."

"I don't mind at all, that is, if you can do it quickly, I think they're making a run for it."

"In that case, your assistance will not go unappreciated, Sir."

"What—this cannot be. Not the French turning their back on us also!"

Oleg looked outside the right side of the jet where he saw a missile streaking toward them. "*Vse* (It's over)."

Chapter 25

Robert retrieved his cell phone and called Brandon. "This is Robert. Tell me what's happening and what you need me to do?"

"Robert we're seeing more fireworks here than I remember the last Fourth of July back home. The General destroyed a private jet carrying members of an organized crime syndicate, and heavy supporters of terrorism."

"Which one?"

"Members of the Pack. I know you worked on this some. We have a lot of containment work. Where are you now?"

"I'm getting into France now," he lied, as he looked upwards.

"That's good. We could use your help."

"Did they get everyone, or are some of the members still on the loose?" Robert started to sweat.

"The only ones left are a few of the ground crew. It appears that all of the rest were killed in the jet."

While Robert smiled, and it appeared that all was as he hoped, he decided to test the waters. He had to know. "What about Victoria and Royce?"

"I'm not sure, but there's a possibility they might have been on the jet." He heard Brandon swallow. "We'll know for sure soon enough. Hurry to the airport and I'll contact you later."

***

Brandon decided it was time to make a call to the General, and he was passed through to his radio in seconds. "Good shooting, General. I heard the news."

"Thanks, Brandon, but I think I've created you a lot of work here."

"Yes, Sir, you have at that."

"I think we'll be landing in a few minutes to try to decide how to proceed, and how to handle this with the French."

"We'll be here to help in any way we can, Sir, and I've one other piece of information I need to share with you."

"What's that?"

"I hate to tell you this, Sir, but two of the occupants on the jet may have included Royce and one of our undercover agents, Victoria."

"Damn . . . I didn't know."

"I'm sorry to have to tell you this, Sir. I learned this myself a few minutes ago."

"I talked to him, and I thought he had escaped."

"I'm sorry, Sir."

Chapter 26

Victoria moved swiftly over to the man she had shot, turning him over on his back. The three men had scattered in several directions, but she knew which one she was going after. After she reached inside the dead man's pockets, searching for his extra clip, she smiled when she located it and several papers inside an envelope.

After glancing around, she stashed them in her bag, and decided to analyze them later. As the sounds of the sirens increased relentlessly, she snapped the new clip into the pistol and headed for the exit on the far right of the hangar.

Since her three inch high heels made running almost impossible, she stripped them off and sprinted toward the door. After edging around the corner, she saw the door to a smaller hangar opening, and a small plane being pushed quickly out of it. She knew it could be him, but since she didn't know absolutely, she decided not to fire immediately, but run to intercept the plane before it entered the taxi lane.

Her lungs burned, as she ran in front of the plane and waved her arms wildly to attract the attention of the pilot. When she heard the engine roar louder, she knew it was him, and that he had every intention of running over her.

She lifted the pistol and steadied her aim. Since there was no change in the roar of the engine, she fired twice. The plane kept coming. She breathed in deep, and fired three more shots. While hearing the bullets hitting the plane, it didn't slow down.

She could feel the sinister thoughts of the pilot wanting to run her down. She dashed three steps to right, stopped, and ran to her left. The movement worked, as the plane followed her dash to the right, and she escaped the plane by a few feet.

As she regained her feet, she smelled the fuel escaping from the plane, and heard the sputter of malfunctioning engine parts. Apparently the pilot noticed it as well, as he stopped the plane and jump to the ground.

After he raised a gun and pointed it at her, he quickly glanced back over his shoulder at the plane which was billowing large black clouds of smoke. She knew he needed to get away from the plane quickly, and didn't have much time to exchange shots, as even a passing shot on her part might cause a possible explosion.

"Drop your gun now," Victoria shouted, as she had no intentions of backing down. The pistol she carried was different than anyone she had ever used before, and she wasn't sure exactly how many shots it carried. She had fired five times, and she hoped it carried nine. While being around sixty feet from the plane, which was a long shot for either of them, she just hoped that she was far enough from the plane when it exploded to be safe.

The pilot turned around and shouted in French. "Go to Hell." He fired twice as he ran toward her. As she heard the bullets fly pass her, the plane exploded before he could fire more shots.

She dropped to the ground, as she felt the blast coming in. With the smoke quickly covering the area, she couldn't see him. "Where are you?" A slight movement on the ground caught her eye, as she saw him raise the pistol again. She responded by firing all four shots, dropping him back to the ground. With her gun empty, she ran to where he was.

"Damn." He was bleeding from several places. She didn't know for sure how much had resulted from the explosion, and how much from her shots, but she immediately kicked his hand holding onto the gun.

He yelled even louder, as he attempted to retrieve it. "You bitch!"

After grabbing his gun, she pointed it between his eyes. "I should kill you right here, right now, but tell me one thing and you can save yourself a bullet."

"Go to hell!"

She fired inches above his head, letting the heat of the powder burn in his face, and the sound piercing his eardrums.

"What the hell is it you want to know?"

"I know the Rapture has a place here in Paris, but this isn't his central place of operation. I need to know where I can find him and who is it he works with."

He shouted. "I know, and you know the Rapture will torture me for the rest of my life if I tell you this."

"You need to tell me right now, or I'll make sure the Rapture learns that you're the one that told us of his place in the 7th ardonietre."

His eyes widen. "I didn't tell you anything."

"Tell that to him, not me." The airport security was approaching fast. "This is your last chance."

He glanced at the car stopping on the other side of the plane. "Okay, it's in Nice. The front is The Royalty Yacht Builders which is located in the central port area."

She smiled. "A word of this to anyone and the deal is off. You understand?"

"Yes." He smirked. "You have to be an idiot to think you can go after him. He has too many connections."

Airport security raced over to them shouting. She couldn't make out the words, but knew to lay her gun on the ground.

***

As the General prepared to land, he received a call.

"General Klinkenberg, this is officer Akron, we captured the helicopter pilot that was trying to escape. Sir, he's not flying the copter that left here."

"Who's flying it then?"

"Sir, we have rescued an agent here also, Sir, and one that we thought was dead. Her name is Victoria."

"Okay . . . I had received word that Royce and Victoria were on the jet that was shot down."

"That is incorrect, Sir. It appears that Royce is the one flying the copter now."

"Royce?"

"Victoria is bringing us up to date now. They escaped from Oleg before the jet took off and killed one of his top men in the process. Royce may have obtained the address of a man known as Raptor."

"Holy Shit!" The General yelled as he pulled back on the controls and thrust the throttle forward, avoiding a landing pattern and going vertical immediately. "Do you have the address?"

"Victoria has it and said that it's on the other side of Paris from the airport. It'll take some time for us to get to the estate, but I suspect that Royce will be arriving there any minute."

"Understood. Transmit the coordinates as quickly as you can to us where I can plug it into the guidance system."

"You'll have it in a minute, Sir."

General Klinkenberg clicked on his radio again. "I need to get in touch with Royce. See if he has his cell phone with him."

Royce answered on the first ring. "I'm listening."

"Royce, this is General Klinkenberg. Boy . . . what in the hell are you doing?"

"Finishing a mission I didn't complete earlier, Sir."

"Listen up; going after him alone is like trying to fuck a

porcupine."

"I'm sure he has received the word on the hell breaking lose here, and he'll head underground again. This may be the only opportunity we'll ever have."

"I understand. Seeing how it is impossible for me to stop you, I'll send you some back up as fast as I can."

"I appreciate it, Sir." The line went dead.

The General maintained a pattern over Paris, waiting, until he finally had Brandon back on the line. "If you haven't heard,

Victoria and Royce weren't on the plane. However, Royce is going after Raptor, and is completely on his own."

"Do what? I'm sure he's well guarded and Royce will be killed in no time," Brandon yelled.

"I'm sure if Raptor knows Royce is after him, he'll be running like hell. Do you hear me?"

"I'm sure if he thinks we're on to him, he'll leave, but I'm not so sure one man will scare him that much."

"It should. Raptor's men personally trained Royce to be one of their best. It's going to get bloody quickly, and I can't say that I blame Royce at all.

"Huh, I didn't know that."

"I'll have the coordinates in a minute from Victoria who has the address. You need to get as much help as you can obtain, and it'll be good to coordinate as much as you can with the French police."

"Will do. I understand Royce has some back history here in Paris, but I don't know the whole story."

"Raptor killed his old girlfriend when he discovered that Royce worked for us. She was tortured for a long time, and abused in a whorehouse until she was found dead there. Royce might not leave a lot for you when you make it there. I would love to have a few left alive that we can talk to, but I'm sure Royce has no intentions of taking prisoners."

Chapter 27

Royce knew he didn't have all of the answers to what was going on, but he did know that this would be his one time to make things right and secure his future. Flying low and as fast as the copter would move, he headed north. He needed to make one stop on the way, but he knew he only had minutes to stay ahead of everyone.

This wasn't the part of town accustomed to seeing a copter landing in the middle of the street. He landed in front of the place Charles lived, as he watched several street people heading for cover. The front door crashed in on his second kick. No one stayed with Charles, and he knew he would not mind at all. In his mind he could even hear him say, "Kill the fuckers for me."

He headed to the back bedroom, and flipped on the overhead light. The mattress and frame soon hit the wall as he shoved them off of the floor covering the trap door. It wasn't a time to be neat. Under the frame he saw an edge to the trap door. A light came on as he lifted it. He smiled, as he viewed the arsenal below. Several backpacks were filled with emergency items designed for such a situation. He selected several weapons from the wall and found their matching ammo bags. Figuring he could hold one more bag, he reached for one containing military explosives. He would have time for only one trip.

His phone rang, but he had no intentions of turning back, and decided to let it go to voice mail. The outside light blinded him for a second while he focused on the copter that had, indeed, attracted the attention of all of the locals.

His straightforward approach to the copter sent them scrambling, as he must have resembled the character Rambo straight out of the movies to them. He had to get loaded and airborne now. The police should be arriving any minute.

As the engine started and he quickly lifted into the air, exactly what he was going to do next wasn't clear to him since they had to know he was coming. He checked the phone and saw where the General had called.

Royce plugged in the coordinates to the house. The automatic directional guidance tried to kick in, but he switched it back to manual. He would reach the estate in minutes.

Coming in fast, he recognized it immediately. Setting on over ten hectors of prime land, the owner had a very formable estate. The grounds were covered with men scrambling with his pass over the top that caught them off guard. He disappeared almost as soon as he appeared.

His phone rang again. It was Victoria. He answered. "I can't talk now. I'll give you a call back in five minutes."

After he spotted a small clearing on the back of a neighbor's estate, he sat down on it, landing hard. He threw the equipment to the ground, flipped the guidance system to automatic, and pulled the throttle back as he bailed out.

The copter rushed directly above him, but obviously out of control, as it darted in erratic circles, but apparently attempting to pick up the signal of the GPS. It would be high enough for the compound next door to see it lumbering toward them. As expected, gun fire quickly erupted from the guards on the side of the house.

He rushed to the wall bordering the side of the estate, and planted his first charge. He quickly moved down the wall, planting several more. The gun fire at the copter attracted the attention from all of the guards moving from the house. While this gave him the cover he needed, he knew it wouldn't last long.

After making it to the back of the estate, he heard the copter sputtered, and saw black smoke filing the sky behind it. They had apparently hit one of the fuel tanks, and it would be over soon. One man stood on the corner on the estate, and directly in front of him. His erratic glances indicated how intent he was on searching for intruders. While he was fifty feet away, and an easy shot, Royce preferred to hide his location as long as he could.

After hugging the wall, he inched closer as a throwing knife slid out of its holder on the side of the backpack. With his pistol in his left hand, just in case, his eyes darted around. He was nowhere to be seen. Where was he?

A shadow suddenly appeared on the ground as the guard moved outside the wall and rushed around the corner. He raised the knife and threw, striking the guard in his chest. The guard reached for the knife, apparently a rib bone had stopped it from killing him immediately. Royce rushed over, grabbed his head, and pounded it into the wall. The man's blood spurted all over Royce as he pulled the body to some bushes.

Now, the hard part. He remembered seeing the back gate from the air, and knew that would be their escape route. He had to get to Raptor before he vanished. Blocking that back gate would be crucial.

A large blast came from the center of the estate. He knew it had to be from the copter exploding on impact. It wouldn't take them long to figure out that he wasn't in it. He removed the detonators, and pressed for the first one.

He heard men yelling, and guns firing. Idiots, he thought. There's no one there, but that's what he hoped would draw their attention, as he inched his way along the back wall. He stopped, and pressed the second button.

Over a small hill he could see men standing outside the

back gate. He pressed the next button and inched forward, as the blast threw debris skyward. Seconds later, he pressed the next one, leaving one more charge for later. The men retreated inside the gate, closing it behind them. Now he had a chance, but he had to hurry.

He rushed to the gate, and planted several more charges at the entrance. He could hear more men shouting above him. Shit, he was now pinned beneath it. He saw a small wall about fifty feet away. It was his chance. Damn, he only needed a small window to make it.

When two more men appeared on the wall, glancing over it, Royce had no choice but to fire several rounds from the sawed off shotgun and run like hell. He managed to jump over the edge as bullets splattered the ground around him.

Other men soon joined in, as the embankment around him had hundreds of rounds exploding around him. He considered pressing the button now, but waited. He sure wasn't going to raise his head to give them a target.

The firing ceased, as he heard the large back gate opening. With the shotgun reloaded and the two pistols setting next to him, he rose long enough to send five blasts from the shotgun scattered randomly at the gate. The return gunfire was intense, but allowed him enough time to disappear behind the wall. It also permitted him enough time to see two cars speeding toward the gate.

He heard one man yell, and instinct told him that the car was passing the gate now. He pushed the button. The explosion threw debris high into the sky, as he heard some men yell, and the gunfire stop. The sound of the blast roared in his ears. He now wish he had covered them, not realizing just how powerful the explosive was.

After glancing over the wall at the heavy smoke coming from two burning cars, he also saw several apparently dead bodies scattered on the ground. He raced to the gate, and peeked around the edge, where he saw several men running back to the main house.

Royce readjusted his position to where he could see several more cars parked at the back of the house and one copter. He wondered why Raptor hadn't left in it, but then again, maybe he had heard about the jet being shot down, and decided against it. However, Royce knew that it was an option that Raptor might try now.

Royce quickly opened the next bag and started assembling a rifle with each part snapping into place with efficient precision. The scope mounted last. He checked the mechanics briefly as he slid in the magazine. By assuming the copter was perhaps two hundred meters away, he adjusted the scope settings, and lowered his body to the ground. He knew he had one shot, maybe two, before he would receive returned fire.

He scanned the copter, looking for a fuel tank. Finding it, he held his breath, and fired. Nothing happened. He reloaded the chamber. The next shot found its mark, making the tank explode. While he saw no cover between the back of the estate and where he hid, except for a few trees here and there, he somehow managed to make it to the house. With a quick glance at his watch, he guessed that he didn't have much longer before backup would arrive.

When new bullets splattered around his location, he ducked lower to the ground, and wallowed toward the back of the gate, where even more bullets whistled in the air pass him. With the shots were coming from all over the place, he was cornered with a small wall at the guard shack providing him very limited protection.

He ran his hand through the bags, wishing he had more room to bring more firepower. He knew the others had to be arriving soon. He quickly located his phone and saw where the General had been trying to reach him.

He clicked on the return button and heard the General respond immediately. "Royce, I've been trying to call you."

"Sorry, Sir. I've been a little bit busy. I'm pinned down." He knew the General could hear the gun fire in the background.

"I'm right above you. You should have some company very soon."

"I'd appreciate that. I have them trapped in the house, but I'm sure they'll be scattering like rats soon."

"I understand. I've been ordered, straight from the White House, not to fire any more missiles, but I do have an idea. I suggest you cover your ears, and open your mouth."

Royce looked skyward as the eagle climbing above him with the engines roaring until it disappeared. The sound caught the shooters attention as the mirage of bullets stopped. A few minutes later, Royce focused his eyes upward, as the image of the jet appeared again directly above him, but coming straight down. However, he heard no sounds of the General's engines.

It only took a second before he realized why. OH SHIT! He grabbed the corners of his jacket to cover his ears as he hugged the ground. The General was coming in faster than the speed of sound, and a hell of a monster sonic boom had to be following him.

The ground shook as the shock wave hit and threw dust and debris in the air around him. With a quick glance over the wall, Royce also saw glass from the windows flying everywhere. Since he now had his chance, he started running for the back of the house.

Royce retrieved two pistols and slipped the knife he had used to stop one of the guards earlier back into its holster. He knew it wouldn't take long for them to recover, and he had over two hundred meters to cover in a very short period of time.

His lungs were burning, as he approached the house. As two men ran out of the back door toward him, Royce fired and connected with the one on the right, but missed the one on the left. Additional bullets flew pass him with an eerie sound as he hit the ground and rolled quickly to one side. When he raised his head, he saw the man running at full speed to his left. He fired several shots at him leaving, but never touched him. "Damn."

He reached the first man he shot and retrieved his pistol, dropping his empty gun. With broken glass and debris covering the ground, the General really did a job on the house with the sonic boom he had created. Royce felt the adrenalin flowing, pumping his energy to the max, but he knew to be cautious. The stillness inside the house bothered him, making him anxious.

He carried a gun in each hand as he moved forward. While he knew reinforcements would be arriving any minute, he wanted to find Raptor before they did. The large room he entered had probably entertained many guests over its life. The large open area led to a kitchen on one side, and had hallways leading off to the left. He decided to move toward the kitchen, letting his eyes flash around the room that remained deathly silent.

The kitchen appeared to be empty, but he proceeded cautiously around the large cooking island in the center of the room. A slight movement next to a china cabinet grabbed his attention. He yelled in French. "Drop your weapon and step out now!"

A tall, slender woman stepped out, her hands in the air. "*Ne tirez pas* (Don't shoot, please)." She appeared to be a maid or a cook.

Royce smiled, and motioned for her to lie down and be quiet. He knelled down close to her and whispered, "*Où sont les autres* (Where are the others)?"

She didn't say anything, but trembled with fear. He patted her on her shoulder.

"*Je ne vais pas vous blesser* (I mean you no harm)."

Her eyes darted toward a pantry behind her.

Royce raised a finger to his lips to instruct her to be quiet. He raised both guns to waist level and edged to the pantry. His steps were small and calculated. A glass on the counter caught his eye, and he reached for it after placing one gun in his pocket. With his back close to the other side of the pantry, he threw the glass at the other side of the room.

Three shots exploded out of the pantry, as a man smashed out of his hiding place. Royce stepped behind him, placing the end of the barrel to the back of his head. "Drop it—now!"

The guy loosened the grip on his pistol, letting it hang limp in his hand. Royce pushed the gun tight against his head before removing it from him. "*Où est Raptor* (Where is Raptor)?"

The man stood silently. Royce backed away from the man and repeated. "*Dites-moi, Où est Raptor* (Tell me, where is Raptor)?" Royce heard a car roaring out of the backyard toward the gate. "*C'est lui* (Is that him)?"

The man smiled. Royce quickly raised the gun above his head high enough to strike the man in front of him on his head, rendering him unconscious. He would come back for him shortly. The car disappeared through the gate, as he raced to the back of the house—he had no time to get a shot off.

He felt someone hit from behind him as they tumbled into the courtyard. Royce kicked the shinbone of his attacker with the back of his heels, but the bear hug only became tighter. He kicked again—no results.

It had to hurt, but only heard the grunting sound of a man determined to squeeze the life out of him. He kicked again—nothing. His head started swirling, he couldn't breathe. The heavy grunting behind his ears increased dramatically.

With one last bit of energy, Royce threw his head backwards into the face of his opponent, striking his nose. The grip softened slightly. He threw his head back again with newfound energy. The big man groaned as Royce slipped free.

Royce gained his senses quickly, as he stared into his blood covered face of the guard with a broken nose. This man who was over six feet tall and built like a large refrigerator wiped his face with his hand and grinned at Royce. Man on man, Royce knew he had very little chance in defeating him.

Royce threw his best punch at his face, turning it slightly to one side. The Russian swung his right open hand across Royce's face, sending him flying across the brick walkway. He stumbled to stand before being stomped on by the giant. He stood again, but the giant knocked him down again.

Royce reached for the knife in his ankle holster and slashed out, ripping open the leg of the monster in front of him. He yelled with pain, as he fell to his knees. Royce stepped back, contemplating what to do. He knew he should finish it now while he had the chance, but the face of this giant changed, reflecting a mind that was more like a little boy.

Several helicopters darted into the backside courtyard of the estate, while several others circled the area. Instructions were being shouted through a loud speaker. Royce didn't understand them exactly, but knew enough to back up and hold his hands in the air.

As the French police swarmed over the area in lightening speed, and established positions around the estate, Royce yelled at the first one approaching him. "*Je crois qu'il y a d'autres personnes a l'intérieur* (I think others may be inside)."

One officer ushered Royce away from the house, and one moved over to the giant lying on the ground. *"Tu dois venir avec moi* (You'll have to come with me)." He yelled at Royce.

Another copter soon landed behind the first one with Victoria and Brandon running from it as soon as it came to rest. When Victoria saw the blood all over Royce, she yelled, "You're bleeding, are you hurt bad?"

He forced a smile. "It's not my blood. I'm fine."

Brandon leaned forward, and slapped Royce on the shoulder. "My boy . . . have you caused one hell of a mess here!"

Royce looked around at the smoke bellowing from all over the estate and the wreck of a house before taking a large breath. "Yes, but Raptor escaped."

"Well, the French police are all over the place and they should have him captured shortly. "You're going to have a lot of explaining to do." Brandon turned to Victoria. "And the same applies to you as well."

Royce glanced toward Victoria and smiled. After all of the long nights and days of thinking about her, and asking himself all of the *what if* questions, the horrid thoughts in his mind evaporated and were quickly replaced with a joy, an inner piece, as he allowed himself to relaxed and take in the reality of what had happened over the last few hours.

Victoria returned the smile, as if to say that she knew she had a lot of explaining to do. After Royce lifted his arms to allow her to come to him, the brief hug confirmed his thoughts of how all of the effort in finding her had been worth it.

The French police continued to yell at the house for those inside to come out. The maid Royce saw earlier emerged, but no one else came with her. Royce moved close enough to hear her talking in French. "All of the bad men are gone," she screamed as terror filled her eyes. "*Mais il y a d'autres personnes à l'intérieur* (But, there are others inside)."

"*Qu'est-ce que tu dis il y a d'autres a l'intérieur* (What do you mean others)?" One police officer yelled at her.

"*Tu vas voir* (You will see)!"

The men glanced at each other. "I think we need to wait. We'll have a special elite force here soon." The officer told Brannon, speaking in English.

Royce turned to Brannon. "I've been half of the way in the house already, and know the layout some. I need to know if Raptor is still inside."

"I'm sorry, but this is a French matter now —"

"Then you have to shoot me in the back to stop me." Royce ran across the back courtyard, hoping for the best. He had to know if Raptor was still alive. He heard the shouting, and men scrambling to rush after him. After he reached the back door, and moved around it, all remained quiet.

After passing the kitchen, he eased into one room that appeared to have been used as an office, but originally built to be a dining room. He heard the sounds of moaning coming from down a hallway as he glanced behind him to see several of the French police following him closely. The look on their face wasn't very happy.

Royce pushed forward with the sound of the moaning becoming louder. He held his breath as he creaked open a door to another large room. "Omigod!"

Royce lowered his head in disguise as the horde of French police swarmed through the house. The sudden influx sent the dozen or so battered souls hidden inside this room into a deep frenzy. They yelled, expressing fears of not knowing if they were to be further tortured, or if this could this be their long-awaited rescue. The sound of weeping mixed with screams of panic echoed around the room, which was covered in dried blood, and various forms of garbage. He had no way of knowing how long they had been here, or what all they've been through.

A small girl, perhaps in her early twenties, looked over at him with deeply sunken eyes. She didn't whine, or cry out loud, but simply lifted her arms toward him. Her single piece of clothing consisted of a partial dress wrapped around her middle. A chain stretched from her blood stained ankle to a central metal beam used for all of the captives.

French police officers hurried pass Royce to her, as they yelled into their radios for additional ambulances. Four other girls cried out in voices that he knew he would never forget. This was one of the many rooms he had heard about, and had hunted for when he had discovered that Lynn had been abducted. The thoughts of her being abused here raced through his mind. *Lynn, I'm so sorry.*

While he felt like he needed to provide immediate relief to these girls that had various signs of abuse and wounds, he froze on the floor, letting the French take over.

He felt a hand on his shoulder, but had no energy to respond. Soon, he realized that from the small size of the hand and its gentle squeeze it must be Victoria. With the last reserve of his energy, he stood to face her. "Wow, I knew for some reason you must still be alive."

Victoria smiled, but didn't utter a sound. As she moved over closer to him, and reached around him, she nested her head into his shoulder. Royce kissed her on top of her head before glancing over her head to see Brandon moving in their direction. He knew that Brandon and others would soon want many answers, but right now, he could care less.

Eventually, Royce stepped back from Victoria, allowing her to turn toward Brandon. He knew that Victoria had been working as a double agent for both the Americans and the

Russians, a fact that might get her executed when she arrived back on American soil.

Brandon's hardened face reflected the stress imposed upon him over decades with the service. It was his remarkable smile, shining through the madness of the room, however, that revealed more about Brandon than either one of them could have guessed as he placed one hand on Royce and one on Victoria. "You two have really caused one hell of a mess here."

A French officer approached them and glanced over at Brandon. "I'm sorry, but we'll have to take both of them into custody."

Brandon's smile shifted back to his rock solid stare. "Both of them have full diplomatic immunity." He glanced around the room. "And from the look of things, it appears that they have completed a task the French haven't been able to take care of now for years. I don't think you really want the general public here to know all of these details, do you?"

The officer glanced back and forth at the three. "I'll leave them in your hands for now, but I'm sure we'll have a lot of question for them later."

"Thank you. I'm sure we'll be in touch with the right people after all of the facts are evaluated."

The French officer turned, and left.

Royce moved in closer to Brandon. "What diplomatic immunity?"

"Keep smiling until we get you out of here." Brandon smiled at Victoria. "You really caused us some problems, but then again . . . I can't believe I'm saying this . . . but you really came through for us, and we're proud of you."

Royce was too tired to concentrate and figure this out. Why was he proud of her? He glanced around the room again. He knew this temporary victory would not last, and that Raptor would soon regroup to be in full operation again. In all of his work here, years ago, he never made it this close to finding him, and he still didn't know exactly what he looked like. No one had any photos of him.

A small rough drawing of a person at the bottom of the wall across from the first girl caught his attention. Royce kneeled down and looked at the girl before asking her. "*Est-ce que tu es un artiste ou, un peintre* (Are you an artist, a painter)?"

She nodded yes.

Royce watched an officer working on her ankle bracelet and the swelling and infection it had caused was beyond his imagination of what it must feel like. "*Avez-vous vu Raptor ici* (Did you see Raptor in here)?"The mention of his name sent a wave of panic over the girl, but she recovered, as she recognized this unknown face might be able to extract revenge. "*Oui, je l'ai vu plusieur fois* (Yes, I saw him many times)." Royce then heard how Raptor and his men had raped all of them there many times. "*Ce sont des monstres.* (They are pigs)."

"*Je comprends. Il ne vous fera plus jamais ça. Je te le promet* (I understand. He'll not do that to you again. You have my word on that)." He stared deep into her eyes. "*J'ai besoin de ton aide.* (I need your help). *Peux-tu me le décrire* (Is it possible for you to draw a description of him)?"

Her eyes glanced around. "*Pourquoi* (Why)?"

"*Il s'est échappé. Personne ne sait à quoi il ressemble. On s'en servira pour le traquer* (He escaped. No one knows what he looks like. We'll need that to track him down)." He continued to study the girl, as he placed his hand on her shoulder.

"*Je peux le faire* (I can do that)." Her eyes were dull, but she bit her lips with determination to proceed.

Royce turned around to face Brandon. "When she

completes this sketch, I want a copy of it."

"Royce, you and I both know that you'll be in this country for just a few more hours. It's best if you forget it."

Royce kept his eyes focused on Brandon. "I want it."

"I'll see, but I highly doubt it." He glanced around at the paramedics, and police pouring into the house. "I think the best thing right now is to get you to the American embassy before they try to check on your diplomatic status."

Royce glances over at Victoria, acknowledging that he was probably right. He reached around her, and together they followed Brandon out of the house. As they walked as fast as possible toward a car waiting for Brandon, a new car suddenly pulled in next to Brandon's car.

After Royce and Victoria slid into the back seat, Robert dashed out of the car, and glanced around before moving around to the front of his car. "Brandon, I made it here as fast as I could."

"I wasn't expecting you here this quick. I'm glad you're here."

Royce knew that Robert apparently didn't see Victoria and him getting into the back seat of the car as he continued to listen to Robert. "I didn't get all of the facts on what happened here. This place looks like a war zone."

Brandon looked back around him, waiting on some of his team to back him. "Yes, you could call it the work of a one man war against terror."

Robert puzzled looked turned to one of shock, or perhaps more like shock as Royce and Victoria emerged from the back seat. "What the hell. I thought both of you died in the Russian jet!" He moved quickly behind Victoria before she could react.

Royce lunged swiftly toward Robert, but stopped short when Robert produced a pistol and pointed it at Victoria's head. Robert's face reflected his predicament in explain his position. "I'm not sure what she told you, but you have to remember that she's a double spy, and one that has double crossed both sides."

Retrieving his own pistol, Brandon trained his aim directly on Robert. "I know exactly who she is. The question is: Who exactly are you?"

Robert had no answer as he glanced back at Royce, who had managed to retrieve one of the pistols he had taken from one of the guards he had shot earlier. "Drop it, Royce." Robert snarled.

Instead, Royce steadied the pistol at Robert's head. "I don't think so."

Robert pulled her closer to him, hiding as best he could behind her. "I don't think you want her dead. I know all about your night together and the hell you have caused by searching for her."

"She won't do you any good. You shoot her . . . and I promise I'll kill you." Royce focused on his eyes, waiting for a moment. He knew his pistol with a three inch barrel was highly inaccurate, even at this close range, but he knew Robert also counted on him knowing this.

Robert tried to back up, pulling Victoria with him. When she struggled, he placed the gun harder against her head. "I mean it, back up now!"

Victoria had her arms pinned to her side as he wrapped his large arms over her shoulder and arms. A smile crossed her face as she faced Royce. After reaching behind her and found Roberts balls, her nails dug in.

"STOP THAT!" He pulled backwards, arching his back, trying to break loose. She dug in harder. "Stop now or I'll blow your fucking head off right here and now!"

Royce could see that she had a grip that she wasn't about to let go of. "Robert, let her go now!"

The pain registering on Robert's red face increased as she

dug in harder with each second. When he moved the gun from her head for a second, obviously wanting to strike her with it and knock her out, it was a bad mistake as he exposed the few extra inches that Royce needed. The bullet grazed the side of his head, stunning him. Robert's gun exploded missing Victoria's head by inches as his bullet cut several strands of hair, while the exploding powder burnt some of her hairs.

Royce fired again, and this time aiming at his hand. Blood splattered everywhere as the gun went sailing.

Brandon lunged to Robert, tackling him to the ground as two other agents jumped on top for extra assurance. "Get cuffs on him now," Brandon shouted. "I need him alive."

Royce yanked Victoria away from the fight, pulling her into his arms, but maintained his gun on the man still fighting on the ground.

When Brandon noticed the gun, he yelled at Royce. "Don't be a fool, we have him now!"

"If I wanted to kill him, I would have put the first bullet between his eyes." He stared deep into Robert's eyes.

Robert remained conscious, but in extreme pain from the glancing shot to the head and the one to his hand. With the officer's rough handling compounding the situation, the French police rushed in, asking questions. Brandon turned to them. "We need an ambulance. This man was a rouge agent that we'll deal with."

One of Brandon's men turned to him. "We can handle this if you want to get those two on to the embassy." He pointed to Royce and Victoria.

Brandon extended his hand toward Royce. "I think I need that pistol of yours."

Royce handed it to him. "Not a problem, I just borrowed it."

Brandon rolled his eyes.

Royce scanned the area, and moved toward the car. He knew that Brandon was right. "Here get in." He reached for Victoria's arm, steadying her into the back seat.

Chapter 28

Brandon flashed his CIA shield as he approached the gate to the American embassy. When the gate opened, they drove in where several guards approached the car fully prepared to escort the occupants inside. "Is Ambassador Arrington here?" Brandon asked.

One man quickly approached them from a side door. "I'm Consulate General Barinski. We've been waiting on you. Come on in."

"Great." He extended his hand, flashing his badge again. "I need a meeting room to use, and we have several more people on the way."

They moved quickly into the embassy, not stopping to clear through normal channels. Royce massaged Victoria's arm. He had so many questions to ask since a lot of pieces still didn't fit. "Are we under arrest?"

Brandon stared at him as he walked. "We'll talk in a minute."

A guard turned the knob to a door, which opened to a small conference room large enough to accommodate twelve people. The three moved around him to have a seat.

Brandon turned to the guard. "As soon as the others arrive, make sure they're ushered in here immediately."

"Yes, Sir." The guard started to close the door behind him, but stopped to ask, "Is there anything else?"

Brandon started to speak, but Royce spoke first. "I could use a change of clothes and a shower. I know we're going to be in here for a long time. I'm sure that Victoria would appreciate the same."

Brandon glanced at Royce's blood soaked clothes and smiled before he nodded his agreement to the guard.

"I'll get right on it, Sir." The guard left the room.

"You're both in very serious trouble." Brandon cracked a smile, glancing from one to the other. "Off of the record, I'd give both of you a damn medal."

Royce's eyes stared directly into Brandon's eyes. "We still didn't get Raptor."

"What you did is blow the cover off of years of work for the local operatives here."

"You mean the ones that let the Pack operate at will, and with no one interested in stopping his torture of innocent people."

"Things aren't always as they appear. You know that."

Victoria remained quiet.

"Yes, I'm in the dark on many things here. Would you like to bring me up to date a little?" Royce asked.

"You know you don't have clearance."

"You granted me diplomatic immunity . . . do you remember?"

"I was bluffing to save your ass, and you know it."

"Perhaps, but the French think that now, and that's all that matters, isn't it?"

"You shot a CIA officer."

"I shot a spy inside your own group. I don't think that will fly, and I don't think you'll even want to try to prosecute me on that one. We both know no court will want to hear this case." Royce added.

Brandon turned his attention to Victoria. "You're the one that started all of this. Perhaps you could tell me what you were thinking."

"You really don't mind if I take the fifth on that one, do you?"

"You're not a United States citizen; therefore you can't

take the fifth. You'll be tried in a military court."

"Since I also worked for you, I'll be asked to answer questions about my work in America as well. Is that what you want?"

Brandon pushed back in his chair. "It'll take a while, but I'll assure you I'll get to the bottom of this."

Royce and Victoria glanced at each other, knowing that he told the truth.

They heard a loud knock at the door moments before the General's massive body stood in front of the group. At six feet and four inches, he was one hell of a big guy.

"I'm glad to see you're still alive." The General studied the blood on Royce's clothes before he continued. "Did you get hurt?"

"Nothing bad." Royce lifted a thumb. "I appreciate the help. That was one hell of a sonic boom."

The General smiled. "Did I do that? How clumsy of me." He glanced at Brandon. "Why haven't the medics taking care of these two's injuries?"

"They'll be treated as quickly as possible." Brandon turned toward the General. "We were lucky to get them to the embassy without any more problems."

"I think they need to be treated now, and if you plan on pressing any charges against them, I hope you have the good sense to check with your boss in Washington."

"I'll assure you that I'll be giving him a call in a few minutes. Since I know he'll want some answers, I thought it was best to have some before I called him."

When they heard another knock on the door, the General moved swiftly to open it for Charlotte who walked into the room, smiling at Royce. "You're not planning on expanding your business into France, are you, Royce?"

Royce shifted back in his seat. "How are you, Charlotte?" A brief coded message passing between Royce and

Charlotte acknowledged their previous meeting.

"I'm fine. I see you finally found Victoria." Charlotte walked over to Victoria and smiled. "That was one hell of a disappearing act you pulled."

"Thanks."

"I have one question to come to mind right now. The investigation into your disappearance was closed. Why did you come back?"

"Things didn't go as I planned, and I had no idea that Royce would pursue it as he did. It wasn't right for me to place him in such danger."

"The last message we monitored from Oleg indicated that he had the code to the information you had provided him, and that he was attempting to upload it to his computer." She turned to face the General. "It appears that his plane exploded after that."

The General looked away, glancing briefly at the ceiling.

Charlotte leaned closer to Victoria. "We need to know what was on that flash drive."

Victoria stood still, refusing to answer.

The French Ambassador knocked at the door before he entered the room. "Gentlemen. What in the hell is going on here?" He glanced over at Royce's ragged, blood-soaked clothes. "Oh my God, you look bad."

Brandon grunted before he spoke. "They're trying to find both of them a change of clothes now."

"I hope so. I have a guest room they can use to shower, and someone can take care of their wounds. We don't need them to look like that around here."

Brandon stood. "I agree. I think both of you know that you'll be answering questions for a long time." He motioned for them to follow one of the guards.

Chapter 29

Brandon returned to his seat at the conference table in the Embassy, and indicated by a hand signal for the General to join him. "I think we have a little time to chat, finally."

The General smiled. "I think we'll both have our hands full in explaining this. I'm not one to beat around the bush, so let's get to it."

Charlotte closed the door, and moved into a seat next to Brandon. "We've more problems than I've had a chance to tell you about."

Brandon glanced over at Charlotte, indicating that she wasn't to say too much.

After noting the coded message, she continued. "I think everyone knows that operations here are severely interrupted and that we'll have to regroup. This will make our chances of making contact inside the Pack very hard in the future."

The General grunted. "I've been in more wars than most men could dream of. The face of war has changed, and for some reason, I'm getting stuck with an office job now. We both know the problem. There are too many agencies, and too much alphabet soup in Washington. The more the politicians try to clean it up, the worse it gets."

Brandon lowered his head. "What do you suggest?"

"I need some information, and you need some information."

"Agreed." Brandon rubbed his hands together.

"I need to know how Royce came to work for you in the CIA."

"We never hired him, and he doesn't work for us."

A look of disbelief passed the lips of the General. "You don't really expect me to believe that crap do you?"

"Royce had a chance meeting with one of our operatives, the girl in here a few minutes ago. Her name's Victoria Zayas."

"I saw her." The General grunted, apparently unimpressed.

"She works partly as a Russian spy, partly as an operative of the Pack, and is also one of our assets."

"That should keep her busy."

"Hopefully, her main allegiance is to us."

"So, what you're telling me is that Royce joined forces with her?"

Charlotte entered into the conversation. "I was in Jacksonville when they met. It was one of those romantic, one chance type encounter. He had no clue as to who she was."

"Then what led him to acting like a one man wrecking crew?"

Brandon quickly entered the discussions. "We had a problem with one of our drops, and we still don't know what happened. Victoria faked her death, and disappeared. Royce never believed she had died, and apparently he was right since she has now reappeared."

"Interesting." The look of the stare by the General indicated he wasn't buying everything.

Brandon continued, "You apparently know our man Royce well. His file was buried so deep we had to keep shooting in the dark."

"Yes, I hired him, and he worked for no one but me."

"Interesting. How did you pull that one off?"

"My job is to win wars, and sometimes the best way to win is to make sure your enemy doesn't have anything to fire at you. This Pack you keep playing with also includes some major arm dealers. The main force that really keeps the Pack together is a small central group that coordinates the meetings, these conventions they are sometimes called, between the various factions."

"Tell us something we don't know."

The General appeared annoyed as he continued. "You send operatives over here as Harvard financiers and bankers. They're on to you before you even book a plane ticket."

"I'll assure you that we do get some penetration."

The General grunted again. "I decided to take a different approach. Various terrorist groups were in France recruiting heavily. The French didn't want to participate in the war against Iraq. They have a large Moslem population here for these members to hide in."

"I understand all of this." Brandon smiled, not wanting to be lectured to.

"They were especially interested in anyone with an American background that appeared to be an outcast. I knew if I could get someone in this group, then I might have a shot at locating the central group."

"I guess that makes sense."

"I learned about Royce on a trip to California. I watched him surf while I had lunch at a restaurant near the beach. He was a great surfer, and wore a swim suit depicting the United States flag. This was just after nine eleven."

Brandon leaned forward.

"A long story cut short here, but we soon had him in training. He roamed the beaches of southern France, surfing on Uncle Sam's dollars for two years until the Pack tried to recruit him." His voice grew rougher, deeper as he continued to tell the story.

Charlotte nodded, acknowledging what she knew.

The General lowered his head. "All was good until they managed to discover who he was, and track down his girlfriend back in California."

Charlotte raised her eye brows. "Sounds like you have a leak somewhere."

"Hum, yes, and a very embarrassing one. I think we'll never know how it happened." His face tightened. "They tortured and abused his girlfriend for months trying to obtain information on Royce. Of course, she knew nothing. Since we were so close on cornering Raptor, the decision was made to not let Royce know about his girlfriend's abduction."

"Since Raptor is still around, I assume the operation must have failed anyway." Charlotte focused her eyes on the General. "What happened next?"

"Royce quit, but was placed in a witness type protection plan for his own safety. His cover was basically blown anyway. The information he provided helped, but wasn't enough to put an end to the Pack."

Charlotte wasn't about to let it go. "So, if Royce quit, how did you get involved with this again?"

"Royce is a marked man. When he travels outside the country, he's followed. I still think he knows information that he hasn't shared with me. I guess I can understand him being mad at his own government for using him."

Charlotte and Brandon glanced at each other, and nodded. The story confirmed what they suspected.

"Now . . . I have some questions of my own." The General leaned forward. "Tell me about Robert."

Brandon leaned back in his chair, taking time to think. "I'm sure you realize that this is an internal problem we have. It'd be hard for me to release any information, or even speculate about it, before we totally investigate it."

"You can tell me what you know now or I can pick up the phone and have the Director order you to."

Brandon and Charlotte glanced at each other, obviously

wanting additional time to analyze the information before making a report of the botched operation. "At this point, as you know, most of what I say is speculation and has to remain that way. Is that agreeable with you?"

"I understand, go on."

Brandon turned to Charlotte. "We haven't had much time to chat about this. I guess this is the time to discuss what you've found out."

Charlotte opened the file she had walked in with. "Robert, as you know, was the last one to have access to the flash drives that Victoria handed over to either the Russian intelligence, or to the Pack. We're now working on ascertaining exactly what he might have been adding to the package."

The General looked directly at him, his eyes piercing. "If you knew she was sending information to the Pack, or the Russian intelligence, why did you keep allowing it?"

"Since it was always fake leads, it was very effective in learning who the information was later sold to. We also know that the information she obtained from them was false. It appears that we were both playing the same game."

"Interesting."

"Yes, very interesting. We're still trying to figure out what they were doing with some of the information. When she disappeared, she didn't make the last delivery. It now appears that she hid it on Royce. When he discovered it, he went to see Victoria's boss, hoping he could open it, and tell him what it was."

"How do you know this?'

"Victoria's boss was shot this morning, along with three of our officers who were blown to bits. Another man was killed that apparently helped Royce into the building where Victoria's boss worked."

"What was his name?"

Charlotte glanced at her notes. "It was a Charles –"

"–Damn. He was also one of my operatives here that worked with Royce. I received a coded message from him, and I thought he may have been shot. He is the one that called Robert by name. " The General lowered his head.

"I'm sorry to give you the news."

Brandon studied the General. "Tell me about the plane you destroyed."

"I didn't take the shot. Someone else radioed me before I pushed the button, requesting to take the shot, and that it would be better politically if he did. I haven't had time to ascertain who it was yet."

Brandon appeared inpatient. "Still . . . you must've known who was on that plane."

"Yes, I knew." His face remained stern. "His name was Oleg, one of the members of the Pack, and a Russian intelligent officer."

"I don't think the Russian government will be too happy about this."

The General smiled. "Once they knew that it was going to be exposed that their government was involved with the Pack, I received a clearance from them to proceed. Oleg must have heard about it at the same time. I think that's why they turned around and headed south."

"Wow!"

Charlotte turned the pages of information in her file. "Now, the problem we have is that we've lost all contact with those receiving the information and we have no idea yet as to what they were doing with it."

"It sounds like you have a lot of work to do."

"When I came in here, I mentioned we have some new problems as well." She glanced at both of them, and waited as they both leaned forward. "Locations of where we had planted seed money to be used to acquire assets are suddenly disappearing. We also have many additional accounts totally missing and money unaccounted for."

"That's not good."

"Tell me about it."

Chapter 30

Victoria's eyes darted around, taking in as much information as she could while Royce held her arm, and lead her behind the embassy guard who was directing them toward the ambassador's private residence. While not extremely well guarded internally, she knew it sufficed for what was normally required.

They passed through the main quarters and into a hall leading to several guest rooms. When the guard stopped in front of one, and motioned for Royce to step inside, a medic rushed in behind them.

Victoria looked over at the guard, and spoke in English. "I need to help him get cleaned."

The medic looked over at the guard, and asked. "*Parlent-ils français* (Do they speak French)?"

Both Victoria and Royce maintained silent faces, as they chatted, hoping to confuse them. Victoria reached for the small bag of medical supplies carried by the medic and motioned for him to go. The guard stepped forward, looked inside and returned outside, but before he could object further, she attempted to close the door. At first he resisted and pointed to a room across from this one for her to use. She shook her head. "No."

The guard shook his head back at her at first, but then finally relented.

Royce pointed to his clothes. "I need clothes." He then pointed to Victoria.

As the guard smiled and left, Royce closed the door behind him. Victoria walked to the center of the room and turned to face Royce as the exchanged stare between them intensified. Victoria spoke first. "I'm so sorry for getting you involved in this."

Royce smiled and extended his arms toward her as she rushed back into them. "For some reason, I knew you were alive."

She smiled back at him. "But how did you know?"

"You never said goodbye."

"Okay, I know I've a lot of explaining to do to you."

He lifted one finger. "We'll have a lot of time to do that later, but I do have one question to ask you now." He paused, and kissed the top of her head. "Why did you decide to come back now?"

Victoria reached for his hand and pulled it slowly toward her stomach. The firm muscles that she had the last time they met were now slightly bulging out. She felt him jerk slightly, as he pulled back to concentrate on her eyes. "I had to come back. You were getting into a situation much worse than you could ever understand, and . . . I want our baby to have a father."

Victoria watched the shock register on his face. She waited, hoping he would be happy with the news. Finally, she felt him touch her stomach again. "Wow. Why did you wait so long to tell me?"

"I didn't want to get you in so much trouble. I didn't know who you were when we met."

"I've been constantly looking for you since that night."

"I know it." She felt the relief in his body as he pulled her close to him again. "I'm so glad to see you again."

"Trust me, Victoria. I've been doing my research on you also. You've had a very interesting life, as well."

"Yes, I have. We have a lot of notes to compare." She glanced at his clothes. "For right now we have to get cleaned up and taken care of." She started stripping off his clothes.

"What are you doing?'

"As long as the guard thinks we're naked in here, they won't come in and disturb us." She had little time to give full details of her plan now. "Do you still have your phone?"

"Yes, but why?"

"I need to connect to my computer."

"How will my cell phone help?"

She extended her hand toward him when he removed the phone out of his pocket. "Now, you get in the shower first, we don't have much time to get out of here."

He glanced at her with a puzzled look, but continued to strip. With him looking so rugged, and just so damn masculine . . . she had to glance away to maintain her focus. "Hurry. We'll have more time later. I promise."

As Royce moved to the shower, he had apparently quit trying to decide what she was working on. She dialed the number she had established earlier that forwarded the call back to America and to her computer in the apartment she had been hiding in. When she heard the buzz of the modem, she spoke slow and deliberately. "Victoria."

Her computer answered back. "Verifying . . . verifying complete. Hello, Victoria."

***

Royce tossed his raged clothes in the corner of the large bathroom decorated with oversized bath towels in the keeping of a theme of prominence that Royce had learned to tolerate. He glanced at his image in the mirror and wondered how anyone could stand looking at him with all of the blood smeared all over his face, and especially the large globs dried in his hair.

He turned to the shower and opened the large glass door. After walking inside the marble lined stall, he studied the gold platted fixtures, and a small shelf holding various soaps, and shampoos. He immediately turned on the water and allowed it to get hot. With the flow of adrenalin slowing, and fatigue setting in, he needed this to regain his energy.

As he scrubbed, and the blood flowed down the drain, he studied a few bruises and scrapes, but noticed nothing else of a major concern. His thoughts turned to Victoria. While she looked great to him, he still had so many questions for her. His main concern quickly focused on getting out of the situation they were in. He knew that until they captured Raptor, they wouldn't be able to rest. The Raptor would surely find out quickly who was behind the raid, that is, if he didn't already know.

After scrubbing, he leaned against one wall to simply enjoy the hot water. He wished that Victoria would surprise him in the shower, but knew she was busy. As he turned off the water and reached for a towel, he knew it was time to see what she was planning.

He saw her walk into the bathroom, as he stepped from the shower. With her hair still a mess, she definitely could use a shower also. He now felt bad about going first and wanted her to enjoy the shower. "Come on in, the water feels great."

"I hope so, I feel gritty." She smiled and walked over to glance at him briefly before she raised her lips to his, kissing him softly.

Royce hugged her tight, knowing that the long search for her was worth it. He had lost one girlfriend before due to the Pack, and he had no intensions to lose another one. "I've dreamed of seeing you again every day since I met you."

"I can believe that. You're an incredible man." She looked around him at the shower. "I need to get in the shower since we've very little time now."

"I think we earned a little time to relax."

"I wish we did, but we're going to be getting out of here soon."

"What makes you think so?"

"I had suspected that we might make it to the embassy if all went as planned. I've a plan in place to get us out of here, but I need to get my shower by the time our clothes arrive. Don't let anyone in here while I wash, and I'll explain everything when I get out."

Royce decided to play along for now. "Okay, I'll get dressed." While she stripped, he couldn't help but stare. She grinned, but motion for him to go to the door and wait. However, he studied her stomach and the small developing bulge when it hit him—he was going to be a father!

Reluctantly, he finally walked outside and occupied the small chair next to the door. The expected knock didn't take long. After opening the door, he saw a guard standing in the doorway with a package that obviously contained clothing for him and Victoria. Royce maintained his body behind the door, hiding his naked body. The guard smiled as he tossed it on the floor inside the doorway. "Merci," Royce said as he closed the door.

Royce opened the package to see a new pair of grey pants and a white shirt inside. It also contained a beige skirt and a white blouse for Victoria. Royce assumed they probably purchased them quickly at a local store, but they were clean. He checked the size and he knew that the shirt was a little large, but it would do. He hoped the size they picked for Victoria would fit.

He quickly dressed and removed his personal items from his bloody pants still lying on the floor in the bathroom. Victoria suddenly opened the door and glanced over at him. "Good, I see the clothes arrived." Royce couldn't take his eyes off of her. She was beautiful. She cocked her hip to one side and glanced at him sideways. "Did they bring me anything?"

Embarrassed for starring, Royce moved back to the front room and retrieved her clothes. "I hope these fit."

"They'll have to do since we really only have a few minutes." She ran her hand through her hair, pulling it back behind her. Her fluffy, blonde hair was now replaced by dark, straight hair.

"Okay, so what kind of plan were you talking about?"

"I have it all arranged. There's a trap door leading to a tunnel that was built back when this street was known as the place of the bitches."

Royce raised his eye brows. "Really."

"It's a long story, but an interesting one that I'll tell you when we have time. It's not what you think."

"How do you know this?"

"Lots of research. I hate to say this, but we need to permanently disappear since it's the best way to secure our future."

Royce shook his head. "The only way we'll ever be safe is by getting to Raptor."

"We can leave that to someone else to do."

"I'm sorry, but I waited on that before, and it will never happen. He has too many connections, and he's protected by too many powerful people. If he isn't captured now, he'll never be."

"What makes you think that you can catch him?"

"I know where he's heading." Royce smiled

"I do also." She adjusted her new clothes. "One of his men told me."

"I heard Nice. What did you hear?"

"Humm. I have the name of the boatyard where he has a boat waiting on him."

Royce nudged her briefly. "You did great."

"Wait, I didn't say I was going to help you catch him."

"I'm not asking you to" Royce glanced around "This is something I'll take care of, that is, if I can get a chance to get out of here."

"I can get us out of here, but I don't like the idea of you placing your life in danger again."

"Trust me. If I don't do this, we'll always be in danger." He hugged her tightly. "I'll come back for you, I promise."

"Like hell." She stood her ground. "If we do this, we do it together, and you'll need my help."

"Why do you think that?"

She lifted the phone. "When I give a voice command to active plan, the power will be cut off for this entire district, but it won't be for long. At the end of the tunnel there will be a taxi waiting on us."

"How did you manage to do that?"

"The computer program I wrote will send a text message to the cab company."

"Nice."

"I'm just getting started." Victoria checked the phone again. "All records of us will also disappear in the government files."

"Very impressed."

"Since they'll have no photos of us to pass on, and no information to build a case against us, we'll be able to start over."

"You're one very smart computer girl."

"I don't know." She paused to give him a quick kiss before she continued. "It's still going to take some luck to pull this off."

"Get us out of here and I can work some magic also. Trust me."

"I do." She raised the phone and reconnected to her computer. "Initiate program."

The lights blinked once and then shut down completely

as a voice boomed through the door. *"Reste dans la chambre!! Je reviendrai après avoir vu ce qui c'est passé* (Stay in this room, I'll be right back after seeing what's going on)."

Royce slowly counted to ten before he cracked open the door. All was dark, with the exception of a small light coming from down the hallway. "This way," Victoria whispered, as she moved ahead of Royce.

Royce saw a door left slightly open down the hallway. Making it to it, Royce pushed it open. "Now what?'

"We need to find the entrance to the tunnel. It'll be on the floor somewhere." The floor was covered with a plush carpet.

"How old is your information?" Royce glanced around the room.

"Very old. The ambassador himself might not even know about it. It was designed to give an ambassador a way in if he was locked out by the French. It was never contemplated that someone might use it to escape. This will be a first."

Royce dropped to the floor and started tapping with his knuckles as hard as he could. It all sounded the same. "There's a good chance the carpet has been added over time."

Next to an armoire used to store clothing, Royce discovered a different feel to the floor beneath. He knocked harder and the sound also was different. He glanced at the heavy piece of furniture. "How much time do we have?"

"Not much, but I'll help you." She moved next to him as he looked for a way to obtain a handhold.

He reached behind the back corner and shoved his weight into it, trying to lift a corner. It barely moved. He made room for her to push next to him. It rose slightly. "Wait a minute." He opened the door to the armoire and started removing clothes, boxes, and unidentified bags at the bottom. "Okay, let's try again."

They threw their weight into the side again and groaned as he lifted. "Now, help me twist it to its side." It moved slightly. "Okay let's do it again." The side barely inched away from the wall again.

Victoria glanced at the door again. "We have to hurry."

Royce knew he had no time left to be subtle. "Get out of the way." He walked to the small space behind the armoire and started to push. When it fell over, crashing to the floor, the carpet muffled most of the crash, but they both knew the loud crash might have been heard.

Royce started looking for a corner or weak point to be able to pull the carpet. With a little luck, he found one and started lifting. As the outline of a trap door appeared below, he knew that they had to hurry.

"Here, let me help. I'll hold this up for you." She lifted the carpet as he worked on the small opening. They saw a ladder attached to one side that disappeared into total darkness below.

Royce grabbed her hand. "You first. I'll hold it open for you."

She didn't hesitate as she entered the hole, and as he moved in behind her, the trap door closed immediately. While he hoped the carpet fell back into place, he knew they would be on to them very soon. "Victoria, where are you?"

"I'm down below. It's a long way down."

He hurried, feeling his way in the dark. Eventually, he felt her hand on his back. Now what?

"We still have a long way to go and I'm sure it might be all in the dark. I forgot about how old this might be. I'm sorry."

"We're into it now, so we need to keep moving." He felt along the edges, looking for a passage.

She found it first. "Over here."

A thought suddenly occurred to Royce. "Wait a minute." He reached into his pocket and retrieved his phone. The slight light emanating from the display worked wonders. "This way, stay close to me."

They walked as fast as possible, considering the small light. Soon, a light glowed in front of them. As they rushed toward it, they found the exit boarded. Now what?

Royce raised his feet and started kicking. They heard a slight vibration with each kick, but nothing else. He tried several more times, while Victoria searched for anything that might help.

"Here, try this." She handed Royce a short board. He wedged it in between some of the cracks and pulled. It squeaked. He tried again and the board moved. He backed up and kicked again. It moved slightly more. He peeked through the opening and saw an opening into a small room.

With enough of the boards removed to slip through, Royce scanned the small room. All remained quiet. "Stick with me."

The room appeared to be a small utility room. He reached the entrance, and cracked it open. He could see another door on the other side, which led out of the building. "Hurry, this way." He gripped her hand, and moved fast.

Once outside, they both glanced around, knowing they wouldn't last long in the open. "VON, VON, VON (THERE, THERE, THERE)." Victoria yelled in Russian, as she pointed down the street to a waiting taxi. The driver standing beside it was glancing around, trying to figure out who had called for him.

They walked fast and almost in a run. While they had to get inside quickly, they didn't want to draw attention to their flight.

The driver smiled as they approached him. "*Êtes-vous la personne qui a appelé un taxi* (Are you the one that requested a taxi)?"

"*Oui.*" They quickly moved to the back door and slid in.

The driver hurried into his seat before turning to ask, "*Où allons-nous* (Where to)?"

Royce spoke first by giving me the address of his friend Charles, the guy that Robert had murdered. While Victoria didn't resist, he felt the tension in her body. This deviated from her plan, he knew, but he had to make one more stop.

Victoria leaned over to Royce once they started rolling. "What are you doing?"

"I have some items stored that we'll need. You'll see."
***

Life in the embassy remained at high alert, even after the lights came back on. "What happened?" Brandon yelled to one of the guards at the front of the building.

"Not sure, Sir. It appears we had a major power failure. It appears to be over now."

Brandon recognized one of the guards standing in front of the gate. "Isn't he supposed to be guarding Royce, and Victoria?"

"We called him to the front when the power went out. It's a stand procedure to show a united force in the front when we have such a situation."

"Okay. But get him back now to check on them."

"Don't worry. There's nowhere for them to go."

"I hope so."

Charlotte worked her fingers over the keyboard of her computer. "Oh crap."

"What is it?"

"Someone had hacked into the power grid and shut it down. The French police are working on it now."

They glanced at each other as they said in unison, "Victoria."

They jogged after the guard who was heading for the

ambassador's residence, taking several other guards with them. When they entered the residence, and spread out, Brandon quickly knocked on the guest bedroom. After they received no response, he motioned for a guard to open it. They found an empty room. "Find them—now!"

The guards spread out, and one soon yelled from the ambassador's bedroom. Upon arriving, they saw the smashed armoire on the floor. "What the hell." This resulted in the guards scattering around the house, searching one room after another, but unable to locate them. The carpet had laid down flat, giving no signs of the trap door below. "They have to be here somewhere—find them."

An hour later, one of the guards discovered the displaced carpet and the trap door below. By then, they knew they had escaped and had a large head start.

Brandon turned to Charlotte as they returned to the meeting room they had been using as a temporary command center. "Get out a description of them, and if we have to . . . contact the French police. We need to find them."

Charlotte went to work on her keyboard. She blinked her eyes, and then entered more keystrokes.

A smile crossed her face that Brandon didn't seem to appreciate. "What is it?"

"I think we underestimated her. Her file has been erased, and I think we'll find Royce's information erased also."

Chapter 31

Royce watched the taxi driver glance over his shoulder at him, and ask, "What was the house number again?"

Royce raised his head before glancing around. "This'll be fine. Let us off at the corner."

The taxi pulled over to the curb. "Are you sure? This isn't the best part of town. I'll be glad to wait on you . . . if you want."

"That will not be necessary. Here, keep the change."

The driver pocketed the money, and moved to open the door on the passenger side. "*Merci.*"

Royce reached under Victoria's arm and quickly walked down the street as the taxi left. The moment the taxi disappeared, he reversed his direction. "We have to hurry."

"Where are we going?"

"I had a friend who lived here. He was the guy that Robert killed at your ex-bosses building."

"I see." She moved along with him.

Royce hoped he wouldn't be recognized, but he knew he had created a scene the last time he was here. While several locals raised their heads to watch them walk by, no one moved toward them. He opened the front door and went inside. The smashed door hadn't been repaired, which surprised him that the place hadn't been looted. Perhaps he had left more of an impression than he had thought the last time he was here.

He shut the door and headed for the bedroom to where the secret storage area was. Victoria's eyes open wide in a deep shock when she saw the size of it. "Wow!"

Royce searched the top of a shelf and smiled as he found a set of keys. He walked over to the front door, scanning the street in front of him. The van across and down the street had to be it. "I'll be right back."

She looked amused. "Where are you going?"

"It's not the best looking ride in town, but perhaps the most inconspicuous."

"I'll be looking over your room."

"Help yourself."

"Do you have any computer in all of this?"

He turned and smiled. "Perhaps. Take a look." He turned, and ran out of the door.

Victoria searched through the shelves, and found much more than she expected. How did he manage to get all of this? She examined the high tech communication equipment, military explosives, and enough weapons to supply a small army.

Royce returned, parking the van in front of the door. "I see you found what you wanted."

"Yes, this'll do."

"Good, now I need a few items. There's no telling what we might need." He started loaded the van with one load after another.

As he completed loading the last of the explosives, he stopped to focus on Victoria. She stood still, almost like a little puppy dog. "I wish I had time to hold you and catch up on what's going on but I know if we don't stop Raptor now, we might never have a chance again. We can't rest until he's stopped."

Victoria moved into his arms. "We don't have to go after him. I have it all set for us to disappear."

"I wish it was that easy." Royce reached a hand around to the back of her head, massaging her scalp before rubbing her silky smooth hair in the process. She smelled so good. His dreams of the time with her before flashed in his mind as he wished it was that easy.

"I know we don't know that much about each other, but I feel connected to you more than anyone in my entire life."

"I understand." He kissed the top of her head. He knew he had to hurry, but he wanted to rest for a minute and hold here for as long as he could. "We have to leave, like now. We both know they'll be after us soon and we need to get out of the city as fast as possible."

Victoria backed away and smiled. "I'm sure they'd love to catch us, but they have a problem right now."

"What kind of problem?"

"I hope you don't mind, but all records of us have been deleted from their files. It'll take a while for them to upload photos of us to send out. Also, since they aren't in very good standings here, I doubt if they'll get much help from the French police right now." She winked at him.

Royce returned the smile. "I heard you were good, but no one has that kind of access."

Victoria handed him the computer. "You're welcome to see for yourself."

Royce realized that she might be right. "Okay, I'll take your word for it. What about the information the Pack has on us?"

"I have most of it erased, but I'm sure not all of it. However, I've reserved us a major bargaining chip to keep them out of our lives."

"It'll be just a matter of time before the American authorities track us down –"

She interrupted him with a small kiss. "Relax, you'll see. They not want to pursue us. I promise . . . you'll see."

"Okay for now, but I suspect that they know about this place and will be here any minute."

She smiled. "This place is amazing, but I'll agree that we

need to leave. Where are you planning on going?"

"We have to make it to Nice. I think he's planning on leaving the country by boat. Since I'm sure he knows that he can't drive across the border to Italy, it would be much easier for him to jump around the coast on a boat."

"I also managed to get this information out of one of his guards before he was shot."

"Good. That confirms the information I received from the pilot."

Royce stared at her with a smile that reflected his admiration for her work. "How did you manage to get it?"

"Staring straight down a barrel of a pistol pointed by a crazy woman leaves little room for stalling. I wish I had more information, but . . ."

"I understand. Let's go." He threw in a box of spray paint primer, some papers and masking tape, as he shut the back of the van.

"What's that for?"

"As soon as we get into the country side, we need to do a quick paint job."

***

Brandon yelled at Charlotte, loud enough for the driver to hear. "How much longer before we arrive?"

"We'll be arriving in a few more minutes. We have a team meeting us. They should be arriving about the same time."

"Tell them not to go in until we get ready."

"If the General is correct with what he told us, Royce will have enough firepower to start a major war. This also accounts for how he managed to dismantle the Pack's estate earlier today."

The street became crowded, as they made it closer. The driver glanced over his shoulder. "It's two blocks ahead."

"Pull over here. I want all exits of this place covered."

"I'm on it." Charlotte jumped out of the car, and opened her phone. "Where are you?"

The group of CIA officers converged on the small apartment. They knew they had little time to stay ahead of the French government that would be right behind them. The team waited on Brandon to give the final word to break in.

Brandon glanced around, and called Charlotte. "Are we in place in the rear?"

"Yes, we are. Well at least as best we can on such a short notice."

"Good, we're going in."

Chapter 32

Taking the autoroute east into Nice, Royce made the exit called the Cote d'Azur, and followed the signs into Nice Centre, and the Promenade d'Anglais. He hoped that the tramway might be finished by now, even with all of the many problems they had earlier in finishing it. Trying to find a place to park a van in Nice is like trying to keep a pet elephant in the backyard and hoping that no one will notice, not to mention the size of the elephant house. Royce knew he had crazy thoughts going through his head, but he had to think of a plan. He headed for the *Port de Nice*, and turned down the *Promenade d'Anglais*. After he passed *La Pérouse,* he glanced around. "We'll check in here later."

"Interesting. You seem to know your way around here."

"Yes, and much more than I want to remember." Royce turned left on the *Quai Lune,* and stared out at *La Basin Lympia* (port area). Raptor could be anywhere in Nice, and in fact with his head start, Raptor could have already left. Still, he thought that it might take a little time for Raptor to arrange for a boat, making him have to hide out in Nice for a while. Royce also knew that if Raptor was there, he wouldn't miss the chance to hit the local night spots. He knew he had a long night awaiting him, since he planned on finding Raptor at all cost.

On the back side of the *Notre-Dame du Port*, he saw a place where he could park. He didn't know how long it would be before it would be removed, but he hoped for the best. "Here, this'll have to do for now."

Royce reached behind him and retrieved a small duffle

bag full of pre-planned emergency supplies. He saw Victoria smile. "Here." He reached in the bag, and handed her a small pistol with a leg holster. "Just in case."

In seconds, he became fully equipped, and they left the van, moving as fast as possible toward the hotel. "I think you'll like it, but I'll let you sign for the room since I lived here for a while and I don't need to take a chance of anyone recognizing me."

She smiled. "What did you do here?'

He returned the smile. "I surfed." She stopped and waited on him to explain. "It was the best cover I could ask for. I'm sorry that I didn't finish the job here the first time." His mood changed as he glanced around. "When you get inside, look for a copy of La Semaine des Spectacles. It'll give us a list of the special attractions happening this week."

"I'll do my best. Don't worry. The new visas we have are perfect. We'll be the perfect couple here planning our wedding."

Royce looked around. "I hope you're right. This'll be one cover that I think I'll enjoy."

"I thought you might like this. I know I will." After smiling and turning to one side, she still maintained eye contact with him. Even at a time like this, she amazed him with her inner humor. He hoped he would be able to explore it much more soon, but for now he had work to do.

After they entered the front door to the hotel, Royce moved to one side, and studied the paintings and other decorations on the wall as Victoria proceeded to the registration desk. He had prepared for all contingencies, he thought. Suddenly on one of the small tables, he recognized an empty pack of cigarettes. Davidoff cigarettes aren't cheap, and they were also the brand that he knew Raptor enjoyed. Damn! Could it be that Raptor was staying in the same hotel?

He scanned the lobby with a newfound interest as he moved around the sides, monitoring every movement and doing his best to memorize every detail.

He heard Victoria talking to the guy behind the front desk. "Do you understand English?"

"Yes, a little," the clerk answered.

"Very good, I'm not sure how long we'll be here, but perhaps for several days. We're here to make arrangements for a wedding in a couple of months." She pointed over to Royce.

It worked as he reached below him and retrieved a key for the room. She handed him her passport for safe keeping. He smiled as he continued in English. "I hope you enjoy your stay."

Royce turned away from the front desk and waited on Victoria to move over to him. "We need to get out of here and hide for a while. I think this might be the same place Raptor is staying." He reached behind her arm and helped her out of the front door and outside to the walkway where they kept their head lowered. While this place had to be staked out later, he knew that for now they needed to change their clothing. He knew the perfect place to go.

"Where are we going?"

"Shopping. We need some clothes, and then we need to check out a few places we need to visit later on tonight." Royce headed to some of the beach shops he remembered from his time in Nice before. He had two totally different looks that he wanted to accomplish. First, he needed to return to the look of the beach bum. These were the people most of the regulars ignored, but often tolerated.

The next style was the one he had little experience in when he was in Nice before. Many of the clubs in Nice that the glitzy rich frequented required this show of wealth to obtain entrance. With the right stores, he hoped to accomplish this before Raptor or his men spotted them. He hoped that Victoria shopped fast.

Royce soon had a business casual outfit, an after hour outfit suitable for dancing, and beach clothes including a swim suit. A large beach hat and sunglasses worked great in hiding his face. "I think this will do fine for me. Now for you."

"I'm hungry. Are you planning on feeding me, or starving me to fit into a smaller size?"

He smiled. "I think you're right. We do need to eat."

"Good."

"However, if you can wait a little bit longer, we can order in our room. We have to stay hidden for a while longer."

She pouted, but soon replaced it with a smile. "Okay."

Royce enjoyed shopping with her, as he helped her select several outfits. The next few days might be very frantic, and he wanted to make sure he had all contingencies covered. When she tried on one of the after five dresses, he felt his heart talking to him, confirming what he knew. How could he be so lucky to find someone so beautiful, and with a personality that glowed so elegantly?

"Do you like?"

"I love it. Just remember when the red hot Frenchmen go after you tonight, you're taken." He lowered his head to look at her slightly below the bottom of his eyebrows.

"I don't know. I'm still waiting on that engagement ring."

"I see. And I think you've learned the way of the American girls very fast."

Victoria glanced at him. "Many Russian girls don't wear one, which is true." She lifted her right hand in a playful motion.

Royce laughed. "I see some habits are hard to break."

"What do you mean?"

"In America, the women wear the wedding and engagement ring on the left hand."

Victoria glanced at her fingers. "Oops."

"We need to hurry back to the room and get some rest since it might be the last time we can for a while. I also need to do some scouting soon, and I'll leave you there for a while after I get ready."

"I can go with you."

"I know this town well and I need to move fast. It'll be better if I leave you for a while."

"We'll see."

"We're going to be visiting several places together later tonight. If you want to help, then check them out on-line and find out if there are any other hot spots that we need to check on. One spot you need to concentrate on rue Droite, but the first place we'll start with is called Distilleries Idéales. It's known to have attracted his attention before as well as many internationals he deals with. It's a great place and you'll love the way it looks inside."

Victoria patted the shopping bag that she carried. "It sounds like it will be one great date."

Royce smiled before returning his face to a serious tone. "At any other time, it would be the most fantastic night of my life. I hope one day we can enjoy such a night."

Victoria stared back into his eyes. "I think you can count on it." She then glanced around the street.

A block from the hotel, Royce indicated for her to stop for a minute. While they had the usual crowds walking past them, Royce still waited. The scene disturbed him, yet he couldn't put a finger on it.

He quickly walked back toward a small shop that he remembered and walked inside. After thinking of some of his favourite niçois food he enjoyed, he asked the girl in front of him for a *tourtart de blea,* which is a thin tart with pine nuts inside.

The waitress placed two in a small bag for Royce as he handed her the francs to cover it. "Merci."

He slowly walked out and moved to the side of the building as a car moved in front of the hotel and stopped. After a man exited the front door of the hotel and disappeared in the back seat of the car, it accelerated and disappeared down the street.

"Was that him?"

"I'm not sure. But it's a possibility." Royce reached inside his duffle bag, and placed a pistol under his shirt and inside his belt. Now may be the best time to make it inside. "Let's go."

They moved down the street and soon ventured inside a vacant lobby. With their room on the second floor and the elevator slow, Royce decided to take the stairs. She followed and closed the door behind her.

He found their room as soon as he exited the stairway. He opened it and rushed her inside. As they looked around, he watched her take several deep breaths before she moved into his arms. Now, maybe they'll be safe for a while. "Ohmigod, I'll be so glad when this is over," she said.

"It'll be over soon, but right now I need your expertise. Can you access the guests list here? I need to know if Raptor is, in fact, here. If he's not here, we need to see if we can locate him."

Victoria smiled. "Not a problem."

"Good. While you're doing this, I need to do some scouting. You'll be safe here."

Victoria grabbed his arm. "I don't want you to go."

"I understand. But it's important that I take care of this—now."

When she looked into his face, the dreamy look that penetrated his own was more than he could stand as he leaned over to her, and prepared to kiss her forehead.

She appeared to have other intentions as she rose on her tip toes and reached for his height. He responded to reward her movement and felt the warm tender kiss from lips that he remembered so well, and had dreamed about for so many months.

In spite of the danger around him, Royce let his guard down for a minute. She parted from him for a second. Royce took a deep breath before lowering his head so that he could reach her lips again, and allow the suppressed passion from deep inside of him to explode deep inside of her anxiously waiting mouth. The taste of her mouth felt much sweeter than he remembered. How could he have been so blessed to have found her again? Now . . . he had to make sure he never lost her again.

Chapter 33

Royce left the hotel and walked down the street, hoping to be undetected with his hair covered by a beach hat and his eyes hidden behind some large circular sunglasses, as he headed for the beach. He wanted to be like the typical beach bum hanging out on the beach, a cover he had used for years before. Looking around, the town appeared to have changed very little, except for the work being completed on the streets, attempting to make them more pedestrian friendly.

He knew the places that would yield the most information, and he didn't have much time to be subtle. If Raptor was here, he wouldn't stay for long. Since Victoria had given him the name of the boating company Raptor had connections with, he planned to make his way over to it soon.

He stopped in front of one of his old hangouts. Most of the cafés were overpriced, but he knew how to sip a latte and watch the crowds strolling by. The waitresses usually had good information for him.

After he recognized nothing out of the ordinary, he ventured inside where a beautiful girl in her early twenties quickly spotted him, and hurried over. "*Ca va* (How are you)?"

"*Pas mal* (Not bad)" He responded. He pointed to a table in the front, allowing him to watch the traffic moving pass the café.

"*Oui, monsieur.*" She moved over to the table, and leaned over to wipe it clean. She had a low cut blouse that opened, exposing her large but firm breasts. He knew that she partially did that for his benefit and partially to make sure she received a generous tip later. Nothing much has changed, he thought.

"*Je m'appelle Jean Paul, et vous* (My name is Jean Paul, and what's your name)?"

She smiled. "*Je m'appelle Christiana.*"

Speaking in French, he continued, "I used to come here a lot, and I don't remember you."

She smiled, and apparently never suspected that he was an American, as she continued to speak in fast French. "I've been working here for a few months. I moved here from Paris."

Royce smiled as she stood in front of him, giving him time to build a relationship. He hoped she would become a fast asset for him. "That is very interesting. I moved to Paris, but had to come back here. This place is fantastic."

"I think so also." She had an innocent, care-free attitude that relaxed him, as he remembered how slow and inattentive most of the waitresses used to be in Nice.

"How long are you going to be here?"

"I'm afraid not too long. I wish I could stay longer, but…"

"What can I get you?"

"I definitely want a latte." He flashed a big smile. "Then . . . I want you to surprise me with a creation that I've never had before."

She returned the smile. "Are you sure?"

"Absolutely."

He watched her turn and walk toward the back. With a little luck she could bring him up to date on the last few days' activities. This was the kind of place that most newcomers stop for their coffee fix at least once. Body guards that protected their bosses worked long late hours, and he knew most of them couldn't resist making a pass at someone as cute as Christiana.

Royce scanned the deep-blue sky. He remembered how the sun shined here almost every day, and how the temperature stayed almost perfect. He wished that he could say the same for the beach, which was covered in blue pebbles. However, this was such a far cry from the beaches back in America, and especially Florida with its soft, white sands.

Christiana soon returned with the latte. "I hope you like it, and I'll have you a . . . *special meal* soon. I'll admit that I turned your special request over to the cook. He's taking it as a challenge, and he told me to tell you that you won't be disappointed."

Royce lowered his sunglasses, and made it obvious that he was studying her breasts. "I'm sure that it would be very difficult for you to disappoint me."

She blushed, but he knew it was for show more than embarrassment, since she appeared to share the fine international art of flirting. With the usual large lunch crowds gone, his timing was perfect, but he needed to act fast.

"Tell me more about you."

"There's too much to tell. I'm simply a waitress trying to get by until my ship comes in."

"Aren't we all? Is anything special happening here in the next few days?"

"Not really. It's that time of year."

"I understand. So, I assume Britney Spears isn't going to be on the beach in the next few days."

She laughed. "I don't think so."

"But . . . I know a lot of important people wander around here all of the time . . . and remain unnoticed."

"Yes . . . and a lot of them stop by here, trying to hide behind large hats, and sunglasses." She pointed at his, making a small frown.

He flashed a larger smile. "Well, you never know."

A larger black car pulled in front of the café, and stopped. She turned to face it, and cussed under her breath. "Damn."

"What is it?"

"I'll tell you later. I'll be right back."

She reached the curb and approached the driver side window. The window lowered, but Royce couldn't see the driver from his angle. He thought that this was the same car he had seen earlier in the morning. The door on the other side opened, and a man walked around the side of the car. Royce reached over, and lowered his head, as he sipped the latte. His eyes focused over the top of his shades while his hand found its way to his duffle bag sitting next to him.

The man stopped at the rear of the car and opened the trunk. Royce couldn't see what he was doing, but kept his eyes focused on him, waiting on him to make a move. He wanted to see a face.

The window rose as Christiana turned to rush inside the café, yelling for the other waitress to help her. In less than a minute, she had a half dozen cups of coffee loaded on a takeout tray. She flashed Royce a quick smile as she passed him. He didn't return it, as he decided to take another sip from his cup, keeping his face hidden.

The window lowered again as she approached the car and handed the tray to the driver. After a few minutes of standing, being patient, he saw the driver hand her some money. As she counted it, he reached his hand out of the car and attempted to grab her butt. With the first touch, however, she swirled and moved out of his range. Even at this distance Royce could hear a crude laugh coming from the car before the window rose again and the car accelerated down a side street that was supposed to be closed, but some rouge drivers ignored.

Christiana disappeared to the back of the café. Ten minutes later she emerged, and smiled, but not with the same flair of being care free as earlier. Royce knew she must have her mind busy working on a solution.

She laid the plate of pasta in front of him. "This is an idea he has always wanted to try. It's a combination of zucchini flower dough that he used to create the noodles from and some cheese from Switzerland that he's been hoarding. I hope you like it."

"That sounds great." He stopped to point to the curb where the car had been. "I couldn't help but notice what happened."

She glanced at the curb again with her face revealing a temper burning underneath. "I'll be so glad when they're gone. I should've poured the coffee in his lap when I had the chance."

"Ouch, that would have hurt."

"I hope so. They arrived yesterday. I think they thought I would love to be a party toy for them, but I want nothing to do with their kind."

"Makes sense to me. Who are they?"

"I think it's the kind of people you just don't ask. They were in here, and sitting over by the bar last night where I heard them talking for a while. Apparently they have some major problems. I heard one of them talking about some of their friends being killed. That's when I decided to have nothing else to do with them, I don't care how rich they are, or what kind of yacht they have."

Royce forced himself to move slowly. She had some of the information he needed, and he didn't want to spook her. "I don't blame you at all. I saw the guy trying to grab your rear." He glanced at her, trying his best to appear to be an open ear and someone that she could trust.

She glanced down at his food, obviously wanting to change the subject. "Tell me what you think?"

Royce glanced down at the pasta and smile. "This looks very interesting and I thought this might be a boring place to hang out. Instead . . . this is one café I'll remember well."

She smiled again. "I hope so."

He raised his fork and ate the first bite. "Hey, this is very good."

She smiled and pointed to the back of the café where the cook was watching them talking. Royce put his fingers together, and tossed a kiss into the air, as if to say this was magnificent.

After he left, she leaned over and smiled. He forced himself to avoid staring down her blouse again, but like wow was it hard. "I'm going out to see what's happening tonight, and I sure hope that I don't have to see these people again. Do you have any idea which places I need to avoid?"

She glanced over at him. "I think anywhere they think they can find women will be a target for them tonight. They told me they were waiting on a boat that'll be here tomorrow morning. I'll be so glad when it does."

"I understand." Since Royce had no doubt that Raptor planned on leaving by boat, this information matched his previous thoughts. He had to find out which boat they planned to use.

Christiana continued, "I have to work late tonight, but if I didn't, I would love to show you what I've learned so far."

"That would be great." Royce grinned. "Do you have a number that I can call you on?"

"Sure. Let me write it down for you." She removed her order pad and wrote some numbers on the back.

Pocketing the number, Royce helped himself to the pasta. "This is great."

***

Victoria let her fingers work the keyboard. She accessed her home computer back in America, and launched several new plans built into it. Royce had changed her original plans, but she had plenty of counters to offset it. The CIA specialist were trying to back track to her, but unable to break through her dummy accounts. She needed a few more days to complete her work.

She managed to get the hotel list, but recognized none of the names on it. Perhaps Royce would when he returned. As she walked over to the window and looked out, the blue water of the Bay of Angels allowed her to lose herself in the thoughts of escaping with Royce. She couldn't get him out of her head. There was so much about him that she still didn't know, but she knew she had uncovered a lot of information concerning his past over the last few months.

When a knock at the door startled her, she moved to the spy hole, looked out, and saw Royce standing on the other side. She quickly opened the door to let him in. After he locked the door behind him, she studied his deep breathing, and the sweat beading on his forehead. "You've been running. Are you okay?"

Royce walked over to the window, avoiding her question. "What have you been able to find out?"

Victoria approached him from behind, giving him a hug, as she felt his sweat. She knew that he must have been running for a while. "I have a list of those registered here. I know none of them, and I can locate very little information about them on the computer."

Royce turned to face her, as he glanced around the room. "We've a very small window to find him. I met a girl that worked at a café who has seen them. She doesn't know it, but she could be in very bad trouble."

"Why?"

"The Raptor, as well as some of the beast that work for

him, have their eyes on her. They stopped by to check on her while I was eating, and I was very lucky that they didn't pay any attention to me."

"Wow, it sounds like it was close."

"Too close." He pulled her closer to him, and kissed her forehead. "You have to trust me on this one. I know we'll be safe soon."

She rose to kiss his lips. "I'm so sorry for all of this." She paused to think. "We don't have to do this. Let me show you how we can disappear."

Royce waited for a second, and then walked to the window. "Here, take a look." He pointed to the car parked down the street. "There's one of the killers that work for Raptor. He has many more just like him that will never stop."

"How do you know?"

Royce pointed out toward the bay. "They have over three ships out in the bay, but they know they're being watched. I understand that he has a special boat coming to pick him up tomorrow. The Pack's much more powerful and connected than you can ever believe."

"I know since I've been studying them for several years, and much more than anyone else knows. They have many weaknesses and they will be glad to see us disappear." She spoke low, but deliberately.

"I hope you're right, but right now we need to get ready to go out."

"Where?"

Royce turned to glance at the clothes they had purchased. "First a wine tasting, and then we need to do some dancing. I need to make sure they're out on the town, and will be busy for a while."

"Isn't this dangerous?"

"It'll be much more dangerous if I don't know where

they are. Listen . . . we need to hurry."

Chapter 34

Royce guided Victoria into the restaurant hosting the wine tasting, and to where a man in a dark designer suit approached them. "*Comment t'allez vous* (How are you)?"

"*On va bien, merci* (I'm fine, thank you)." Royce pointed toward the bar where he saw a consultant setting up for the wine tasting.

The man bowed and let his arm flow in that direction, indicating his understanding of their intentions. While the elaborate polished wood inside accented the entrance, many leather chairs encircled several small tables on the way to the bar where most of them were taken by couples enjoying themselves, laughing and nibbling on small plates filled with various cheeses and fruits.

The bar, equally as polished, reflected the glow coming from the rolls of liquor neatly placed behind the bar tenders. An arrangement of lights of various shades of colors accented the expensive liquors. The wine consultant uncorked the wines, and smiled over at them. Royce knew they would let them breathe for a few minutes. He had planned on arriving at this wine tasting early to ensure that he had a good place to sit, as well as to be able to watch for Raptor or any of his men. He wanted to remain unnoticed as much as possible, but had to make sure they were out on the town and not at the dock or warehouse.

Places like this required a certain style to obtain entrance. The patrons dressed in beautiful clothes, much like you would expect from a country that boasts so many fashion shows and where everyone wanted to be a clothing designer.

Victoria pointed to a table at the back side of the bar where the lights were low. Royce nodded his head, as a waitress followed them to the table. After helping Victoria into her seat, he turned to this girl. "*Je voudrais le plateau de fromage, s'il vous plait* (I want a plate of cheese, please)."

The girl smiled and asked what they would like to drink in a strong nasal French. After accessing their new clothes, she appeared to be unimpressed.

Royce allowed his French to flow smoothly. "I think some water for now. After we taste some of the wines tonight, I'm sure we will buy a bottle then."

"*Tres bien* (Very good)." She turned and walked away.

The table that they had selected had a wall behind them, but allowed them to be able to turn to each other and hide their faces if they needed to. "Keep your eyes open, but don't make eye contact with anyone." He watched Victoria smile, as she scanned the room.

Several people wandered over to the bar, where the host had started pouring. The waitress returned with their wine glasses for the tasting, as Royce leaned over to kiss Victoria. "Since it's early, we'll take our time."

She nodded in agreement.

Several more couples entered the bar, looking for a chair, and thus leaving very few empty. Royce lifted their two glasses. "I'll be right back."

He soon stood behind a short couple who were speaking in Italian. While she expressed interest in the wines, he appeared very bored. The designer suit he wore fit perfectly, obviously tailored produced from a fantastic fabric. When the man turned, Royce studied his tie. The style was fresh and new—perhaps Gucci. The gold watch he wore looked expensive, but not a Rolex. He guessed it to be a Cartier.

After this couple was served, Royce walked forward, and

faced a male host with a big smile who spoke in a deep French nasal voice. "Tonight, we have several wines I hope you will like." He glanced down at the two glasses, and let his eyes roam to the table Royce came from, where he studied Victoria who had remained in her chair. "The first one is from the champagne region. It's not a Krog, but I think it might even taste better."

"I'm sure it'll be good." Royce accepted the pour, and turned to make it back to his table. That's when he saw several men walking in, scattering out, and covering the room. Royce moved toward Victoria while preparing to draw his pistol on a minute's notice.

Victoria had lowered her head, but kept her eyes active. Her hand remained close to her purse, which was hanging on the side of her chair. She casually turned toward him, as he handed her the drink. She patiently waited on him to have a seat before she touched her glass to his. After they sipped the wine slow, but deliberately, she slowly leaned over to give him a kiss. The men had to be convinced that they were a couple deeply in love with each other, and no threat to this group of men scouting out the place.

One of the men nodded to the others and walked out, apparently satisfied. He returned with two other men. Could one of these be Raptor? Royce waited, straining his ability to hear any clues.

The two men wandered over to a small table not far from where Royce and Victoria sit. One of their men walked over to the host, and obtained two glasses of the champagne.

Victoria leaned over, and whispered, "Is that him?"

"There're no photos of him, but I know that he has a very ruddy skin that is full of old acne marks and some scars. It's too dark to tell from here. I'll get us some more wine while you watch my back."

He retrieved her glass and stood as one of the men stared

in his direction. Royce didn't glance back, purposefully ignoring him, since he wanted to pass quietly by the table while they were talking. While many rich people frequenting this restaurant had body guards with them, they usually had less than this. He heard them laughing, but their conversation remained in small whispers.

The host smiled, as Royce extended his glasses toward him before asking in French, "How was it?"

"My wife loved it, and we would like for you to put one to the side for us. Can you do this for me?"

"Absolutely!"

Royce extended his glasses for the next wine, a white one. "This is a pinot from Tuscany. I'm very interested in hearing what you think of its crisp, clean taste."

"I'll let you know."

As Royce turned to leave, he saw one of the men standing behind him. When he moved to one side to walk past him, he heard whispering, but the only part of the discussion that he could make out referred to the price of boat fuel. Just before walking out of the range of hearing, he heard the words "the yacht".

Victoria accepted the wine and smiled, playing her part perfectly. Royce leaned over, but instead of explaining the wine, he whispered, "It's not Raptor."

"Are you sure?"

"Yes, the face is too smooth. However . . . I think they may be connections of his."

Victoria sipped the wine. "This isn't bad."

Royce leaned over and kissed her cheek. "One day we'll have a good wine cellar."

Royce forced his attention on her, making small talk, hoping to keep her calm. He felt proud of her ability to make light of the situation that could explode at any moment. Royce knew that he was the most hated man that the Pack had encountered in a long time. "Are you ready for number three?"

"Yes, I have this funny feeling about this place."

Royce smiled and walked back over with their glasses. Several couples were in front of him as he approached the tasting spot. When of the men in the group walked over next to him, Royce knew that he had decided to check him out. If this man discovered he had a gun under his coat, he would have to move fast.

After the couple in front of Royce received their pour, he moved forward. "How was it?" the host asked.

"It was very good, thank you, but I've several cases close to it and I'll pass on it for now." Royce knew that his French was good; after all, he had received the best language instructions in the world. To make his cover earlier, he was required to have no accent. He had lived in Nice for several years before they had allowed him to do any serious work.

Royce walked pass the men again. This time he became lucky, and heard one of them mention a night club, as he glanced at his watch. The other one forced a laugh, as he pointed to the girls around the bar.

After returning to the table, Royce handed Victoria the next wine as he leaned toward her. "I think I know where they're going next." He kissed her cheek again, but knew he had to stay out of sight for now and wait on the two men to leave before they did.

***

Victoria walked pass Royce, as he closed the door to their hotel room. "That was close tonight."

"Yes, but I'm sure he's out there somewhere, and if he's going to stay out late partying, it may be my one and only chance to get into his warehouse and look around. If possible, I'd love to check out a few of the boats in their boatyard as well."

"I need to go with you."

"I'm sorry, but this is one of those times that I need to go on my own. I might have to climb some walls and I can hide much better than both of us can. Don't worry since I can maintain contact with you on the cell phone."

Victoria reached for her computer and then for her bag where she retrieved a small box. "Here take this with you. I, at least, want to know where you are."

Royce resisted at first, but then finally accepted it. "You need to get some sleep. I'll be back as soon as I can."

"I'm going to keep doing some research. You know . . . we can't stay here too long since it's just a matter of time until Brandon finds out that we're here. I'm sure he's already checking out the possibilities of how we plan on leaving the country."

"Don't worry about it. We'll think of a solution."

Victoria smiled, and kissed his cheeks. "When you can slow down for a minute, I'll let you know what I've already worked out."

"Okay, but first things first." He moved to the closet and retrieved a different pair of clothes, one much more suited for the mission tonight. She knew that she had to trust his instincts on this one mission, but she would definitely be glad when he completed it.

***

Royce reached down, unfastened his belt, and unsnapped his pants. He watched her studying him, smiling, and showing her brilliantly white teeth. "What is it?"

She walked over to him while she kept her eyes focused on him. "Royce, I was thinking about how we have been on the run the entire time that we have gotten back together . . . and well how it's so interesting that we feel so comfortable with each other." She glanced down at his pants falling to the floor.

Royce smiled as he stepped out of them. "I'm sorry. If I embarrass you, let me know, and I can go to the bathroom to change."

She laughed again. "Not on your life. I think you look great." She made the last few steps to him, but stopped inches from his lips, allowing him time to study her eyes. The beauty in them remained so perfect, so pure. His stare increased, as he knew she constantly was waiting on him to do something, to do anything, yet he waited. This moment was one that he had dreamed of constantly while he had searched for her.

He felt her place her hands on each of his arms, sliding them up toward his shoulders, and massaging as she progressed. He allowed his eyes to close briefly as he pressed the images of her eyes into his brain. As the rush of happiness overflowed his heart enough to where all bad memories suddenly disappeared, he felt like he had penetrated them enough to see inside her soul.

With his eyes closed, he leaned forward, and felt her gentle breathing. The air from her warm and smooth breathe provided a comfort of knowing that she was, in fact, alive, and not a figment of his imagination or a sordid dream. Finally, he whispered, "You feel so good."

He felt her hold her breath. He edged closer until he felt the warmth of her lips before he even made contact. The slight touch electrified his senses, as her moist lips quickly expressed an eagerness to accept his own. As he pulled her extremely tighter to him, he moved his head to one side. "I thought you would be alive. You had to be." He felt the silky smoothness of her hair against his face, while enjoying its wonderful smell.

As her lungs expanded, he knew she was about to speak. He let her pull from him momentarily. "I'm so glad you're not mad at me. I truly had no idea what you would do when you found out that I faked my death. I never intended to get you into trouble."

He kissed her forehead. "You don't have to say a word. I understand much more than you know."

She breathed out as he felt her body relax. "Thank you." She kissed the side of his neck, which tickled even his spine. The warm kiss slid to one side and back to the other. With the engrossing feeling of affection growing with each new kiss, he had a new reluctance to leave. He felt his mind floating, wanting to stay, but he knew that he had to complete his mission in Nice.

He forced himself to think, to speak. "I want you so much . . . not just now, but forever."

"Me too, and we will. This will all be behind us soon."

He knew better. He knew. He pulled away from her slightly. "Unless I get Raptor now, he'll never quit. I know."

"He will quit. He'll not have a choice in it. I've −"

"I know what you're saying, but . . ." He leaned over to kiss her lips again.

It was so tempting to tell her more, but it was best if she didn't hear it. "You have to trust me now. Soon, we'll compare notes, but later, when all is safe."

He felt her wanting to speak, but rushed to intercept. "Hush . . ."

She quickly gave up, and fell deeper into his arms. He, in turn, ran his hands through her hair, hoping he was telling her the truth. This feeling of submission made him relax. Her hands moved from his shoulders to the back of his neck, as she now pulled him closer. Her lips immediately explored his, and he could feel a passion inside of her that she must have been restraining for a long time. Yes, he knew that she must have been through a lot the last few months also.

He pulled her closer, and now felt the full size of her breasts against his chest. He allowed his hand to slide toward her stomach, as he suddenly thought of her being pregnant. A small smile erupted, as he realized again that yes—he was going to be a father.

She guided his hand to her stomach, apparently understanding exactly what was on his mind. "I hope this is okay with you. I considered an abortion at first, but I could not force myself to do it."

Royce realized that she had been in a very tough spot, and wished he could have been there for her. "Don't even think about it. I couldn't be happier." He reached her stomach, and rubbed the small bulge. The last three months had passed so fast in some regards, but so slow in others.

"I'll make you happy one day. I'll be a good mother and wife, if you'll allow me to."

Royce looked at his pants around his ankles. "I think I need to finish getting ready."

She smiled. "Perhaps I can still talk you into forgetting about this." She moved her hand lower and cupped it over his manhood, squeezing it slightly.

Royce smiled. "I wish we had time. I really do." However, he didn't try to remove her hand, and the more he stared at her, the more beautiful she became. Her gentle massage to his manhood brought instant reactions. With his pants on the floor, the thin boxers allowed her to wrap her fingers around his shaft and strobe it, as it became larger, and stiffer.

In a moment of weakness, he considered taking time to stay with her since it would be a long night. As she continued to massage, to stoke him, he leaned over and kissed her again, but with much more force and passion than before. It apparently excited her as she quickly reached to the top of his boxers and slid her fingers beneath them. With the touch of her skin on his sending increased spurts of electricity through his body, it became harder for him to leave. But he had to. Damn it!

He saw her glance at the bed and back up, pulling him with her. As he stepped out of his pants, while following her, she stopped and kneeled to be able to lower his boxers all of the way to the ground so that he could step out of them also. As she remained, knelled on the floor in front of him, she looked directly at his bulging hard dick. When she glanced up at him, he waited to see what she would do. After she glanced back at his stiff erection and moved closer, he had one quick thought about asking her to stop, but it disappeared quickly as she kissed the tip of it for him. "Ohmigod." He moaned, letting her know that it felt good–real good.

After he saw her smile up at him, she lowered her head again and leaned forward to take the entire length of it into her mouth. He felt it sliding smoothly inside her mouth. He thrust his hips forward, completely involuntary, and completely with a loss of control. After she continued to take him in and out for several minutes, he rubbed the top of her head before he finally managed to reach over, and grab the side of her blouse to pull her upwards. As she rose, she made it clear she was happy in doing this for him, and at any other time he might be unable to resist, but not tonight, as he forced her up and into his arms, where he kissed her lips as soon as she was high enough.

He reached over and lifted the bottom of her blouse up. She did not resist, and let it come over her head. The bra soon unhooked in the front, which allowed him immediate access to her breasts. He reached over, and used his fingers to graze her nipples, one finger at a time. After he heard her moan, he let her sit on the bed.

He knelt on the floor and reached for her skirt. The snaps quickly gave away and she pulled it first to her ankles before finally allowing them to hit the floor. As the white panties she wore slipped off with ease, he studied how she was still clean shaven, just as he had remembered from before. Since her body had no flaws or marks of any kind, he studied just how beautiful she was to him. How did he ever get this lucky?

She pushed back to the top of the bed, and toward the headboard, allowing him room to join her. After he removed his shirt and climbed in on top of her, the full feel of her naked body against his intoxicated him, driving him further and further from the reality of their situation. He had to concentrate. There were men that wanted both of them dead, and these men might even be in the same hotel.

Still, she moaned, as he covered her body. With her firm breasts pushed up against his chest, and her silky smooth skin allowed him to slide over her easily, he shifted his weight. While she spread her legs wider, making it easier for him to center in on top of her, his mind focused on her stomach against his. "Being pregnant . . . hum. Is this okay? This is all new to me."

"Don't be silly. You're not going to hurt the baby, or me." He now felt silly about asking, but had never been with a pregnant woman before.

As he inched higher and felt his shaft inch up higher on her leg and toward her crotch, he felt the sight twitches in her body as he progressed. He remembered this feeling so slightly from before, as the memories returned slowly. "Are you feeling okay?" He wanted her to acknowledge him.

"Yes, this is fantastic!" She kissed his neck, waiting on him.

After feeling her pubic bone on his lower stomach, he made one last movement higher and felt his throbbing shaft touching her. He felt for the opening where she was wet, very wet. As he slid inside her, he heard her moan in ecstasy, erasing all thoughts of Raptor and his men disappear, and leaving his guard completely down for now. With the world of reality disappeared in a dazzling world of enchantment, and one he had never experienced before, he reached over and turned the lights out.

Chapter 35

Breathing hard, but with a newfound energy, Royce returned to the warehouse he had located earlier. This time he would complete what he should have done years ago. The quiet of the late night and the many dark corners allowed him to move around easily. Now, he needed a way to find his way inside. As he walked around the building, looking for an easy point to break in, he approached a door at the rear that was secured by a padlock.

While he could see no tell-tell signs of a security system, he smiled and cautiously located his tools. After he removed the lock and moved inside, he saw a single light down at the end of a hallway. He quickly passed by it and into the open area of the warehouse, which was covered with boating parts and several large machines. He glanced at several cars parked on the far side of the warehouse, but kept moving.

He saw a small office on the far side and worked his way to it. Without warning, a large black object rushed at him with a deep growl breaking the silence. While his first instinct was to shoot, he grabbed his knife instead and pointed it in the direction of the attack, forcing it under the snapping jaws. At first the dog knocked him backwards, but as he pushed harder he felt the knife punch through the dog's skin. When the dog snapped at his arm, Royce twisted the knife, opening the wound, and making the attack quickly end about as fast as it had begun. So, this was their security system.

He pulled the dog to one side, trying to find somewhere to hide it. After a piece of canvas caught his eyes, he quickly hid the dog under it, while his breathing became deeper and stronger. His arm continued to bleed slightly, but appeared to be okay otherwise as he pushed on toward the office, where he cracked the door open slowly.

Royce removed a small light from his side pocket which illuminated the sides of a room full of old papers. The desk in the center had an old chair behind it, but there were no chairs for visitors. While the musty smell suggested that the office hadn't been used much lately, the guard Victoria had received the information from specifically mentioned this warehouse. He glanced around, hoping to find out more.

On the desk were several files. He glanced at them, but nothing looked new. Behind the desk he saw a small red light coming from the floor. He moved closer, and studied the multiple connectors of a wiring system. He followed the wires to a cabinet, and opened it. When an unexpected bright light suddenly blurred his vision, he quickly re-closed it. He glanced around, hoping this hadn't given his intrusion away.

He found some papers to help shield the light, as he opened it again. Several computers servers and communication type equipment were hidden behind the door. Interesting. Okay, now he wished he had taken Victoria with him.

He quickly found his cell and called her. She answered immediately. "What is it?"

"This place is practically abandoned . . . with the exception of some cars that are stored here and one office that looks like it has seen better days. However, I stumbled into something I need your help with."

"You name it."

"I found some computers, and large ones that I think are servers."

"OHMIGOD."

Royce examined the computers, continuously wishing he knew more about them. "What do I need to do?"

He heard her take a large breath of air. "This is going to take a few minutes, and it's very important that you do exactly as I say."

"I'll do my best." He glanced around, and hoped to be able to find some tools.

"Royce, the first thing you need to do is plant one of your charges close to it. This is, I think, a backup storage computer of the Pack's files. While it'll be very important to destroy it, but, before we do, I'm going to try to lead you through some programs that'll allow me to access it. Do you understand?"

"Is this going to take long?"

"Royce, if you need to get out of there, let me know. I love you too much to let you die now."

Royce held his breath. "I was going to pick a much better time to tell you this, but I love you too."

"Good, very good. But now we have to hurry."

Chapter 36

With the last explosive finally placed at the warehouse, Royce reattached the padlock and headed down the street where the early morning signs of the sun coming up glowed along the eastern sky. He needed to hurry back to the van and move it to somewhere else for a while.

All remained quiet as he approached the back door and slid in his key. WHAM! The door suddenly smashed into him, knocking him backwards. He raised his pistol instantly to see a sawed off shotgun pointing at him, and at point blank range. As the door opened further, he blinked to make sure he recognized things clearly. Christiania, the girl from the restaurant, was tied and gagged next to the guy holding the shotgun. Her eyes, which were full of fear, darted around. Royce steadied his hand, as his mind raced.

"*Jettes ton arme* (Drop it now)," a voice yelled out of the van, giving Royce no choice but to comply.

The man jumped out of the van and motioned for Royce to get inside, where a much larger man waited for him inside. He immediately tied Royce's hands. "*Il y a quelqu'un qui souhaiterait vous voir* (We've someone that wants to see you)." After the door slammed shut, Royce heard the keys which had been left in the keyhole being removed.

Royce looked over at Christiania, who had her hair ruffled, and makeup running down her face that also had a large bruise under her left eye. With the dress she wore earlier now torn, revealing her bra underneath, he wondered what other injuries she had sustained. The man with the shotgun checked her gag and laughed.

Within minutes, the van circled around to the back of the warehouse. When the back door opened, they were yanked out, and Christiania hit the floor hard. Royce tried to help her, but was knocked down beside her. "Stay there."

He had no choice. He heard a man talking to Raptor on a cell phone, calling him by his name. Is this the way it was going to end?

A few minutes later, a Mercedes pulled into the warehouse. Several men quickly exited from the car and walked towards them. A shorter man lumbering ahead of them suddenly shouted, "*Levez leu* (Stand them up)."

Several more men moved over and forced them to their feet as Royce finally was able to stare directly into the face of the man he had hunted for years. The descriptions he had received fit perfectly. Raptor stood at around five and a half feet, but stocky, and well built. His face was covered in scars, some from apparent knife fights, and others from a bad acne problem he must have had as a youth. He wore a French cap that hid his hair, giving the impression he had a balding head.

"*Vous n'abandonnez jamais, n'est-ce pas* (You don't give up, do you)?" He glanced over at Christiania. "*Je vois que vous avez une nouvelle amie copine* (I see you have a new girlfriend)."

Royce remained quiet, wishing he could have one more chance to get to him.

Raptor continued in rapid French. "You had the balls to make it here. We could have become your family, but no . . . you decided to destroy me instead. Who in the hell do you think you are?" He reached out and kicked Royce hard in the stomach. He went down, but Raptor's men hauled him back to his feet.

Raptor glanced at the van. "I understand you had enough

explosives in there to take out a small army. It's too bad you didn't have time to use them . . . and we do appreciate the gift. It's hard to get high quality military explosives. The sleepers we've placed in America will love them." He motioned for one of the men to load them into one of the cars. "Take these explosives to the boat. We'll be along in a minute."

Royce maintained his eye contact on Raptor, only to be rewarded with a new kick to his knee. He yelled, as he went down.

"Now, this isn't the girl you left with from Paris. I assume you know where she is. It's too bad you'll not be able to warn her. From what I heard, she's a very good looking girl also." Raptor's phone rang, and he turned to answer it.

Royce looked over at the girl, and wondered why she turned him in, and knew that his look was immediately interpreted by one of the men. "She went looking for you last night. She had no idea who you were, but provided us with enough information to let us know that it had to be you. We knew you had to have driven here from Paris, and it didn't take long to find a Paris tag that looked out of place." He smiled at her. "I also knew that Raptor would love to see her, she's not bad." He laughed as he watched the girl cry softly, falling limp. The man holding her would not let her have the pleasure of falling to the ground, as he forced her to stand again.

Raptor returned from the phone call. "Our boat is almost here. I hope you don't mind us not asking you to join us. Just the same, I'm going to enjoy watching you die before we leave."

He looked over at the girl again. "Sweetheart, I'm so sorry, but we don't have much room." He walked over to her and smiled back at Royce. "I would have thought that after hearing what we did to your first girlfriend that you'd become a little smarter."

He walked over to Royce again, and slapped his face. "Yes, the American government did a great job in hiding your file and your new life. It's too bad you had to throw it all away, isn't it?" He laughed like a mad man. "Perhaps I should show you what happened to your first girlfriend since we do have a few minutes." He walked over to the girl being held by his men and further ripped her blouse before forcing a kiss on her, and fondling her breast with one hand and yanking her head back by her hairs with the other. "Sweetheart, you picked the wrong guy to be a girlfriend with."

Suddenly, a loud voice coming from behind them overrode Raptor, "She's not the girlfriend–I am!"

The men turned to see a slim girl with a big gun pointing at them. She wasted no time in further discussion, firing five blasts into the crowd of men, sending several bodies backwards and the others scrambling.

Royce grabbed one of the fallen men's pistols and fired at the retreating men as Victoria reached him. Raptor and one of his men jumped into the Mercedes as Bullets from the pistol fired by Royce ricocheted off the bullet proof window. The car raced toward the door, with others following.

Royce reached for his pistol holster and found the small compartment on its side. The designators were exactly where he had left them. He pushed the first button and an explosion threw one car on its side.

"Royce–behind you!" He ducked as bullets ripped pass his head. She joined him, firing the last of the clip.

The men were in the far side of the building, but he knew they would quickly regroup and come after them. "Here, duck as low as you can and cover your ears." The three huddled close as he pushed the next button, which designated the explosions he had planted earlier next to the back wall. After the explosion, Royce glanced over the cover they hid behind. No one could survive that kind of blast.

Royce yelled at Christiania. "Come with us, they'll have reinforcements here soon." She didn't move. After he shook her, he saw the blood and where she had taken a bullet to the back. "Damn!" The anger raged in Royce as he reached for an extra pistol that Victoria carried.

They rushed toward Raptor's car lying on its side, approaching it from two different directions. Was Raptor dead?

The driver had blood covering his face and with part of the top of his skull missing. After Royce searched the rest of the car, he realized that Raptor had disappeared. He quickly ran outside to see the other car retreating—the one that they had also transferred more of his explosives to.

Victoria ran back inside toward her computer. "We have just a few minutes before the French police arrive, but I have an idea."

***

The French police had quickly surrounded the building and had a copter circling over head. While their instructions shouted over a loud speaker remained unanswered, they waited. Several shots suddenly came from the warehouse, and they all hit the ground. They had a standoff.

They heard the voice of an American yelling from inside. "Don't come inside! We're well armed. We're American and want to surrender, but only to the American CIA."

The French police repeated their call, and ordered them to come out with their hands in the air. No other sounds came from the warehouse.

***

Brandon was finishing his third cup of coffee when his phone rang. "Yes, this is Brandon."

"We have a situation here. There's an American barricaded in a warehouse, demanding to speak with the CIA."

"Where?"

"In Nice."

"I'll be damned, who is it?"

"You tell me, most of the building is destroyed already."

Brandon motioned toward Charlotte "I think they found Royce. We need to get to Nice—now."

Chapter 37

While wearing only her white bra and panties, Victoria slipped into the water and started to swim. Royce followed, wearing only his boxer shorts, but carrying a small plastic bag protecting some of their electronic gear. Now, he wished he had taken the time to have her explain her plans to him, but with no other plan available, he swam after her, as sirens were now screaming from everywhere.

She turned to him. "It's not far, but we have to hurry." She pointed to a location on the beach.

Royce saw two surf boards on the beach next to a small tent. "Are those ours?"

"The crowds aren't on the beach yet, so this is the best I could do."

They rushed into the beach area, as Royce remembered how he hated feeling the rough pebbles under his feet. As he noticed the small plastic bags taped to the top of the surf boards, he smiled. "What's this?"

"You're not the only one working all night. This we'll need when we get to the other side of Angel Bay. It's four miles. Are you okay?"

He grabbed one board and headed for the beach. His knee hurt like hell, but he decided not to let her know how much right now. They had to keep moving. "I've been here many times before."

It took a while, but they finally reached the shore where the beach ended. Royce opened his package and slipped into his clothes as he watched Victoria jump into her outfit. This would buy them a little time, but not enough. They needed to get out of the country. "Now what?"

"We need to get to the airport." She showed him two passports. "We have tickets waiting on us there."

"You're amazing." He reached over and kissed her. "How did you manage that?"

"Until I met you, the computer was my best friend."

Royce looked out toward the bay. "I wish we had captured him. We were so close."

He lifted his designator, and tried one more time. "He has to be out of range or he discovered the way I rigged it."

"I have an idea. Let me see your phone."

He handed her his phone. She connected with her computer and started searching for the number of a local radio station. "There, this'll do."

"What are you doing?"

"I'm calling in a special request." The on-line radio host answered. She pressed the button next to the cell phone microphone. No one heard a noise, not them, not the station, or all of their listeners, but . . . she knew.

A boat that had circled its way around Cap Ferrat, past the golden triangle, and into the bay of Villefranche exploded. Even from that distance, they soon saw the signs of smoke in the air. Now, all they could do was hope that this time Raptor had received what he had coming to him.

They exchanged smiles. "There's only one last item to take care of," she said, as she leaned over and kissed him. "This will complete what I hoped to do last time. There'll be no turning back. Are you sure you want to always be on the run?"

"Do it." She moved the trigger to the last explosive. As the warehouse exploded, she could only imagine the French police hitting the ground. Seconds later, she saw a new massive black cloud rushing into the sky.

Royce held her in his arms. "I love you."

"I know."

***

Brandon's copter approached Nice, as he saw the black smoke in the distance. "Damn, the boy does like to create a scene." He strained to see through the smoke, as the copter raced closer. The remnants of the warehouse lay on the ground, and fire trucks fought the last of the remaining flames. "Get us on the ground." He looked out at the bay, and studied another rise of black smoke in the air. "What in the hell is that?"

Charlotte glanced out of the window. "I'm not sure, but I think a boat's on fire."

The copter landed, and they were met by the French police. While Brandon had a lot of explaining to do, he also wanted answers.

Chapter 38

As the French police searched through the remains of the warehouse, several firemen searched for any remaining hot spots, as well as any evidence of the cause for the explosion. Other specialists were collecting samples from many parts of the warehouse. Brandon recognized the remains of an office and pointed toward it, just enough to alert Charlotte.

The French officer in charge of the investigation approached Brandon. "We have five dead men here, and one woman." He studied Brandon, waiting on some response.

"Tell me again . . . who owns this warehouse?" Brandon wanted to receive information, but not volunteer it.

"It has been abandoned for a long time, but an Italian shipbuilder uses it to keep spare parts in."

"Have they been contacted?"

"Not yet. It'll take a while to determine who these people are that died in this blast. And one other thing. Two of the men, those over there, were shot multiple times."

"Do you think that the explosives were used to cover that up?"

"No. If they wanted to do that they would've placed the bodies closer to it."

Brandon walked over closer to the bodies of the men that were covered with blankets for now. "May I?"

"Be my guest. It would be great to have them identified."

Brandon raised the blankets to see one body guard after another. All of them were large men with dark business suits on, but their faces were in too bad of a condition to make any positive identification. He didn't want to give away the fact that he was looking for Royce and Victoria. He knew that Royce's blond hair would be an important clue, but none of these men had such hair. The last blanket covered the woman that had been killed. Brandon held his breath for a long time as he studied her. A small possibility existed that it might be Victoria, but he had no way to know for sure. He felt his stomach tightening. He had seen all he wanted to see.

"Do you know who she is?" The Frenchman stared at him, waiting on an answer.

"I'm not sure." He walked around the warehouse again, letting the officer follow him and giving Charlotte more time to examine the office area.

"I'm not sure anything in here could cause such an explosion. If I had to make a guess, it had to be a military type explosive. We'll know soon enough."

Brandon suspected that it was such when he first saw the warehouse from the air. "I'd be interested in hearing what you find out."

The French officer stopped, and turned toward Brandon. "There were several explosions in Paris a few days ago that matched this one. Since you're here, I'll assume you think there's a connection. I need you to tell me what you know."

"We do have a common enemy, and as you know, I'm very limited on what I can say."

"Understood, but this is France and I can have you held until I get some answers."

Brandon only offered a smirk. "You can try." He moved over to the other side and waited for Charlotte.

Another French officer approached them minutes later. "The fire on the boat has been put out. There are more casualties. About six or seven bodies were blown to bits in an explosion on the ship."

"Keep me informed." He turned to Brandon again. "Tell

me what you know, or I promise you'll live to regret it."

"I'll make this as simple as I can, and I expect it to remain as quiet as possible for both your government's sake, and ours."

"I understand, but I need to know what's going on, and I need to know now."

"We had two ex-CIA officers that the Pack had tracked down, hoping to get more information out of, and to extract a little revenge. They picked the wrong two to pick a fight with."

"Are you telling me that two renegade agents caused all of this damage?"

Brandon looked around. "They didn't pick this fight, but it looks like they damn well finished it."

"I need a full description of them."

"I think one of them might be the woman you have over there, but can't tell for sure. Also, I can't tell from the bodies of the other men, if the other ex-agent was one of them, or not. If they're still alive, I do need your help in finding them." He pointed to Charlotte. "She'll give you a description as best she can. It appears that they have accessed our computers and erased all information we have on them, as well."

He waved over at Charlotte to come join them. She approached them, stepping over the debris scattered all over the ground. "There's very little left here," she announced loudly.

Brandon glanced over at Charlotte. "They're going to help us find them if they aren't in fact dead here already."

"If you're looking for a description, it might be easy, or it could be hard. They both are in their mid thirties, and both have blond hair, but probably hiding it. They may be passing themselves off as beach bums, or surfers, but they could, just as well, be strolling around as one of the super rich. I wish I had a photo to give you, but that's about it. They would have arrived in Nice yesterday."

"That's not much, but we'll check with the local hotels. I think they had to spend the night very close to here last night." He turned to make his way out of the warehouse.

Brandon waited until he knew he couldn't be overheard before talking to Charlotte. "What did you find out?"

"I suspect that an office was there, but an explosive attached to it destroyed anything that might have been useful. Since we both know that Royce went after Raptor, I think he might have succeeded. One of these men or one of the men on the boat may prove to be him. I'm not sure if we'll ever receive full co-operation from the French Government. It'll be an item that the politicians will have to work on from here."

They walked around the warehouse for the next hour, looking for any more evidence of what happened. The French officer in charge of the investigation suddenly came back over to them, moving at a rapid pace. "I think we might have found your renegades. Please come with me."

***

The French policemen were already in place at various points around the hotel when they arrived. They heard conversations with various snipers in place on several adjoining buildings being coordinated, as several police cars directed traffic away from the street in both the front, and rear of the hotel. The French officer in charge of arranging the assault team came over to the investigating officer that had Brandon and Charlotte in tow. "Stay close to me and let us handle this. I need you to identify them, but it's our job to take them down. Is that understood?"

"Understood."

Brandon and Charlotte followed the officer into the main lobby, where no one was left to cover the desk. Apparently he had already been rushed out of the hotel. Two different officers moved to both sides of the stairs, while another one remained by the elevator. Brandon followed the investigating officer. "How do you know it's them?"

"They checked in yesterday and they match the description. The clerk noticed how they acted suspicious, and how the woman did all of the signing in. They didn't have any suitcases when they checked in, which was also very unusual. Since they also had no reservations, he knew immediately that they fit the description."

"Do we know if they're in there?"

"He hasn't seen them all day. We'll know soon."

"It might be best if I call them out. We don't need any more shooting."

"I brought you along in case you could help, but we're prepared to storm the room if we have to. My boss has my head on a block this time."

"I think they'll listen to me. All I ask for is a chance to talk to them."

They were finally in place on the floor, and slightly down from their room. The officer completed a call on his cell phone, and then handed the phone to Brandon. "I think it'll be best to call the room first. The call will appear to be from the front desk. You don't have much time to talk some sense into them."

Brandon accepted the phone, and heard it ring several times, but no one answered. He turned to the officer, and shrugged his shoulders.

"I understand. Let's get closer to the door." They walked closer to the door while several men took positions around them. While one of them held a battering ram, they all were in riot gear, expecting the worst. Even Brandon and Charlotte had been issued bullet proof vest for protection.

Receiving the go ahead from the French officer, Brandon

stood, and stepped forward. "Royce, this is Brandon. Are you in there?"

They received no answer. The French swat team glanced at each other.

"Victoria, if you're in there with Royce, you need to let me know. The building is surrounded and there's no way out. I'm your only hope."

Still, they received no answer. The French officer motioned to the man holding the ramming device to move forward.

"Royce, Victoria, This is your last chance. Answer me!"

No answer. The ram moved forward and smashed open the door with ease, allowing several officers to rush inside. In seconds word came out. There was no one there.

Brandon and Charlotte walked in, and looked around the almost vacant room with the exception of a few clothes and a lap top on a small table. Charlotte walked over to the computer, and turned it on. "I think this was left here for our benefit."

The screen soon flashed in front of them, and a video appeared on the screen. "Hello, Brandon."

Charlotte smiled at Brandon. "This'll be interesting."

His smile revealed the fact that he wished he could open it in private, but knew the French officer would insist on seeing what was left. "Let's see what kind of message she has left for us."

Charlotte clicked on the screen to see a message quickly appear. "I know you have many questions, and I hope this answers some of them for you. I intended to remain dead, but I had to come back to get Royce. It appears that he's going to be a father. The last flash I delivered to the Pack will be the very last. It was reprogrammed to introduce a virus into their system which will erase the benefits they have accumulated for the last several years. They were not interested in tracing the seed money as you assumed. That was never their intentions. I didn't know exactly what they were after until I disappeared and completed more research. Robert always managed to add more information that he obtained from the banks by encoding in it what was referred to as useless data files. Those useless data files of foreclosed properties and bad loans are what they were really after."

Charlotte clicked on the computer to lower the screen. "Most of America's enemies know that the Americans largest source of riches lie in its real estate. The housing crisis has given them a way to accomplish many objectives and if they can aggravate it by increasing its downfall, they win. However, there is much more. By knowing where these properties are, they were actively purchasing them from people eager to sell and not ask many questions. Not only are these great investments for them, but a place to plant sleepers for later."

Charlotte glanced over at Brandon. "Wow!"

She continued to scroll down. "As I mentioned earlier, they downloaded a virus when they thought it would contain more of this same data. So while they own many properties in America, they have no idea where they are now. In return for doing this for you, I think you need to work on returning these properties to the rightful owners."

Brandon laughed. "She's much better than I thought."

Charlotte continued to scroll down the page. "In the warehouse not far from here was a backup computer. I have copies of it, and I know they would love to have it back. That was one reason for destroying it. At this time, we aren't sure if Raptor was killed, or not. If not, I hope you continue the search for him, but it's not our battle any longer. One last item: the files you tried to send to the Pack and the Russians were always known to be false. The correct files have been downloaded, and are ready to be sent. You will also see several of your bank accounts missing, just to confirm to you, that like the Pack that has lost access to their files, the same can happen to American files."

Brandon whistled softly, as Charlotte scrolled down further.

What do Royce and I want from all of this?

DON'T COME HUNTING FOR US AGAIN–EVER. IT'S OVER.

THE END

310